THE
BE

THE GRAVE BELOW

PATRICK HANSMA

The Grave Below

PatrickHansma.com

Second edition 2024.
First edition 2020.

Interior & exterior design by Jenni Hansma.
JenniHansma.com

Cover photography by Patrick Hansma.

ISBN: 978-1-7357350-3-0 (paperback)
ISBN: 978-1-7357350-2-3 (hardcover)

Dedicated to—

The Damage Boys
(Silas, Luke, & Caleb)

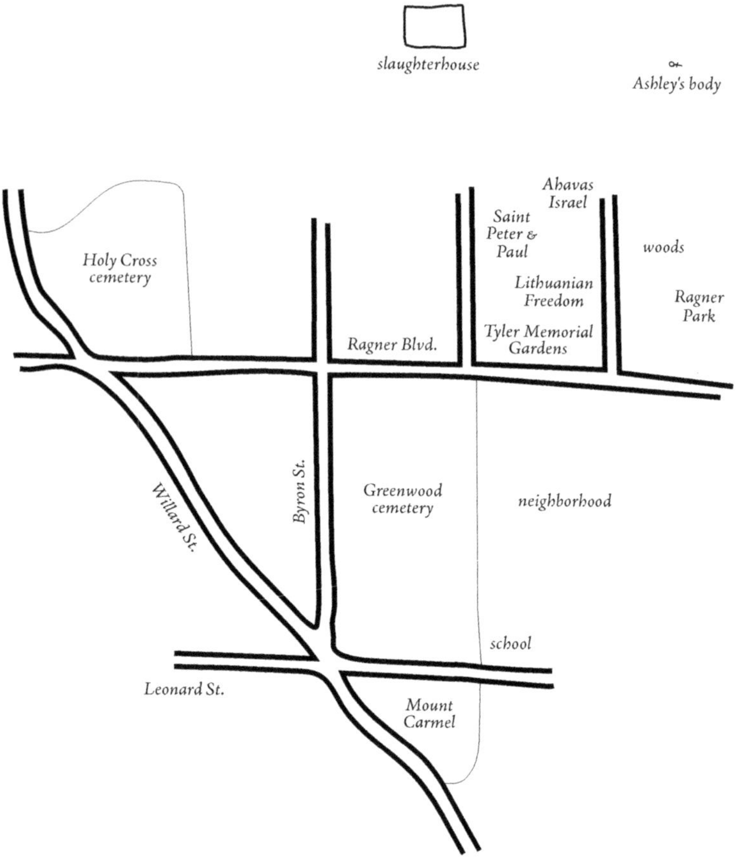
slaughterhouse
Ashley's body
Ahavas Israel
Saint Peter & Paul
woods
Holy Cross cemetery
Lithuanian Freedom
Ragner Park
Tyler Memorial Gardens
Ragner Blvd.
Willard St.
Byron St.
Greenwood cemetery
neighborhood
school
Leonard St.
Mount Carmel

Greenwood cemetery Map

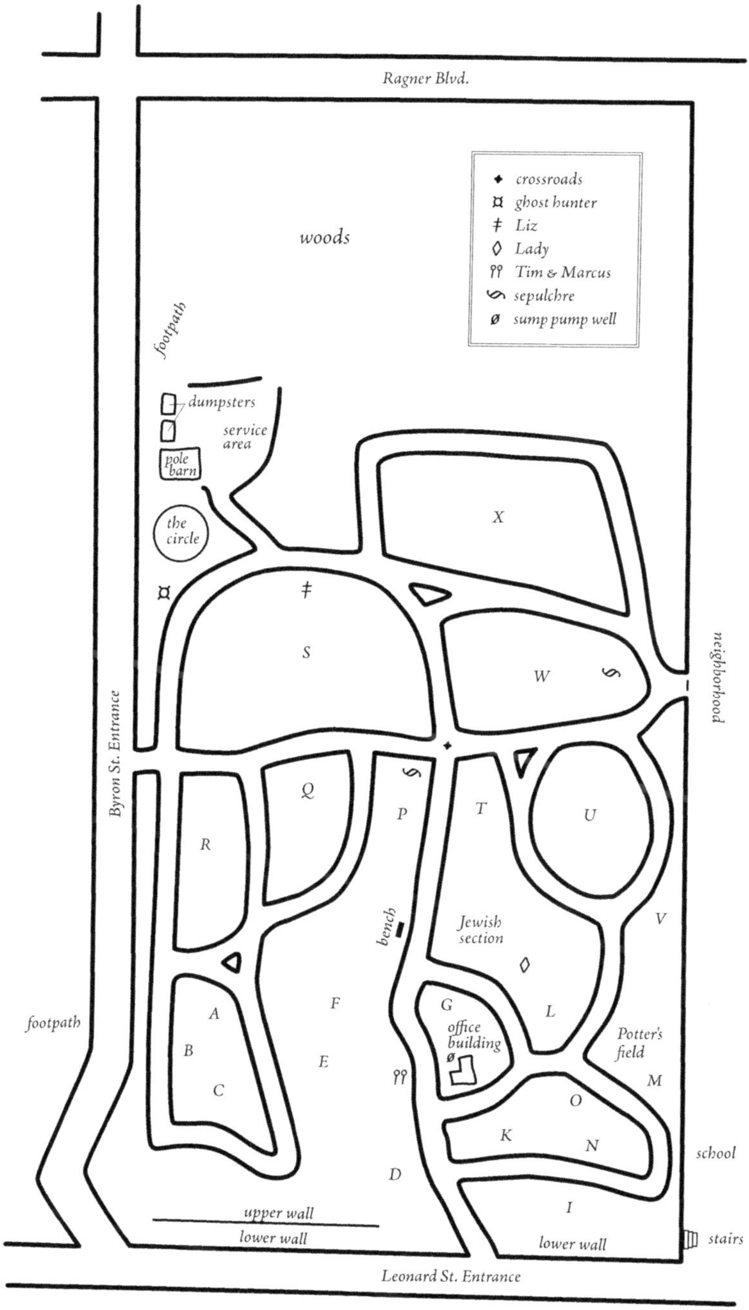

For the earnest expectation of the creature waiteth....
For the creature was made subject to vanity,
not willingly....

...the creature itself also shall be delivered from the bondage of corruption into the glorious liberty of the children of God.

For we know that the whole creation groaneth and travaileth in pain together....

– Romans Chapter 8
(Authorized Version)

Chapter I

"Do you think it's really haunted?" Tim asked.

"Shhh!" Marcus whispered. "Of course it's haunted!"

"Well what are we doing here, then?" Tim whispered back.

"Do you want to be a kid for the rest of your life? Or do you want to man up like Matt said? He dared us, man. We gotta prove we aren't cowards!"

"How are we supposed to do that?"

"Look. Just go ring the buzzer." Marcus gave Tim a slight push out from the tree they were both hiding behind.

"I don't want to ring the buzzer! The place is haunted!"

"Just go do it!" Marcus gave Tim a firmer shove.

"Alright, alright! Lay off!" Tim nearly shouted.

Tim slowly stepped out from behind the tree and looked in terror at the old building decaying before him. There was an extinguished jack o'lantern on the porch glaring back at him. He turned to look back at Marcus.

"Why don't you go ring the buzzer?" he asked.

"Because I'm not the one who's scared. You gotta do it because you need this."

"What if we go together?"

"Just go ring the buzzer!"

Tim briefly looked to his right down the long drive toward Leonard Street. It was a million miles away. Even if they ran they would never make it out of this graveyard before being eaten alive. To his left the path crested a hill and meandered deep into the cemetery. Several lighted jack o'lanterns glowed in the darkness among endless trees and graves. He trembled inside as he looked back at the building in front of him. Matt had told them it was a witch's house. The roof was steep and the shingles were crumbling. There was a spooky old lightning rod at the top and ivy over much of the outside. The exposed brick was faded yellow and there were no curtains or blinds in the windows. Tim didn't know why there would be a house in a cemetery. It had a black mailbox at the bottom of the steps with faded letters that read "Office." Tim had never seen an office that looked like this. Maybe it used to be a house, he thought. Maybe they put the cemetery around it because no one would live in a house where a witch used to live. He looked back at Marcus one more time, but Marcus just gave him a dirty look.

It was just a few steps across the cemetery drive, and four long stone steps up to the door. All he had to do was ring the buzzer. He drew one long breath and cautiously began to walk toward the old house. Marcus watched in amazement from behind the tree as his friend approached certain death. His mouth gaped. He couldn't look away, though he was terrified by what he was watching. This was the best Halloween ever.

Tim scanned every window on the front of the house. It was all dark inside and no movement. He looked at every bush and tree nearby. He was certain there were zombies or ghosts lurking among them, but he kept walking, though slowly.

He reached the steps alive. Of course the wind raised a gust just then. Tim shivered with fright. Summoning all of his courage, he put one foot up onto the first step. He froze there and stared at the window. Did something move inside? Something moved inside. He was sure of it. His heart raced and he breathed more quickly. He wanted so badly to run away, but he knew Marcus was behind him watching. He didn't want to be called a coward. Marcus might tell Matt. Then he would never hear the end of it at school. Gathering the last of his courage he ran as fast as he could up the steps and smashed his hand against the button. The buzzer gave a loud and horrible tone as Tim turned back to see the look on Marcus' face.

But he saw no one.

"Marcus?" he whispered.

Just then the door behind him swung open and he was yanked inside. The door slammed immediately shut again, and the cemetery was dark and quiet once more.

The clouds churned silently above and the darkness grew thicker as the night wore on. The graveyard was empty and expansive. No moon could be seen through the gathering storm. The fallen leaves rustled in the night air, blowing helter-skelter across the graves, and gathering at the bases of the headstones.

Hours later, through this blustery Halloween night, a man walked casually passed the office building, but stopped to look at the darkened jack o'lantern on the steps. Ryan had been operating a clandestine business out of Greenwood and other local cemeteries for several years. Police routinely patrolled the graveyards for vandals on Halloween, but Ryan always made at least one pass through Greenwood, just to check for more nefarious things which might threaten his business.

This was the first time he had seen pumpkins in the cemetery.

He had passed several of them as he walked the paths, and wondered who did it and if they would be back. He did not want unnecessary attention or activity in Greenwood. Hopefully this was a one-time scheme from some neighborhood kids. But since all else seemed quiet, Ryan continued down the path, out of the graveyard, and disappeared down the road. Gradually October gave way to the eerie gray dawn and a dismal November morning.

Chapter 2

With the sun rising behind thick clouds, a bright yellow truck rolled into Greenwood and up to the office. The driver was a newly-hired city employee named Sal. This had been his first week on the job, and it wasn't going well. He hated mornings and this graveyard job. His coffee was cold and he was already in a bad mood. He was seriously considering quitting when he got out of the truck, and was stopped by what he saw. There was a jack o'lantern on the steps. Its face was partially blackened by candle soot. Sal sighed. It was one more thing to clean up.

He walked up to the door and found it unlocked. Pausing, he looked around to see if any of his coworkers had arrived. But he saw no one. Something wasn't right about this. He slowly pushed the door open and stepped cautiously inside. All seemed as it should be on the ground floor. He walked up the stairs to the attic thinking he might find some vandalism. Nothing wrong there though. He turned and walked all the way down to the basement, since that was the ground floor on the back side of the building with its own door to the outside. Clicking on the light, he turned and stepped off the grimy old stairs into the unfinished basement. Then he realized why the stairs seemed even more sticky than usual.

He was surrounded by blood. It was spattered all over the steps, across the floor, onto the walls, boxes, folding chairs, and on the plumbing. It dripped from the ceiling. It was on the light bulb. It was even spattered on some of the spiders lurking in the corners. And now it was on the soles of Sal's boots. He ran back up the stairs, out the front door, and vomited repeatedly. After he lay in the grass hyperventilating for some time, he made his way back to the truck, called his boss, and quit his job. When pressed for a reason why, he gagged again several times before he could explain the situation.

It wasn't long before the police arrived. They made an extensive search of both Greenwood and Mount Carmel—the Catholic cemetery across the street. The bodies of two children were found in the dumpster by the garage at the back of Greenwood. Their throats were deeply lacerated. There was some insect activity on the corpses and they were already in the earliest stages of putrefaction.

In Mount Carmel, strange symbols were found scrawled in chalk on the concrete. Neither the police nor the caretaker could make any sense of them. They had no apparent organization. None were English nor were they Catholic. The caretaker wanted them removed as quickly as possible because this was holy ground. Regardless, the scenes were documented per the typical time-consuming protocol, with little regard for what the caretaker wanted. Everything was photographed, surfaces were dusted for fingerprints, notes were made, and the dumpster was impounded for further analysis. The office doors were locked and the basement was roped off. Police tape was stretched about liberally. People in neighboring houses were questioned. Eventually the lead investigator left to notify the families of the deceased while the bodies were sent to the medical examiner's office. As they packed up the last of their equipment, a cold rain began to fall. The jack o'lantern, still sitting on the office steps in Greenwood, began to fill with rain water. The strange chalk symbols across the street slowly dissolved and were washed away forever.

The remainder of the day passed uneventfully at the scene of the crime. But on the second day of November, Ryan sat on the upper retaining wall of Greenwood watching the traffic go by on Leonard Street below. He had heard about the murders on Halloween, and having been there that same night, he felt he should survey the scene himself. This was exactly the type of thing he feared would threaten his business. And it was all the more striking that the crime happened inside the office building. The groundskeeper, Mike, who facilitated Ryan's comings and goings for a cut of the money, had stopped by earlier and unlocked the office building for him. Ryan was impressed by the amount of blood in the basement, but otherwise, there wasn't much to see except residual police tape here and there. So he lingered on the retaining wall to consider how this would affect the body trafficking business.

As he sat in contemplation, he noticed an unmarked police car roll in from Leonard Street. Unfortunately, Ryan made eye contact with the driver as the car turned in. It parked near the office building. This was exactly the sort of thing he was concerned about. Ryan casually rose and pretended to move on, but quietly worked his way toward their car to listen to the conversation. It quickly became apparent that they were the detectives assigned to the case and, for whatever reason, had now returned to the scene.

"Were you able to attend the autopsies of the two boys

yesterday?" Detective Malli asked.

"I was there for hours," Detective Jameson sighed.

"Who cut the cases?"

"Doctor Rezek did both autopsies on our vic's. He said they both had irregular sharp force injuries of their necks. Both boys had lacerated jugular and carotid arteries," Jameson replied, flipping though his note pad.

"I thought you said they were sharp force," she quipped.

"Yeah," he was quick to respond half annoyed and half confused.

"Lacerations are blunt force injuries. Weren't you listening at the forensic conference last month? Dr. Rezek said it like twelve times in his lecture," Detective Malli explained.

"Well whatever."

"What does irregular mean?"

"So he said they were penetrating injuries, probably sharp force but not classic incised wounds like a knife would typically make. They were also obscured by insect and maggot activity from being in the dumpster," Detective Jameson went on.

"Any kind of pattern? Did he have a weapon in mind that could have done it?" Detective Malli continued to query.

"I asked. He said no. He said they sort of resembled bite marks, but would not be textbook examples, so he doubts that's what they are. He swabbed the injuries for saliva but said he doubts it will be of any use because of the maggots. I forgot what he said about any defensive wounds though. I'll need to call him back about that."

"He doesn't use that term," Detective Malli interrupted.

"Why is that?" Detective Jameson sighed once more.

"He says it doesn't mean anything. Having injuries on the hands doesn't automatically mean you were defending yourself."

"OK, well, anyway I got some good info about their night. The two boys go to school together and they each live about a half mile from the cemetery but in different directions. They were supposed to be trick or treating and then Marcus was going to spend the night at Tim's house. Marcus' mom says she doesn't think they ever go to this cemetery but she remembers Marcus asking about it once. Couldn't recall when, but it was just kid stuff. He asked about it being haunted. We're going to have to do considerable canvasing to see if anyone in either of their neighborhoods recalls seeing them Halloween night. We still don't know if they mentioned going to the cemetery to any friends. Maybe they were brought there by the killer or maybe they went on their own and the killer happened to show up."

"Or was already there," Detective Malli interjected. "Any thoughts on the symbols in the cemetery across the street?" She motioned toward Mount Carmel.

"No idea. I sat down to do an internet search but realized I don't even know what to type."

"Same here. I got nothing. So wait a minute. It's November. How much insect activity could there possibly have been in that dumpster? I mean I know we saw a few on the bodies when we pulled them out but it didn't seem like there were that many."

"Yeah that's what I thought too. Doctor Rezek says that all the bugs and bacteria in the dumpster might cause it to be like a slightly warmer microenvironment in there."

"Microenvironment?"

"Yeah that was his word. October was not particularly cold I guess so the bugs in the dumpster were probably just still active and protected from the weather," Detective Jameson explained with a tone of incredulity. "And I was thinking most of the critters probably scattered when we moved the bodies anyway. Mostly just a few very small maggots were left behind."

Ryan had not seen the symbols they were talking about, so he set about scouring Greenwood for them. He made a wandering route at a brisk pace, scanning tombstones, trees, and sepulchres for any new graffiti. But he found nothing. Though October had not been particularly cold, November was already getting colder and the winter would likely begin early. He wondered if there would be any breaks in the case before Spring. This situation made him wish he worked at the medical examiner's office rather than as a diener assisting autopsies at a local hospital. Then maybe he would have access to the actual facts in the case. He would have to rely on his usual channels for information, however, to stay abreast of this in the coming months. But in the meantime, he needed to get to work.

CHAPTER 3

Idelette walked with purpose through the crowded mall, past the Macy's, and up the escalator. She was a pale woman who stood about five foot six, prettier than not, and looked to be about thirty-five, but was slightly older. As she moved among the groups of people, she carefully noted the trends in the various portions of the mall. It was a Saturday in the summer and the place was chaotic. Teenagers were all around her. Businessmen and housewives were scattered about. But having passed the computer and clothing stores the herd had thinned substantially and she found a pillar to lean against which was nicely triangulated between Nobility Books, the Fine Chocolatier, and the Hot Gothic clothing store. Various 14-year-olds scuttled about, texting each other as they went and complaining about their yoga guru mothers or whatever other idiotic thing overwhelmed their pathetic lives. Some of the people noticed Idelette leaning against her station, left boot to the floor, right one raised against the pillar, but most were too consumed by their phones to notice anything around them.

Her coat was long and black—an unfortunate stereotype. Her blonde hair fell in front of her eyes and an unlit cigarette floated on her lips. Lung cancer had missed its chance with her, but she didn't actually smoke anyway.

With her right hand she grasped an aged book in her coat pocket. It was a fifteenth century leather-bound Bible. It was small but very thick and the boards were fastened with two clasps. She contemplated its significance but kept her resolve focused on the people passing by. It was a little like fishing while surrounded by fish. She just had to decide which fish she wanted to bite. As she raised her left hand to brush her hair behind her ear, she noticed a security camera near her. She looked directly at it for a moment but wasn't worried. For some reason, she was always blurry in recordings and photographs. She never had figured out why though. Turning her gaze back to the crowds, she observed a brooding teenage girl with purple hair ambling with several equally attention-addicted friends. Written in ink pen on each of the girl's forearms were the words "as above" and "so below" for some reason. The group laughed and bantered on as they strolled out of Nobility Books and into the Hot Gothic clothing store. Pulling the cigarette from her lips and placing it behind her ear, Idelette sighed at the thought of mall goths and then followed the group into the store.

Cyberpunk Euro trash 'music' blasted needlessly through the store and stupid teenagers shuffled about amongst the over-priced concert shirts and various metal accoutrements. The aesthetic was faux brick and gun-metal grey. The carpet was blood red. Idelette listened through the music, studying the conversations around her. The purple-haired girl wanted to try on some things, but her friends wanted to go to the Apple store at the other end of the mall. Agreeing to meet up at the Orange Julius, the group left their pariah comrade behind.

Idelette stood between them and the exit, requiring the group to split up awkwardly to either side of her as they passed. She took no notice but watched the girl with the purple hair. She was shopping for a new skirt or something—it didn't matter.

"Can I help you?" the clerk behind the cash register to the right of Idelette inquired. She didn't even blink and she certainly didn't acknowledge him. She merely used his question as her cue and she walked to the back corner where the purple-haired girl was browsing. The girl held two skirts and a corset in her arms and was just about to cross the store to the dressing room when she was intercepted.

"Excellent selection," Idelette commented on the corset with indifferent monotone,"I have one very similar," (no she didn't) "but I didn't try it on before I bought it, and it turns out it doesn't fit."

"That sucks. I'm just about to go try these on actually," the purple-haired girl replied with an affectation of annoyance.

"Make sure you lace it correctly otherwise you won't know that it's right for you, and you'll waste your money. I'm headed to the dressing rooms too. I tell you what, you put it on over your t-shirt and come out to show me. You really need a friend to give you an honest opinion before you buy something like this," Idelette calmly insisted as she maintained eye contact.

"Uh, sure I guess. Thanks," the girl found herself unable to refuse and just a little surprised at her answer. The two passed behind the black curtain and into the hall of stylized dressing rooms. They stood before a mirror at the end of the hall as she held up different combinations in front of herself. The girl studied herself in the mirror, strangely indifferent to Idelette. She was almost fully mesmerized at this point.

"What's your name?" Idelette asked just as she was about to enter a dressing room.

"Cheryl," the purple-haired girl replied, startled at the broken silence.

"Tell me, how old are you, Cheryl?"

"Seventeen."

"Listen, Cheryl, I think you should come with me. Your friends obviously ditched you. And you seem like someone who is actually worth hanging out with. I'm parked close to here—we should get out of this mall. Don't you feel like your friends ditched you?"

"Yes," Cheryl replied softly.

"Do you like cool old graveyards?"

"Yeah, actually," Cheryl's voice escalated just slightly.

"I figured as much. They always do. Well, that corset isn't for you and those skirts won't work without the corset. I say we forget these things and I'll take you to the coolest old cemetery you have ever seen. It's not far."

"Um, ok." Cheryl said blankly as she stared at their reflections in the mirror.

"Perfect," Idelette smiled and tossed the clothes into a dressing room. She led Cheryl out the employee exit at the back of the store, through the empty service corridors and out a fire exit near the dumpsters in the Sears parking lot. Stopping just outside the door she looked about studiously and assured herself that no one was nearby. Then, with new intent, she turned and stared at Cheryl.

"Still with me?" Idelette inquired.

"Yeah, of course," Cheryl replied as though they were old friends.

"Good," Idelette declared and with that hollow remark she stretched out her left hand and grabbed Cheryl by the throat. She lifted her from the ground, and slammed her against the back of one of the large green dumpsters. Cheryl pathetically tried to fight back but was helpless. Idelette forced her body against the girl and sank her teeth deep into Cheryl's neck. Blood spurted on the rusty metal and across Idelette's chin. She drank deeply for many moments as Cheryl's attempts to struggle slowly subsided and her breathing became more sporadic. When the flow of blood had slowed substantially, and Cheryl was limp and unresponsive, the vampire broke the girl's neck and threw her lifeless body—or nearly lifeless (she didn't know or care)—into the dumpster.

"See, O Lord, and consider, for I am become vile," she whispered as she turned away. Then, wiping the blood from her own chin, she reached her right hand into her coat pocket, reassured herself that the Bible was still there, and with a shudder at the thought of her inmost being, walked across the mall parking lot toward town.

It was a beautiful day. The skies were mostly cloudy and the sun was covered more often than not. There was a gentle breeze out of the north and yesterday's rain was now only a few puddles here and there. Idelette followed the highway—passing through yards and various other lots—from Jamestown toward Grand Blanc, but she changed her course at Chicago Drive. She went down into the trees where there was more shade. From there on she followed the Grand River. The water was turbid and the road she walked was still quite damp. She didn't really notice though. Her right hand had instinctively gone back to her pocket and her fingers were studying the Bible therein. She had a perfect mental picture of it but she analyzed it yet again as she walked. The book was perhaps six inches high and four and a half inches wide. It was thick too, over three inches. Her finger tips explored its smooth brown leather boards and the raised bands on the spine. She felt the metal clasps and contrasted them with the worn edges and rounded corners of the soft rag paper leaves. And as she walked her thoughts melted to memory.

Centuries vanished away and she found herself once again walking the dirt road from the countryside to her village. The trees rustled with the summer breeze and the grey sky overhead threatened a storm. It was the year of our Lord Fifteen Eighty, Idelette was 36 years old, and she was still mortal.

Chapter 4

Lost within the Germanic regions of the Holy Roman Empire, Idelette's village was quiet and comfortable most of the time. A church was situated within a small graveyard near the western aspect of the village. Its doors opened to the east, and the path at the foot of the steps led straight through the cemetery toward the homes which were mostly arranged at the center of the village. A large barn and pastureland were located on the north end for when livestock needed to be brought in. An ancient wall—really just a large wooden fence—surrounded the village. Its gate was at the southeast corner. Beyond the wall were primarily farmland and pastures. The soil around the village was fertile and the grass and trees grew lush. Beyond these comforts sprawled a dense and wild forest which extended for many miles. Several paths meandered and intersected between the trees, as did a winding river. The roads all eventually turned toward the king's highway, which was hidden far away among tall pines, beyond the hills that rolled deep within the southern aspect of the forest.

Idelette walked casually through this countryside, along the dirt road to the open gates in the wall. The wind was blowing. A storm was gathering on the eastern horizon. She was not concerned though. She was eager to get to the church where she had an appointment with the cleric, Dom Calmet—an elderly Frenchman of the Benedictine Order who was sent by Papal writ to replant a church in this village. He was the most learned person in the village—able to read and write in several languages and in possession of nearly two dozen books.

Idelette, a devout Christian, was deeply attached to the cleric. She was the child of tragedy. By far the younger of only two siblings, her parents bore her in advanced age. Her father was a wagon-maker. Her mother had occasionally taken odd jobs as a seamstress, but had mainly tended the home and raised the children. Unfortunately though, they each died of phthisis when Idelette was a young girl. Her brother, 20 years her senior, became head of the household and worked in his father's stead. Restless in later life however, he sold the business and all his possessions to fund an extended pilgrimage to the holy land. Not to forsake his little sister though, he put in place a trust for her (which Dom Calmet managed) to see that her basic needs were met until she married. Their house and property taxes were securely managed but other than that, Idelette was undeniably poor. Last year Dom Calmet had received a letter that Idelette's brother had died of cholera in Nubia. And it was not certain how much longer the trust would last. Betrothal would likely save her from future ruin. She had had two suitors in the last few years. One died of pneumonia after having his foot crushed when moving an anvil. The other drowned while trying to save some sheep during a flood. Now, there were few eligible suitors left in the village and Idelette's poverty did not make her a particularly attractive marital prospect, despite her pleasant appearance.

Knowing all this, Dom Calmet favored the woman and treated her with exceptionally close attention. He had even been teaching her how to read and write, which was the nature of her appointment with him today. There were few others in the village who were literate, but she was not proud or boastful. In fact, no one else knew that she was getting an education. She merely wanted to learn. It was not exciting work learning to read and write but she loved it all the same. She would copy pages from books while Dom Calmet worked himself into a frenzy over the nature of the Protestant movement and the future of the Holy Church of Rome.

Wondering what he would rant about today, she laughed to herself as she continued along the dirt road through the village to the church. She crossed the churchyard swiftly, with little thought to the graves around her, threw open the doors, and proceeded directly to the cellar below the sanctuary, where Dom Calmet kept his office.

"Ah bien. Copiez cette page. Ah, good. Copy this page," the cleric insisted and handed her an open book. Idelette sat down immediately at the table and began her work. She began with: 'That which is acquired by single combat is acquired with right.' • The language was Latin. She didn't understand this statement and she wondered who the author was because she thought perhaps she disagreed. The title at the top of the page was De Monarchia. She turned back to the title page for clarification. It read Opera Omnia—the author, Dante Alighieri.

"Was ist dieses Buch, denn? What is this book?" she inquired with a frown.

"Ah, young lady it is the work of the most famous of Italian poets. This book is somewhat more obscure than what you are probably used to, but I thought it was time to make your mind truly labor, not just learn."

"What other books do you have in your collection, Father? I suspect that this is merely an essay on politics. You know I haven't the intestinal fortitude for politics. Can't I just continue scribing the Scriptures? Where did you put the Novum Instrumentum Omne?"

"A fair line of questions indeed; let's see what we have," Dom Calmet conceded. Turning to a shelf he began pulling books down and reading aloud the titles. "You have already suggested The Holy Bible and certainly that is the best choice. But it is not the only choice. You have foolishly turned down Dante so... I have Almagest by Ptolemy. Oh, but better still, I have On the Revolution of the Heavenly Spheres by Nicolaus Copernicus. My copy is appropriately redacted according to the instructions of the Index Librorum Prohibitorum, mind you, lest we find ourselves in a spot of bother. I have Malleus Maleficarum by Kramer and Sprenger. That is an important work certainly! Hmmmm.... Vigiliae Mortuorum Maiores &c Minores Secundum Chorum Ecclesiae Maguntinensis, that would be laborious for sure. Ah ha, here is De Exorcismis et Supplicationibus Quibusdam. Have you read that one yet? Or perhaps—"

"Dom Calmet! Dom Calmet!" Voices screamed from above them and frantic footsteps shook the boards over their heads. "Dom Calmet, come quickly!"

The cleric rushed up the stairs and Idelette followed closely behind—almost forgetting to put down the volume of Dante which was still in her hand. She turned back a moment to drop it on a table and then raced up after her priest.

"What is this commotion? This is unusual church behavior!" Dom Calmet insisted as he reached the top of the steps.

"He's dead! He's been murdered!" shouted one of the members of the frantic crowd that had suddenly descended upon the church and now filled much of the back of the sanctuary.

"Will you ever learn to hold your tongue? We don't know that at all!" interrupted another.

"Exactly! Who are you to say anybody's been murdered?" yet another joined in.

"He's dead, is he not?" someone argued back.

"He's more than dead—he's torn apart!" another shouted.

"It wasn't human! It was some sort of devil!" someone yelled.

Everyone began talking over each other again and the whole situation devolved into noisy chaos.

"Stop right this instant!" Dom Calmet interceded quickly. "I need each of you to remain quiet and just one of you to tell me what has happened. Who is dead?"

One of the more sensible men in the crowd, Conrad, came forward, and detailed to the cleric his understanding of the situation. Conrad was a handsome and generally quiet man. He had a strong frame, dark features, and commanded respect as an honest, working man. He had been the first to happen upon the body and so his information was the most reliable. He was returning from the forest with a bundle of firewood when he came upon a mess of blood on the trail. It was evident that something had been injured and dragged through the ferns and creepers deep into the trees. He let fall his bundle of logs, and with axe in hand, bravely followed the trail of clotting gore into the recesses of the mossy woods. Far in the shadow of a great canopy of thick pine he found himself staring down at the mutilated corpse of a man. It was Benjamin, a man well known to all the villagers, who had been returning from the river with fish. His throat was deeply lacerated, his torso spread wide open, and his entrails disturbed and torn. Deep lacerations were present over his face and limbs. His bundle of fish lay on the ground a few feet away. Conrad hurried back to the glade where he had been chopping wood and gathered his companions who were still working. He told them of Benjamin's corpse and together they hurried to the village. A crowd gathered with them as they entered the gates. Seeing there was something amiss, people entreated them in the commotion—but only confusion resulted. Conrad led the mob to Dom Calmet and that was how the matter stood up to this moment.

"Thank you, Conrad," the priest said. "This is clearly a very serious situation and I need all of you to contribute by obeying my orders. A small group of us must go tend to the body; the rest of you should go on about your business until we return."

Dom Calmet selected several men from the crowd to accompany him: Conrad, a couple men who also had been out in the forest, and another pair of men to pull a cart which would serve as Benjamin's bier. Idelette was not invited. So she silently invited herself. She didn't know why she was so curious to see but she couldn't ignore the internal urge to satisfy her curiosity. She simply had to see for herself.

Once the rest of the crowd had been dispersed, the assembled team gathered necessary provisions and walked directly out of town and into the forest. With all the talk and commotion no one seemed to even notice that Idelette had accompanied the group without invitation—no one except Conrad that is. A few yards out of the village he made a point of catching Idelette's gaze and holding her in a silent stare for a few moments. Her eyes admitted her awareness that she was there without explanation. His eyes informed her that he had definitely noticed but did not disapprove. So, on they walked, beyond the fields, through the wood, and into that mass of pines where the body of their neighbor Benjamin lay exposed to the corruption of nature.

Once there, Dom Calmet immediately began to assess the situation. He knew that many questions were already brewing in the hearts of the villagers. He also knew that he was not the ideal man for this task. But no one more qualified was to be found among them. So, as the spiritual shepherd of this bewildered flock, he accepted the burden without hesitation. Everyone readily saw how Benjamin's body was greatly broken. His flesh was torn in many places. His clothes were tattered over the wounds. His fish, though, were still lying on the ground. Everyone noticed, and everyone had the same thought on it.

"This was no animal," Idelette whispered as she stared at the bundle of uneaten fish near her feet.

"No. This was likely not an animal," Dom Calmet conceded, but he was too consumed in his thoughts to notice who had made the comment. "This appears to have been murder, though the reason is beyond me. We all knew Benjamin. He was a man free of vice and had no enemies. He was killed certainly without cause—and swiftly too! This was a frantic attack. This was savage. This was the evil work of some fiend not yet perceptible. Some sinister man or demon is responsible and we must all be certain to pray fervently about this tonight and in the days to come. Fail to do so and the Devil may gain a footing among us."

Overcoming their disgust, the men loaded Benjamin's body onto the cart. A blanket was placed over it and the whole assembly returned to the village. It was a slow procession as the wooden cart wheels bumped down into divots and up onto mounds scattered about the dirt path. Finally they breached the tree line into the fields, bringing their village into view. A carpenter, who had hastily prepared a wooden coffin while the group was away, met them at the gate. Benjamin's body was placed in his pine box. The lid was nailed shut and he was not seen by mortal eyes again. They slid the coffin onto the cart which previously carried his corpse, and the procession continued through the village toward the church. Everyone assembled in the graveyard. A new plot was dug near the church and a wooden marker was temporarily placed until a stone one could be fashioned. It was now late in the evening and the sun was approaching the horizon. Dom Calmet began to read the holy rite:

"Udi maledicte satana, adjuratus per nomen aeterni Dei, et Salvatoris nostri Jesu Christi Filii emus, cum tua victus...."

No one could actually understand him but they listened, crossed themselves, and genuflected on cue. The rite having been read, and holy water sprinkled, the priest committed Benjamin's body to the soil and commended his soul to Almighty God. As they lowered the coffin into the grave and began to bury it, people cried and prayed—petitioning the Lord for mercy on Benjamin's soul and mercy on their town. They prayed for deliverance from the evil one who had committed this sinful act.

The funeral came to a close just as the sun set. Darkness began to fill the village and the mourners went their separate ways. As Idelette walked alone out of the graveyard she looked out to the forest and beyond. She noticed how frightful it all seemed and yet still how beautiful. The trees were almost endless, but the forest was punctuated here and there by small clearings with low grasses and shrubs. As her eyes scanned these familiar features of the countryside, now with new fear of what evil was lurking in the benighted wood, her gaze was suddenly arrested by movement in the increasing darkness. Out on the hills the last few rays of sunlight distinctly revealed a figure passing through one of the clearings amongst the trees! Idelette stopped and watched in indescribable terror. She could not breathe but only stared desperately out into the night which was rapidly stealing the sight from her. She was certain that she saw something—some sinister man or ghoul—though now it was too dark to see anything at all, save only the moon and the stars.

Cassiopeia, the so-called queenly flux, was partially visible in the north and beyond the cityscape the Eagle was low in the eastern sky. Saturn had passed Leo and was now with Virgo. Idelette noted these heavenly shapes and realized that the storm clouds were miraculously gone—she had reached her destination. She had walked from the mall in Jamestown to Grand Blanc without giving any thought to her surroundings or to the traffic on the roads she crossed—nor had she thought about Cheryl's body in that miserable dumpster. The street lights cast their artificial hue and traffic had dissipated. She deviated into Greenwood cemetery and seated herself on a bench. At last she pulled her Bible from her pocket. Her right hand had not let go of it the entire time. Unfastening the latches, she opened to the Psalms and began to read, temporarily forgetting about Benjamin and the terror-filled moment when she saw that mysterious figure lurking outside her village so many centuries ago.

Chapter 5

Night was well established and the street lights spread a soft orange glow over the neighborhood around Ragner Boulevard. Even though it was June, Ryan wore a long coat to conceal the various contraband that he would carry out of the cemetery. It was merely uncomfortable now, but in a few hours, after working up a sweat digging, he would begrudge that coat completely. He tried to consol himself that at least it was June in Michigan rather than August in Louisiana. Whoever was doing that work must be crazy. Maybe the pay was better there. That thought was little consolation, however. Still wishing it were a slightly cooler summer, Ryan walked through Tyler Memorial Gardens, then west down Ragner toward Greenwood.

The city of Grand Blanc is heavily laden with cemeteries. There are city cemeteries, private cemeteries, active cemeteries, defunct cemeteries, hidden cemeteries, and lost cemeteries.

The oldest city cemetery is Fuller Street cemetery on the east side. Several city founders are buried there and it is fenced in.

The trees are tall and dense. It is notorious for vandalism every year on Devil's Night. The largest cemetery is Oak Hill. It occupies two sides of the road at the intersection of Hall and Eastern on the southeast side of Grand Blanc. The monuments and sepulchres are massive and elaborate.

The northwest side of Grand Blanc has the densest population of graveyards. It is a blend of city and private cemeteries. The southernmost is Mount Carmel, which is on the south side of Leonard Street. Directly across Leonard is Greenwood. It is 79 acres, but the northern 20 acres are woods waiting to be deforested for future grave sites. Greenwood is hilly and has a lot of trees among the graves. Its southern border is a large two-level retaining wall rising 30 or 40 feet above Leonard Street. Northwest of Greenwood is Holy Cross. Northeast of Greenwood is Tyler Memorial Gardens. The northern boundary of Tyler Memorial is confluent with Saint Peter and Paul, Lithuanian Freedom, and Ahavas Israel Cemetery.

This roughly one square mile of the norwest side is like its own borough, and some call it cemetery alley.

And right in the center of this is where Ryan found himself again, all alone, walking toward Greenwood to rob another grave. When he was about 50 yards from Byron Street he crossed Ragner and walked directly into the woods which occupied the northern acreage of Greenwood. Just inside the tree line Ryan kicked away a small heap of leaves and located the tools he had left there that morning before sunrise. Things had changed in the past few years. Ryan's usual partners in crime, Sarah and Calvin, were often working overtime at their day jobs, so he frequently worked alone. This meant he had to be picky about the jobs he took. He needed to take more precautions and work longer hours. And if Sarah and Calvin were specifically not available at the beginning or end of the season, that shortened Ryan's season as well, because he could not contend alone with the frozen ground of early spring and late autumn. It was just too exhausting trying to break through that much frozen dirt alone. But even though Ryan was increasingly tired, he remained focused, alert, and disciplined. He still enjoyed the work and he still considered himself the best in Michigan, though others were capitalizing on jobs that he was now forced to turn down as a solo outfit.

Ryan picked up his bundle—a shovel, wrecking bar, and an old backpack which contained various supplies such as rope, a tarp, glow sticks, and a few other well-kept secrets. He hastened south through the woods toward the developed part of the cemetery. The moon and stars glowed brilliantly above and his surroundings were well-illuminated. As he walked, Ryan became increasingly certain that tonight was going to be busy. It was like some kind of sixth sense he had developed over the years. Somehow he always knew ahead of time when a night in the graveyard would be more eventful than usual. He remained focused on his task though, pausing only once to appreciate how creepy this would all seem to anyone unfamiliar with it. There he was, walking alone in the moonlight through the woods, into a graveyard, with shovel in hand, to dig up a skeletonized baby.

After traversing the woods he came to the small slope of ground which descends out of the trees to the drive in the back of Greenwood. Before proceeding down onto the path, he looked around for a few moments and made sure all was quiet and still. Assured of his solitude, he stepped out of the trees and continued straight south through the graveyard. He followed no roads or paths but proceeded over the grass and graves directly toward his destination, watching his surroundings carefully as he went. The lights from the neighborhood to the east were no significant threat. Ryan knew how far the lights penetrated the cemetery so he stayed just beyond visibility.

Concealed in darkness, Ryan advanced undaunted. He had his techniques well entrenched into muscle memory, such as checking all drives that he must cross as he approached them so that he never had to pause to see if the coast was clear. He could just keep walking. This saved precious seconds. He also had virtually every stone, root, bat, and insect in Greenwood memorized. It was home court advantage. He could navigate it blindfolded. These little things made him better than his competition in the resurrectionist business.

Comfortable in his natural environs, he did not stop or deviate until he reached his destination: the small section designated for the graves of children, located on the northern slope of the hill northeast of the Jewish section. This slope of Section T curved until it paralleled the main drive at the center of Greenwood. This meant that Ryan had minimal visibility of anything to the south or the west—which happens to be where each entrance into Greenwood are located. To the north and east there was essentially no cover from the neighboring houses. It was a risky spot to dig and things could get out of hand very quickly. Ryan knew that he had a long night ahead so he lost no time dwelling on what he could not change.

He found the grave he was seeking and got immediately to work. Though he hated to do it, because he couldn't cut and run quickly if someone happened upon him, he took off his coat, set his provisions nearby, and began to dig. When it is an adult grave, the whole process is extremely time-consuming and physically exhausting, especially when done alone. Fortunately, this was a child's grave from 70 years ago, so it did not require digging a large hole. Plus the grave was likely shallow, and there was probably not much to find inside anyway.

Doing this properly is something of an art form. It's all learned technique. But Ryan was well-practiced. He first used his shovel to cut a rectangle of grass and sod which he lifted away from the grave in one piece. He placed this on the tarp which lay spread out next to him. Then he dug the hole. As he dug he kept circling the hole so he could monitor different parts of the cemetery without having to turn around or look away from his work. Though he never saw anyone else he was certain that he was not alone tonight. Moreover, he was sure that he was being watched (he knew tonight would be eventful!). He analyzed the possibilities while he worked. Whoever was watching him must have been doing so from a great distance, and was not interfering. If they objected, they would have already called the police. But since all was quiet, he just kept digging.

After a couple hours Ryan hit old metal which split when struck by his shovel. He cleared away the rest of the dirt and hoisted the rusty coffin up out of the grave. It was a small casket designed for a child, but still quite heavy from years of water and earth seeping into it. These were crucial moments which demanded skill and haste. If the police were to arrive at this moment it would be very difficult for him to hide everything (and himself) before being observed. He quickly forced the hinges with a large flat head screwdriver and began sifting through the remains while gripping a glow stick in his teeth. There was not much left of the child—only a couple of intact long bones, a mandible, and a few other fragments. He gathered all that there was into a leather pouch and put that in his backpack. He replaced the coffin, shoveled the dirt off his tarp and back into the hole, then carefully replaced the rectangle of sod. He then reached up with his shovel and struck a tree branch above the grave, causing a few leaves and twigs to fall to the ground over the site. This would help conceal the cut lines in the grass so it would look even less disturbed. It was also helpful if the sprinklers came on in the early morning, or if it rained heavily the next day, because the lines would vanish as the soil turned to mud.

Having accomplished the crime, he gathered his tools and began to walk back toward the woods. It was now well into the second watch of the night and Ryan pondered the Scylla and Charybdis he now faced. He was certain he was being watched. How could he just leave the cemetery without investigating that fact? But he was carrying tools and a child's bones in his backpack. How could he just leave them somewhere unattended while he pursued whoever was watching him? Recalling that Odysseus braved the waters nearest Scylla because she was a more limited threat, so too Ryan decided that hiding his contraband for a short time while he investigated the cemetery posed a more short-term risk than leaving Greenwood without figuring out who had been watching—perhaps they intended to sink his entire ship!

With his mind made up, he hurried north through Section U, then W, then X, and deposited his possessions on the far side of the slope which descended into the woods. Free of his load, Ryan turned swiftly back into the graveyard, his keen and experienced eye monitored far into the darkness. He knew every gravestone and every tree. He knew every sound. He could practically hear the occasional bat echolocating above him.

From the bench by the Jewish section, and too far away for mortal eyes to see, Idelette watched Ryan closely as he walked southwest toward her. She contemplated relocating but he suddenly changed direction. She grasped the Bible in her pocket as she watched him advance directly west into Section S and confront a young lady sitting on the bench there.

"What are you doing here?" Ryan asked an old friend he was definitely not expecting to meet.

The young woman's straight blonde hair glistened in the cool moonlight as she turned toward his familiar voice. Zoe was pale, thin, and rather anemic. Some might say she looked a bit sickly. Yet she was still relatively pretty. Perhaps 'frail' was the best word to describe her. She and Ryan had been friends in high school—long before he became a grave robber. As with most friends from the previous decade though, they had drifted apart. Now they hardly ever saw one another except rarely by chance.

At the sound of his voice she raised her head to meet Ryan's brown eyes, then immediately leapt to her feet. "I don't really know why I'm here actually. I never come here anymore—haven't for years. But I was bored tonight and wanted a good scare. So I thought I'd come to Greenwood all alone and see what might happen."

"And so far have you seen anything that scared you?" Ryan probed, not particularly convinced by that explanation and wondering if she saw him working.

"No, not yet; I only just got here a few minutes ago," Zoe lied.

"I see," he allowed. "Why here though?"

"Oh I don't know. It's stupid but I was watching a crappy horror movie and I was thinking my way down memory lane. I remembered years ago that you used to get into mischief in here with friends. Then I remembered hearing from others that you still come here sometimes. So I naively thought to myself, 'if I go to Greenwood maybe I'll get a good adrenaline rush, like maybe see some ghosts, or maybe I'll run into Ryan. Maybe both.' Stupid, huh? But I was right."

"So far. Not sure I can provide ghosts though. Come on. It's a pleasant night for a walk, particularly with an old friend." In feigned chivalry he offered her his elbow, still unconvinced by her response, and the two strolled, with interlocked arms, among the graves.

Engaged in small talk, they ambled northwest toward the old reservoir which lay at the top of a hill in the trees north of

Section S, east of Byron Street. Everyone who knew about it called it 'the circle', but it was actually a concrete basin, perhaps 50 feet across, and recessed into the ground with a large rusty pipe at the center. It was about 6 or 7 feet deep with a flat earthen bottom. An incomplete fence circumscribed most of it. There was a fallen tree trunk and large pile of dirt at the north side of the circle which formed a natural ramp down into it. At one break in the fence the concrete was engraved with the words "capacity 75,000 gal." Zoe and Ryan chatted as they walked, but all the while Ryan pondered the situation. He was unconvinced that Zoe had only just arrived a few minutes ago. Nor could he convince himself that she was the one who had been watching him—but if not her, then who else could it have been? They climbed the slope up to the circle and looked down into it.

"What has been going on here?" He wondered aloud.

"What is all this?" Zoe added.

Ryan clicked on a flashlight and shined it along the inner circumference of the circle to get a better view of the graffiti. It had long been vandalized with various gang-related artwork, but clearly it had recently been painted over with something entirely different. Where there had once been previously familiar gang signs and drug-related art, there were now numeric sequences, odd text, and strange symbols—some astrologic, some overtly Satanic, some not identifiable. The ground had been cleared of leaves within much of the circle and there were remnants of candles and burned fragments of paper scattered about.

"Well, I gotta say this is all new to me, but it looks kind of witchcrafty, don't you think?" Ryan spoke at last. "Then again, what do I know?"

"No, I agree. It definitely looks like that. Like a seance happened here or something. This is crazy. And kind of scary too. I'm a little freaked out right now."

Ryan jumped down in and investigated some of the burned paper.

"Can you read anything?"

"No. There are words but it's all too burned. I can't read it."

"Maybe those are just incidental."

"Maybe." Ryan paused, still looking around, then muttered to himself, "'stand fast in your enchantments and your many sorceries, with which you have labored from your youth; perhaps you may be able to succeed; perhaps you may inspire terror.'"

"What is that?"

"Isaiah 47:12."

"You just happen to have that memorized? Oh, that's right, you grew up going to church, didn't you?"

"Sure did. Still have quite a bit tucked in my memory, too."

"What did you say that one was? Isaiah 47:12?"

"That's the one."

"You know what, this stuff is all a little intense. Witchcraft. Bible prophecy. Maybe we should go."

"Yeah, we've seen it; no sense in staring at it all night."

Ryan let the scrap of paper in his hand fall to the ground. He climbed back out of the circle and they walked back among the graves toward the crossroads near the center of the cemetery.

"I've read that crossroads are the most haunted places in the world," Zoe noted.

"Well then we better avoid it. Didn't you say it has been a little too intense in here tonight? Come on, let's turn off the path and I'll walk you out."

"Oh you don't have to do that."

But Ryan insisted that he at least walk Zoe toward the exit. He did not again offer to walk her out of the cemetery though. He secretly did not want to stray so far from his things he left in the woods. She declined his offer, however.

"I'm parked at the gas station. It's not far and I'll be OK. Where are you parked?" She insisted.

Ryan replied indifferently, "North."

She gave a perplexed look.

"Just trust me."

"OK, well, have a good night. It was good to see you again." And with that remark she walked west toward the Byron Street exit.

Ryan sat on a headstone and watched her until she was out of sight, then sprinted back to the woods to find his stuff. It was undisturbed. Now, approaching the third watch of the night, he walked out of the trees and back to his car. There were no cars on the road at this hour and all the houses were dark. He kept the shovel tucked partially in his coat, but there was little risk of being seen. All that was left to do was bring the bones to the morgue at St. John's Hospital. They would be picked up after sunrise by a mortician and money would be left in an envelope for Ryan. That being accomplished, he could go home and get a little sleep.

Idelette had watched their entire interaction with great interest. After Ryan finally disappeared into the woods she went to investigate the circle to see what had delayed them so long there. She stood along the perimeter with a grave expression on her face as she stared down at the peculiar symbols. After a protracted amount of time spent committing it all to memory, she could only sigh as she pondered the evil all around. She had heard the conversation and Ryan's quotation of Isaiah echoed in her mind as she walked. Her hand grasped her Bible even more tightly as she finally turned away and descended the slope out of the trees and traipsed back among the graves. The cemetery was completely still except for the vampire. Her boots dragged as she walked toward the office building. Nearly there she located the iron lid covering a concrete well which was about four feet deep and similarly broad. It contained a sump pump that was seldom used. She lowered herself down into the hole and pulled the iron lid back over the opening. She could sleep here through the daylight with little threat of being discovered. In her last moments of wakefulness, she pondered what she had seen tonight. But as she fell asleep her dreams brought only terrible memories of her village and the days following that first murder.

Chapter 6

"Dom Calmet," Idelette stormed into her priest's office, "I saw someone last night. Someone was out on the hills. I saw him pass through a clearing in the trees!"

"Are you sure it was a person that you saw? When did you see this?" The cleric replied, looking up from his missal.

"It was last night as I returned home from Benjamin's funeral. I stopped and looked out at the forest. I am sure that I saw somebody. Who could possibly have been outside the village wall that late? I think it was the murderer."

"That is a tremendous leap that you are making. Are you even sure that it was a person you saw? No doubt it was very dark. It may have been an animal."

"It was not an animal. I'm certain of that. I think it was the murderer. Most of the people in the village are saying that Benjamin was killed by a phantom or goblin. They say it was certainly the Devil. What if the Devil really has come to our village? What if—"

"What do you know about the Devil, Idelette?" Dom Calmet interrupted.

"I know that he was once an angel. But he fell and now he is evil. He is determined to undermine Christ's efforts."

"Good. What else?"

"I know that he has no power over Christ. And I know what you are doing, Dom Calmet. I know that the Devil is weak and that his ruin has already been decided, as you have preached in your homilies. But what about Benjamin? What explanation do you have for all of us who are scared for our lives?"

"The Devil does not have authority to kill. His influence is everywhere, Idelette, but he is only one—albeit the worst—of many evils in the world. I don't know what killed Benjamin but the answers are in prayer. If we petition Heaven with prayers, Christ will deliver us."

"Do you believe it could have been a goblin?" Idelette probed. "What if it was a witch? Or a vampire? I've only heard stories and I don't know what to think; you are educated, Dom Calmet. What do your studies tell you about the phantom world?"

"Idelette, I am convinced of the reality of such creatures, and am certain that they exist to distract Christians from their faith in God. I have seen and read of many things that have unusual explanations. Recently I read of little flames spurting up from the graves of churchyards. Though they appear supernatural, it seems the flames are actually the result of vapors being emitted from the bodies below, which then ignite when exposed to the heat of the sun. Still, other phenomena defy explanation. I have read about turning lead into gold by using incantations," he rambled, barely on topic. "I have read of malformed people with no body, but their arms and legs arise directly from their enlarged heads. I have read of witches directing venomous effluvia from one village to the next, causing great suffering and death. I have read of still stranger things which I need not burden you with. All manner of phenomena exist and the spirit world is a reality, Idelette. Evil is a part of this world. Do not think on it—pray about it. It is as I said; Christ will deliver us."

Conceding, though still not fully satisfied with the answer, the young woman left the priest to his missal. She vacated the church and ambled toward home. As she passed through the church yard she took greater notice of the dark tombstones. Many were greatly worn and tilting. Their inscriptions were faded and patches of lichen covered the letters. She watched the ground closely for any little flames, but she saw none. Why had she never seen such a thing before? Her morbid curiosity provoked her. She watched Benjamin's grave closely as she walked because his corpse was the most recently buried. Perhaps it was the most likely to emit combustible vapors. She saw no flames over his grave though. Entirely distracted she stumbled over a tree root. She managed not to fall, but this brought her mind back to reality. Suddenly the events of the previous night rushed through her brain. She turned her eye toward the forest beyond the village and scanned the trees and the clearings for anything unusual. But she saw nothing.

Shortly before reaching her home she saw Conrad approaching from the opposite side of the village. He appeared to be returning from the forest with hares. Their eyes met briefly and they came to a stop before one another. It was obvious that they had been thinking about each other. And likely they were both thinking about the events of yesterday. Idelette thought for a moment about her appearance and tried to quickly brush her hair out of her face. She hoped he hadn't seen her trip on that root a few minutes ago.

"Hello, Idelette," Conrad spoke first.

"Hello," Idelette replied softly, looking up just enough to make eye contact.

"Are you doing alright since yesterday? It was a gory scene and not something a woman needs to see with her own eyes," Conrad continued.

"I'm fine. Though, I confess that I am a little frightened by the whole situation. The entire village is talking about it. Everyone is certain that some monster or demon has come to our village. Dom Calmet told me not to think on it. He said just to keep praying. But I can't stop thinking about it long enough to pray," Idelette confessed.

"Listen, I think the people are right to be concerned—and so are you. Benjamin wasn't just killed. He was mutilated. You saw the condition he was in. Who would do something like that? It was no animal because his bundle of fish was untouched. A bear or wolf would hardly resist the temptation of freshly caught fish. It could not have been a person who committed this atrocity. Why would they? No one begrudged Benjamin. He was highly esteemed. And even in murders of rage I've never heard of a person mutilating another the way he was. Wicked people may murder strangers, or even their neighbor, but they don't mangle them as though in a frenzy. I think you are right to dwell on these things and to fear that this may be the Devil's work. If not Satan himself, some Hellish minion of his may be lurking in that forest. I have heard stories, Idelette, about vampires and wolfmen which heed no commands from Heaven and which commit such evil acts. I fear for the people of this village. I think there is even more evil approaching. I agree with Dom Calmet; don't think on it. Pray."

"I don't even know which saints to petition for something like this," she sighed.

"I'm not sure it matters. I have to return to my work though."

And with that he abruptly departed.

Many long hours elapsed as Idelette whiled away the melancholy day. She accomplished some various chores but her mind was never on what she was doing. In her distraction she found herself needlessly repeating several tasks. Finally, recognizing it was futile, she quit trying.

The yellow sun rolled across the sky and the shadows crept from west to east. Clouds drifted in and hung mysteriously low over the village. A dark sky had formed in the east as the now-orange sun was nearing the western horizon, when suddenly a distant and visceral scream aroused Idelette from her sullen thoughts. She rushed to her window and looked to see what was transpiring. Men were running from all directions toward the apparent source of the noise, and women were gathering children into their homes. Idelette dashed out of her house and sprinted down the path, desperate to know what had happened.

Having joined the crowd, she ran beyond the gates, across the fields, and up to the forest's edge. It would be dark soon and the storm clouds had now covered much of the sky. The red sun had set low enough to shine below the clouds and cast ghastly shadows through the trees. In that eerie light everyone stopped and silently stared at the macabre spectacle strewn before them.

Two bodies lay in the ferns just inside the tree line. Their flesh was severely torn in several locations. But there was something strange about the corpses. Dom Calmet arrived last, as his age did not permit him to run swiftly with the young men. Once he regained his breath, he again assigned two men to return to the village for a cart to transport the bodies. He also instructed them to notify others to prepare graves, coffins, and markers. Then he began to inquire into the situation at hand.

"Who screamed?" Dom Calmet asked.

"I did," an elderly woman, named Mrs. Freiberg, spoke up.

"I was out gathering kindling. Conrad happened upon me and suggested that we head back into the village because the weather was turning dark and stormy. We were almost out of the trees when we happened upon the bodies. It took me a moment to recognize them as Martin and John, but when I did.... I didn't even realize I had screamed. But I suppose I must have, and it must have been awfully loud."

"Thank you," said Dom Calmet. "Conrad, is this correct? What were you doing in the forest before you crossed the path of Mrs. Freiberg?"

"Actually, I wasn't. I had seen her walking out here while I was still in the village. I came out here looking for her specifically because I was concerned for her safety," Conrad noted.

"You are a true neighbor to us all, Conrad." Then, turning from the crowd, the priest mumbled to himself, "now let us address the nature of this crime. These bodies are greatly torn and their skin is pale. Yet, where is the blood? The ground and the ferns remain completely clean," he muttered his thoughts aloud to no one, although everyone could hear him.

"Their blood was consumed!" Idelette exclaimed suddenly. "Dear God help us! These men were our friends! I stood near them at Benjamin's funeral! Now look at the evil that has befallen them—and us! Dom Calmet, we all know what drinks the blood of good Christians. What shall we do now?" The crowd murmured and grew restless as her words sank into their collective psyche.

"Dear girl," Dom Calmet soothed, "do not be alarmed. I do confess that I fear you are correct. But, I tell you again, do not be alarmed. This sin is treacherous and a vampire would use our fears to undo us. So do not let yourself succumb to it. Be clear-minded and self-controlled so you can pray."

The crowd felt fear creep upon them. The sun was rapidly sinking below the horizon and the starless sky was overtaking them in darkness. People mumbled and muttered about what was to happen to the village. Stories of vampires were common in Europe and sundry versions of them had reached their ears from neighboring villages. Now the nightmare was upon them. And so was night.

Presently men came with a bier for the bodies. The mob of people walked swiftly back to the village with the gruesome cargo in their midst. People watched in fear as they approached the village wall. As they passed through the gate the whole village joined them in a procession to the graveyard.

Dom Calmet read the mass as Martin and John were buried near the spot where Benjamin's corpse also now reposed. A somber silence had overtaken the whole of the village as they watched the interment of their departed friends. Then suddenly someone spoke up.

"Suppose they become vampires now! What are we to do?"

The whole crowd erupted in pandemonium. Women wept on their husband's shoulders and children clung to their mother's dresses. The men tried to feign courage but everyone felt the same fear overtaking them. Someone suggested salt should be poured over the graves. Another said that they must be overlaid with iron. Still another insisted on beheading the corpses and wedging large stones in their mouths. Someone else suggested destroying the hearts. As this debate continued, a barn owl suddenly flew out of the church belfry and over the graveyard. Everyone stopped arguing as their attention was immediately arrested by the bird flying silently over them. The owl was ghastly white and glowing. Glowing! With a soft blue hue emanating from its feathers it glided over the crowd, out of the village, and into the forest. The ghostly glow of that phantom owl was an omen of conviction.

Everyone knew that it was the fabled will-o'-the-wisp which carried the souls of the recently dead away. All their arguing about the bodies was now too late! This otherworldly creature soared over the tree tops until it disappeared in the pines beyond a clearing. That particular point rendered the experience all the more terrifying to Idelette. The owl vanished precisely where she had seen the murderer before!

She grew faint at the thought, then swooned and fell hard to the ground. Blackness overtook her. When she awoke she did not know where she was. She felt trapped in oppressive darkness and the air was close. She gradually recognized the concrete walls around her and the sump pump beside her. She slowly lifted the heavy iron lid above her and confirmed that it was again night. The day had passed uneventfully. She climbed up out of the hole and looked to the stars above the office building in Greenwood. Her right hand slid instinctively into her coat pocket and confirmed that the Bible was still there. She was thirsty and there were distant voices in the graveyard—then a camera flash. Idelette cringed with disgust.

Ghost hunters.

Chapter 7

Detectives Malli and Jameson traipsed through a landfill toward the spot where a body had been found. They were too well dressed for this sort of thing and their shoes were definitely suboptimal. The squishy puddles of rank garbage spattered foul-smelling drops onto their pant legs from below. Seagulls, still mysteriously circling in the night sky, threatened to soil their clothes from above. It was warm out. Flies were everywhere. Every time one landed on Detective Jameson he wondered what putrid place it had just left.

"People worked here all day but we don't get dragged out until after sunset?" Malli muttered to Jameson as she shined a flashlight down into a puddle to keep her partner from stepping in it.

"I called my supervisor as soon as I saw it," the employee responded as he led them to the body. "It was the end of my shift though and the sun was still up then."

"Do you think it arrived here today?" Asked Jameson.

"No, probably not. I think this trash was dumped in the last day or two though."

"Any way of identifying where it came from?" Detective Malli followed.

"Not likely. I can narrow it down to the garbage routes for the last few days from the various municipalities we serve, but that is still a very, very large area."

"Well maybe we can get an idea based on what else is around her. In the meantime we need to call the medical examiner's office. And while I do that my partner can start searching the system for missing persons," she replied.

"Are you pretty confident this garbage was dumped here yesterday or the day before?" Detective Jameson chimed in.

"Yeah, I think so. I know trucks were unloading here, and the body is not too far in among the debris. How are you going to get her down and out of there? Do you need us to bring around an excavator or do you have crime scene people who do that?"

"We'll make that decision after everything is photographed and the MEI has done their job. The law says we can't move the body until they give the OK."

"MEI?" The man asked with a puzzled expression.

"Medical Examiner Investigator," Malli sort of explained as she dialed her phone.

While Detective Malli called the medical examiner, her partner called the station to ask if there had been any missing persons reported in the last three days.

"I have a potential hit," Jameson shouted to Malli. "A girl went missing from the shopping mall a few days ago. Purple hair. Could be her. We can easily find out when the dumpsters were picked up from that mall."

"What's the name?"

"Cheryl something or other. I don't remember. They're emailing the report to me."

"Who reported her missing?"

"Her parents. She had been shopping with some friends. Apparently they parted ways in a clothing store for a while, lost track of her, and eventually called her folks to see if she had come home," Jameson added.

"Well, it would appear that she hadn't. The MEI is texting. She is on her way."

"How long until she arrives?"

"She's 20 minutes away," Malli sighed, still looking down at her phone.

"Ask her which doc will get the case."

"Does it matter?" she quipped as she typed.

"Not really I guess."

"She says the autopsy will be tomorrow and Dr. Rezek and Dr. Millard divide the cases in the morning."

"Well, for now let's find out about trash pickup from that mall," Detective Jameson suggested.

"Is there anything we can do to keep these seagulls away while we process the scene?"

"Not much. Running the engines on the dozers helps a little but wastes gas and you have to put up with the noise," the man replied.

"Since when are seagulls nocturnal, anyway?"

"They will settle down as the night cools but they always stay active later here because the machines have finally shut off."

"What can we cover her with?"

"When I found her she was under a big sheet of cardboard. I could just see part of her face under it. That's probably why the birds and bugs hadn't found her yet."

"Well where is that sheet of cardboard now?"

The man pointed behind him. There was a large piece of cardboard now mostly laying in a putrid puddle several feet away.

"Do you have any tarps or anything?" Jameson sighed.

"No. I suppose you can search for one in the heaps of garbage if you want."

"Not a chance. We at least need to keep the critters away from the body as much as is possible. Stand right over there for me would you? Maybe that will help keep gulls away while I call the city waste management department and figure out when they pick up trash from the mall."

"Anything?" Detective Jameson asked optimistically a few minutes later. He saw the frustrated look on Malli's face however as she hung up her phone.

"The main number goes to a voicemail. Unions, right? We'll need to get security footage from the mall. I suppose we can probably narrow that down after we speak to the friends though. Hopefully they still remember where they parked and which stores they went to."

"It's a little hard to see from here but she looks mostly intact," Jameson shined his flashlight up onto her face. "Looks like her face is pretty clean, what of it I can see anyway. No significant injuries at least. I bet we'll be able to just do a visual ID."

"I hope so. If not though, maybe dental. I would prefer to avoid asking the family for DNA swabs."

"Does the ME do their own identifications?"

"Sometimes. We can ask about it when their investigator gets here and the body is accessible."

Chapter 8

Listening to the banter halfway across the graveyard, it occurred to Idelette that the hour must be later than she had thought. Over the years she had noticed that, for whatever reason, ghost hunters typically wander into cemeteries around midnight. It seemed to be residue from high school readings of Edgar Allan Poe smeared across their collective psyche. Unfortunately, any genius in Poe they may have encountered clearly never made its requisite cerebral dent. The ghost hunting routine was consistently a spectacle of ineptitude. Idelette had seen it many times and only cultivated more disdain with each new exposure to it. In the seventeenth and eighteenth centuries it consisted of bells on string tied across doors, and flour poured on the stairs. In the nineteenth century seances and daguerreotypes were added to the debacle. Things were really not any more impressive today. The modern routine had become predictable and equally ineffective.

Teams of charlatans lug cameras and recording equipment into houses, factories, and graveyards. They always have gadgets that supposedly monitor electrostatic activity, but can't explain why or how they know that it proves anything. As a consequence of the previously-mentioned Poe residue, they usually try to have their equipment set up before midnight—apparently that is a very active time for the dead? The results of these ridiculous escapades are generally a bunch of audio recordings with no content (though the occasional whisper from one of the group members may be pawned off as a voice from beyond the grave), hours of video showing nothing but malnourished people smoking, and a lot of out-of-focus photographs accidentally capturing passing moths and dust which are then claimed as conclusive evidence of spirits in the form of orbs. Idelette found these people insufferable. Presently, though, she was thirsty. And the opportunity was now.

She wasted no time but turned toward the crossroads at the center of the cemetery. She hastened toward her prey. There were three of them, dressed in the usual black t-shirts, black hoodies, and black jeans. They laughed and bantered loudly as they took pointless photographs while meandering down the path toward the back of Greenwood. Idelette noticed that their car was parked inside the cemetery. She paused to glance inside. There might be even easier prey still in the car. She could carry them off without the other group even noticing until they returned to their vehicle. Seeing that it was empty though, she continued to follow. The vampire approached them from behind. Her boots were silent on the path. Her right hand grasped the Bible in her coat pocket. Two of the ghost hunters led the way while a third was just a few steps behind. Idelette could easily kill all three but there was utility to be had in only killing one. She selected her victim as she picked up pace, rapidly attaining inhuman speed.

Silently closing in on the group, she accomplished the last few yards in an instant. At the last moment she relented her grip on her Bible, and withdrew her right hand from her coat pocket. She grabbed the lagging man by the hair, covered his mouth with her left hand, and without slowing down, changed course by 90 degrees. She dragged the man off the path—soaring among the headstones—and in a few seconds they were in the grove of trees which bordered Byron Street. Having thrown the man to the ground, she put her knee on his chest, then paused for just the briefest of moments to look him in the eye. Unable to strain against her remarkable strength, his eyes darted about until he could only stare back at her with a bewildered expression.

Before he could even attempt to speak, she broke the silence, "'Do not long for the night, when people vanish in their place.' Then she held his head back, and sank her teeth into his throat. He writhed for a few moments but rapidly weakened from lack of cerebral perfusion. His hyperventilation became erratic with lengthening periods of apnea between uncoordinated breaths. He died helplessly. With the dead man's blood dripping down a few strands of her hair, Idelette rose feeling replenished and repulsive. Stepping over the corpse and out of the trees, a shudder went down her spine as she reached her right hand into her pocket and once again grasped her Bible.

Meanwhile, the other two ghost hunters had only just noticed that their companion was missing. They had walked merely ten or twelve yards in the time it took Idelette to kill him. Now they were nearly in the northern most recess of the cemetery. Idelette watched from near the crossroads as confusion and frustration began to overtake them.

They called out for their friend, shouting things such as "this isn't funny," and asking "where could he have disappeared to?" as they searched in vain. Bewildered, they wandered about the entire graveyard for nearly an hour, calling out again and again to their dead friend. They received no answer. With unlaughing sarcasm, the vampire thought maybe they should have clicked on their electrostatic gizmo to see if he was a ghost. The confounded ghost hunters considered calling the police but after some deliberation felt they would only bring suspicion on themselves—after all, it must just be a prank. Idelette returned to the crossroads at the center of the graveyard and climbed to the top of a sepulchre. She lay there looking out at the stars. Her hand probed the Bible in her pocket and she listened to the two fools slowly give up and return to their car. They turned onto Byron Street and went south. Idelette knew they would return to retrace their steps. It was a guaranteed meal in the near future.

Ryan also watched. He had heard them calling somebody's name as he walked in from the southwest. Their voices moved about randomly but he soon located them. He sat up on a large family headstone and watched them eventually give up. As the two drove away he hopped down and proceeded north. He did not know what had happened but he surmised that the lost individual was in the trees somewhere north of the cemetery—not amongst the graves themselves. Most ghost hunters are actually too spineless to cross the tree line that forms the northern boundary of Greenwood cemetery. This missing person was either dead or intoxicated in the woods. Ryan entered the trees at the northeast corner and worked his way west toward Byron Street. He was not certain that he would find anyone but this path would take him to the circle. That was the real reason he came back tonight anyway. As he stalked through the woods he considered what had happened and wondered how it all fit into the events of last night. Maybe those responsible for tonight's disappearance, and those who tagged the circle were the same. But who were they? Had he encountered them already in his resurrectionist work but didn't even know it? The circle had clearly been used for some sort of rite. He hadn't seen anything like that while grave robbing before. Something new was happening. He had sensed someone watching before. Someone was watching now, too.

Ryan emerged from the trees, crossed the service drive at the back of Greenwood, and was about to ascend the slope up to the circle when he observed someone walking toward him along the path from the Byron entrance. She was quite aware of him also and he was momentarily on open ground. So much for quiet observation.

She was blonde, pale, and rather thin. Prettier than not, she wore boots and a long black coat, and was looking right at Ryan. She looked to be in her early thirties. Conspicuously keeping one hand in her coat pocket while the other arm stayed at her side, the woman walked confidently up to him.

"Do you know what time it is, exactly?" Idelette initiated the interaction.

"A little after eleven," Ryan replied. This was the person who had been watching him last night. He knew it but didn't know how he knew it. More importantly, he thought he smelled blood.

"Really!" She exclaimed at the news about the time. It was earlier than she had thought.

"What's your name?" Ryan calmly asked, keeping his demeanor.

She hesitated for a moment. "Idelette. What's yours?"

"Ryan." He paused. "Do you smell blood?"

Startled by the question, she was struck mute. It was a provocative thought. Her senses were aroused at the mere mention of it. Who would ask such a question? How could she possibly respond? She had just fed and yet this mere question brought on powerful thirst. He was all alone. It would be an easy kill. Why not a second victim? Yet, she knew he was here for something important because he had been so disconcerted about the witchcraft in the circle. She was disconcerted too. Maybe it would be prudent to leave him alive. She wanted to see how that situation would ultimately unfold. Who were these witches? Who was Ryan? She gripped her ancient Bible with impassioned self-torment.

"Should I smell blood?" she finally said in a voice that betrayed her thoughts.

"I'm going up to the circle," he conspicuously ignored her question. "Would you care to join me?" motioning his eyes in the intended direction.

"No, thank you. I've seen it. And it is concerning." With this remark she walked past him, up the service drive, and out the foot path that connects to Byron Street.

Ryan continued up to the circle, noted that nothing had changed since yesterday, and then listened for his new acquaintance. But she was gone. He realized he had not checked the trees along Byron. That was the direction Idelette had approached from. He hastened to the spot and searched among the trees. He knew he smelled blood. As he searched frantically, he suddenly felt flesh. He quickly brushed away piles of old dead leaves and found the body of the missing ghost hunter. There was a gaping defect on the left side of his neck. He couldn't ignore the fact that it sort of looked like a bite mark. There was a small amount of blood spattered on his chin and shoulder but none in the leaves. His thoughts raced to put all the pieces together. Who was Idelette? What had been going on at the circle? Idelette knew about it but apparently didn't know who was involved. Why had Zoe been there so randomly the night before? Her story about thrill seeking in the graveyard was obviously a fabrication. It actually sounded scripted. And then Idelette again—she likely killed this ghost hunter. But why? That couldn't really be a bite mark though. That's nonsense.

Reigning in his tumultuous thoughts, Ryan reburied the body under the leaves then headed for home. He had not found what he was looking for in Greenwood, but the story was clearly evolving.

Meanwhile, Idelette was in a frenzy. She was completely overcome by the craving. She could normally go a couple days without blood and feel only minimal thirst. There was something in the conversation with Ryan that sparked it though. And now she needed it! She had to find a second victim and fast. She hurried down Byron, turned right on Ragner, and entered Tyler Memorial Gardens on the north side of Ragner, near the park. Her right hand felt the clasps on her Bible. She just needed to collect her thoughts, that's all. She just needed to calm herself and work through it, as she had so many times before. But then she saw them.

An extremely large, rather dim looking individual in his late twenties was standing near his pickup truck parked at the back of the graveyard. With him was a small blonde girl who looked to be about sixteen. Idelette ran straight for them. The trees and tombstones blurred as she crossed the cemetery in an instant. She grabbed the girl's hair with her left hand, yanked her head back, and sank her teeth into the girl's neck. The warm blood flowed quickly and forcefully. She sucked it down frantically.

The man fell back against his truck and sank to the ground, dumbfounded and panic-stricken at what he had just seen. Idelette let the girl's nearly bloodless corpse fall and then she looked at the hyperventilating man who peered up at her. There was blood all over her. She stared at him for a long moment. It would be too much to kill him too. Three bodies in two cemeteries in one night would be a lot. The police search would go on for days and days. But this guy looked pretty easy to mesmerize and could prove to be useful as a scapegoat.

"Now then," she said at last to the still silent and trembling man, "I will dispose of the body, but what am I to do with you? I think you know how to save your life. Your silence is not enough. I need your cooperation. I don't work miracles. I can hide her body but I can't make it disappear. If it is found though...what are you to do? Someone probably knows that she was with you tonight. If the body is found and the cops come asking, you will confess to the murder. Pay attention now! You will confess. Because if you don't, I will be forced to kill you too. So the choice is yours. One, you can leave and hope that nothing happens. Two, you can leave and if she is found you get to keep your life, but keep it in prison. Or, three, you can die right now—painfully. Look at the dead girl and look at her blood on me. I will let you live, but you will confess if anyone comes asking."

The dim-witted man agreed but he did not know why. Something in him was compelling him to cooperate. He knew it was all wrong but he submitted anyway. He got in his truck and left for home, still alive and still terrified. Idelette picked up the body, slung it over her shoulder, and carried it north through the woods. She left it on the banks of the creek north of Ragner Park as she set her coat on a branch and waded in to wash the blood off herself. She knew the girl would decompose quickly in the moist environment and the summer sun. Even if the body was found, the soft tissue evidence would be gone soon, thanks to the robust insect activity. That done, she grabbed her coat and followed the trail along the stream to the old abandoned slaughter house. It was merely a doorless, windowless, concrete infrastructure now, covered in graffiti and infiltrated with plant life. But it was a popular place for criminal activity.

Entering the building she found only two meth-heads just starting their trip. She picked them each up and threw them out the door behind her. They landed about 50 feet away. Terror-struck, despite their altered state of mind, they ran. Idelette did not watch. She put her hand in her pocket to let her fingers study the Bible therein while her eyes surveyed the graffiti on the walls. It was just like the graffiti she had seen in the circle in Greenwood. Old gang symbols were painted over with satanic and wiccan symbolism. Having seen it, she climbed up onto the rooftop and sat down to contemplate the disheartening situation. The night was young yet—only a little after 1:00 AM—but she needed to think.

Idelette listened to the nearby brook, babbling as it passed under the old railroad bridge, and stared up at the stars. Saturn was in Virgo. It was thirty years since it was last in Virgo, and would be another thirty years before it would be in Virgo again. Its astrological symbol is that of a sickle, implying seasons, and it is a marker of time and mortality. Most mortals would not live long enough to see the completion of three Saturnian years. Idelette had seen far more. A gentle breeze rustled the leaves around her and brought her mind back to the present. She turned her attention to recent events, thinking long and hard about the evil around her. She cringed with an overwhelming feeling of self-loathing as she considered her own actions and she lamented her existence.

"I have seen affliction under the rod of your wrath, O you who lives forever," she began to pray. "You have made my flesh and my skin waste away, and have made me dwell in darkness like the dead of long ago." She took the Bible from her pocket and was about to open it when suddenly she realized people were approaching.

From Byron Street a hearse drove to the lot behind the factory and parked. A man in a suit got out and walked the two-track to the clearing by the slaughter house. Simultaneously, four girls crossed the railroad bridge from the east and entered the clearing opposite the suited man. Idelette felt a foreboding uneasiness creep upon her mind. She felt the oppressive presence of sin. Then she realized she recognized one of the girls. It was Zoe, the girl who spoke with Ryan last night. Idelette eased herself down the back side of the building and entered it through a window. From there she watched. One of the girls walked in to make sure the place was empty. Idelette could move faster than a person can turn their eye in its socket. Staying ahead of the girl's peripheral vision she darted silently around the room as the girl scanned her surroundings. Satisfied that the building was empty, the girl walked back out. Idelette returned to the window and studied the situation.

The four girls approached and surrounded the man. He was apparently a mortician, judging by attire and hearse, though she could not see his face due to several branches in the way. He presented them with a package and they gave him an envelope in return. Zoe was visibly uneasy. None of the other girls seemed to be similarly agitated. Idelette noticed her persistently looking about with grave concern during this brief exchange. It was as though she knew something the others did not, and it troubled her, like an animal that seeks shelter from a coming storm before humans notice any change in the weather. No discussion took place during the transaction. As soon as they had swapped parcels, the four girls walked urgently back the way they had come, and the man returned to his hearse and drove off. Zoe turned and walked backward for several paces, all the while looking about with a discerning intent, she almost looked paranoid. But then she turned again and caught up with the other girls as they vanished down the trail.

Idelette felt like a great burden had been lifted. It was as though the devil himself had passed by amid that rendezvous. She realized it was time for her to leave too though. She was too near the body of the girl she left by the stream. And after what she had just witnessed, it was likely that a strong police presence was impending before morning light. Something nefarious was afoot. And Idelette was leaving a trail of bodies that crossed these girls' path, literally. There was no way that police would not be involved, and soon. Scent hounds might come during the search, and she hadn't gotten all the blood off of her clothes. So to keep the trail circular and seemingly futile, she doubled back to Greenwood. She walked to the office building and noticed that a small pane of glass was missing from the window at the back of the attic. She climbed up to it, put her arm through the opening and unlatched the window. She climbed in and settled under a tarp behind some old boxes. It was only 2 AM but she still needed time to think. She set her mind towards unraveling this enigma as she again pulled the Bible from her pocket. She missed Dom Calmet and her thoughts drifted back through the centuries to the night when she first saw the glowing owl.

Chapter 9

Waking with a gasp, Idelette sat up immediately. She collected her thoughts as she studied the room around her. It was very dark but for a single candle. She smelled old paper. As her eyes adjusted she recognized Dom Calmet's office and she began to remember what had happened. She had seen that terrible owl take flight as everyone stood around the graves of the recently buried dead. She had fainted and Dom Calmet must have brought her into his office. It appeared that he had prepared a bed for her using a pair of benches and some blankets. But she was certainly alone in the room and did not even know how much time had passed.

She rose from the impromptu bed, took the candle in hand, and slowly proceeded up the winding stairs toward the sanctuary. The candle seemed to make every stone move in the dark and it terribly hindered her night vision. She held it low to her side so she could see beyond the flame, but then it caused her shadow to lengthen on the wall and this filled her with fear. Scared of her own shadow, she set the candle on a stand at the top of the stairs and cautiously tip-toed across the back of the sanctuary toward the door. Faint starlight was shining in through the gaps between the doors. She now faced a long walk across the village back to her home—and she did not know which was worse—beginning this terrible journey by stepping out immediately into the graveyard, or having her back to the graveyard the rest of the way home. She drew a long soft breath and was about to open the doors when she suddenly noticed someone on the steps! She gasped just a little.

"Dom Calmet?" a male voice inquired in a low tone.

Idelette knew that voice. It was Conrad. She was sure of it. What was he doing here? She opened the door just enough and slipped out of the church and onto the steps.

"Idelette!" Conrad exclaimed in little more than a whisper. "Are you alright? I was worried about you." And, indeed he looked deeply troubled as he spoke.

"Yes," she responded in tones lower than a whisper, "I'm doing just fine now—but what hour is it?"

"It is nearing midnight. You have been asleep for only a short while."

She remembered that twilight was just beginning to creep in when they all saw the owl. The owl! She turned her gaze to the forest and strained to see the clearing in the distance. It was too dark. She turned back and looked to the graves of her recently-murdered neighbors. The graves appeared undisturbed. She looked to Conrad.

"It's alright. I've been here the entire time," he consoled.

"What happened after I fainted?"

"Please, sit with me here on the steps and we can discuss many things."

The two of them sat down beside one another on the top step and looked out across the graveyard to the village. The night air was cool but not uncomfortably so. The sky was becoming mostly cloudy, and only rarely would a star show itself through the firmament. The forest rustled softly in the distance as an occasional breeze passed among the dark trees. The village was obscured in deep darkness as well, with only a few scattered windows admitting soft candlelight. They sat in silence for some time.

"I've never seen such a fearful night," Idelette interrupted the silence. "It is as though I have found myself in a nightmare. Have you ever seen such things as those which transpired tonight?" She looked to Conrad for his reply.

"It is a lonely night but for you," Conrad responded without looking at her. "And it may be a nightmare, indeed. I apologize. I owe you an answer to your earlier question. After you fainted Dom Calmet urged everyone to return to their homes. It was not an easy thing to convince people that they should part company from one another. I suppose there is comfort to be found in a crowd. I picked you up in my arms and carried you into the church as Dom Calmet ushered everyone out of the churchyard. No one knew how to proceed. Even a simple thing like walking from the church to their homes had become a strange and daunting task. They constantly shifted their eyes from the forest to the graves and back again. They muttered and mumbled and shuffled about. Some of the women were crying—and many children too. I think it frightened the youngest ones to see their mothers in tears. Once everyone had finally dispersed, Dom Calmet came into the church and directed me down the stairs to his office. We placed two benches together and laid you upon them with some blankets."

"Thank you," she interjected.

"You're welcome. Dom Calmet said he would stay up to see you when you woke. I told him I would be happy to watch over you and he should get to bed. Too much falls on his shoulders. And he is not a young man. He reluctantly agreed and retired for the night as I stepped out onto this porch and set my mind to the task of pondering what is yet to come."

"I shudder to think."

"Not one of us knows with any certainty what we are up against. Not one of us has ever been confronted by a vampire. People are terrified. But having now had a chance to grapple with the matter, I have reached some possible conclusions."

"How can we conclude anything?" Idelette interrupted. "If none of us have ever experienced anything like this? I've never even read about such things—only heard stories from travelers passing through."

Conrad looked her in the eye briefly, surprised to learn that the young woman could read. "Well, I have heard numerous tales as well. And though I have never encountered a vampire, some years ago I spent a few seasons in a village which was plagued by attacks from some other menace. People swore that they saw the creature. Some were convinced it was a werewolf. I don't know whatever became of it because I moved away after a short time. But I did see how people were stricken with fear and panic without reason. So, I have seen what we should not do."

"Were you not also terrified?"

"You and I have seen corpses drained of their blood. Now an unknown person or thing has apparently begun to abide near our town. Can there be any doubt that there is a vampire in our presence? And yet, you and I are sitting here unharmed. The same was true in that other village with the so-called werewolf. I took confidence in our numbers and the randomness of the attacks. I felt confident that I would not fall victim."

She was struck by his logic. "So what do you feel is to happen here? What do you know about vampires and how shall we protect ourselves?"

"Are you certain that you want to have this conversation, Idelette? My thoughts on this are not pleasant."

"I am certain," she nodded.

"Very well. But please do not hold my words against me. I am not in the habit of speaking on such vile topics with a beautiful woman." Conrad noticed a blush come over her on hearing these words. "I do not wish to sour your thoughts of me but if you are certain then I will proceed."

"Yes, please continue."

"Very well. I have heard that a vampire is an insatiable creature. It craves human blood at all times and will murder indiscriminately. Vampires are the cursed dead perpetuated in their sin. And because they are dead, they are not easily killed. The vampire will survive in its undead state even after sustaining many mortal wounds. It is swift and strong. To kill the fiend, you must decapitate it or pierce or burn its heart, and—once it is dead—stuff its mouth with garlic—which is poison to it. However, they also have weaknesses. They burn in sunlight, cannot tolerate Christian artifacts, and must sleep on soil from their native country. And while sleeping after feeding, some lie engorged in blood like a saturated sponge. Blood seeps from them. Have I said too much?"

"No. Please continue." Idelette had been listening intently. Her mouth gaped slightly in astonishment.

"As you wish. I think this vampire is here for no other purpose than to drink the blood of whoever it so pleases. It is irrational and does not care what town it happens to find or what innocent people it causes to suffer. Doubtless it moves throughout the land and indulges its murderous cravings. It will keep killing people as long as we allow it to survive."

"Conrad, if you are correct, and all these things are true, then what are we to do? What can we do?" she interrupted, looking deep into his eyes.

"We must prepare. That is precisely what I have been scheming as I sat here alone. We cannot presume that this will eventually pass us by. We must ready the entire village. We shall strengthen the wall around the town. We will arm the people with whatever is available. And we shall pray, just as Dom Calmet has always instructed us to do."

"I'm so glad that you are here with me tonight," she sighed. "I have been sorely afraid since this all began. Thank you for being so bold while I wrestle with my fears."

"I am glad for your company as well. And I think your words betray bolder thoughts than you are willing to admit. But should I not get you home? It is late and you have so much weighing on your heart. You should sleep. Come, let me walk you."

She consented and the two traversed the village to her home. The night was terrible and every dark space in the village seemed to be a cauldron of evil. Idelette was comforted by Conrad's company but she wrestled with a strange mixture of emotions. She could not stop thinking about what horror each moment might bring, but she also recognized a strange new affection for Conrad. He delivered her safely home and went his own way once she was inside. It was such a pleasant feeling to be cared for. But how could she have such thoughts during such dark times? Still, she could not deny a certain attraction which she felt for him. In fact, she suddenly realized that she could not stop thinking about him.

Amid her thoughts of Conrad she opened her front door again to peek out across the village. Perhaps she could catch a glimpse of him still on his way home. But when she opened her door, she was surprised to see someone else right outside her home.

"Oh. Good evening, Kurt. How are you?" Idelette asked politely but somewhat reluctantly.

"I'm doing very well, thank you. I was just passing by. How have you been, Idelette?" Kurt was a shorter but strongly built man who occasionally spoke with Idelette, but she was never particularly comfortable with him. He was very kind but every interaction was awkward. She wondered if he was really just very shy and didn't know how to approach people. But he never seemed to hesitate to speak with her, so how shy could he really be?

"Also very well, thank you." She paused. "Well, have a good evening." She began to step away.

"It's been a frightful time, has it not?" He detained her. "It has not been long since the first of our friends so strangely died. Now there have been two others as well."

"True. True. And it is rather frightful," Idelette granted, "but Dom Calmet will soon get to the bottom of this mystery."

"It seems, too, that Conrad stands at the ready as well. He is a bright and capable man, and possesses the youthful vitality that our priest may lack."

"Yes, indeed. He seems prepared to act. It is most courageous and charitable of him. He is genuinely concerned for each of us."

"Courageous. Yes." He maintained eye contact with her in his usual awkward manner. "Well then, if I can be of any service to you, no doubt you know where to find me. I seldom leave the barns. There is always a calf to deliver, or a tool to sharpen, or hens to feed."

"Certainly. Thank you, Kurt. You are very kind. I believe I will try to get some sleep now though. Good night."

With that remark, he smiled and walked away toward the other side of the village, in the same direction as Conrad. Idelette was not sure what to make of that unexpected conversation. But she closed her door and a thousand additional thoughts rushed back into her mind. The hour was very late and she needed sleep, but her own thoughts defied her. To calm her mind, she lit a candle and, as she lay in bed, attempted to read from some pages she had borrowed from Dom Calmet.

Chapter 10

"Do you ever see Ryan anymore?" Zoe changed topics to end an uncomfortable pause in the conversation.

"Barely. He practically lives in cemeteries and frankly I get a little bored with it. I don't understand what constantly draws him back to graveyards again and again. I don't get it," Lydia confessed as a waitress refilled their coffees.

Zoe had asked her to meet over coffee so the two of them could catch up. They were school friends and it had been a while. So now they sat in an overpriced French restaurant on the northwest side, making awkward small talk. There were few other customers though people did come and go now and again. The floor was tile and the metal chairs scraped obnoxiously whenever a customer slid one out from under a table to leave. The manager behind the counter looked like he was thirteen, and he had safety pins through his earlobes. He was ogling Lydia. She was used to ignoring that. She was both blessed and cursed with an impressive figure and she knew it—but never flaunted it.

In fact, she tried hard to hide it. Dodging the drooling manager's inappropriate stare, she looked about the room instead. The pastries under the glass looked dry and cheap. She scowled at a gallon of milk left out unrefrigerated.

"Yeah, I actually saw him for the first time in a long time just the other day. He was in Greenwood, of course, since you mention it," Zoe replied.

"How was that?" Lydia returned her attention to her companion.

"We caught up a bit but it was late and I couldn't stay long."

As they spoke, a pair of girls came in and sat down at a table near Lydia and Zoe. They made conspicuous eye contact with both of them prior to resuming their conversation. Lydia wrote them off as just weird. But while she and Zoe chatted more girls steadily showed up, some individually, and some in small groups. They took seats at various tables but all looked at Lydia. She was growing increasingly uncomfortable with it.

"Listen, we are starting something and I want you to be a part of it," Zoe changed the subject.

"Is this your posse I've heard about? Your new group of friends? Rumor has it you've got some kind of club going or something. What do you do, play with Ouija boards and tarot cards? Light candles and wish you had boyfriends? Come on, it all sounds so pre-teen angsty."

"You should join us, Lydia," Zoe ignored the insult. "It's the right decision," she pressed the matter.

"Join what exactly?" She looked around at the other girls. "I see a bunch of girls who don't have a clue why they are even here or what any of you are trying to do. Seriously. What do you do?"

"We can show you," the waitress said as she handed Lydia her bill. It had strange symbols doodled on it. Lydia looked perplexed at it for a moment then shook her head slightly.

"I remember you were into this stuff years ago, Zoe. You tried putting curses or whatever on guys who wouldn't date you. I assumed you grew out of it. Your little hexes and pseudo-hoodoo never worked. And I was never all that interested anyway."

"This is nothing like that," Zoe snapped with slight irritation in her voice. Then relaxing her tone, "but your assumption is actually correct. I have outgrown all of that. I grew into something much, much bigger. Just watch. Zoe silently mouthed some words and stared out the window at the sky. Then she turned to look back to Lydia as the sky darkened and raindrops started to hit the window. "See?"

"See what? The rain? You expect me to believe you made it rain?"

"You watched me do it."

"It was cloudy to begin with anyway. I don't believe any of it. Just fortunate timing, that's all."

"Very well. I'll cause that man out there to get hit by a car."

"Even if that happens how do I know it's not just coincidence? Pedestrians get hit by cars. It happens. I don't believe you can do magic and I am not joining your dumb little coven. Besides, if you do make that happen, I have to report you to the police as criminally insane and a danger to society."

With that, Zoe and the rest of the girls all rose simultaneously and left the restaurant. Lydia watched the previously-mentioned pedestrian become distracted by the girls and get clipped by a side view mirror as he was attempting to cross the street against the traffic signal."

Lydia rolled her eyes and sighed.

Chapter 11

"Is that a man or a woman?" Detective Malli asked as she leaned in over her partner's shoulder and pointed to a blurry figure on the screen. They were in the police station downtown working on the case of the murdered girl who went missing in the mall and was later found in the landfill.

"I don't know. I've watched almost all the security footage available. This person is blurry every time he or she is on camera. It's like watching Bigfoot footage," Detective Jameson sighed and began the segment of footage over again.

"That's really weird. Why would it do that? You think this has been tampered with?"

"There's no indication of that. But the tech guys haven't analyzed it yet. I will send it down the hall to them when I'm done. In the meantime, you can watch the blurry person with me too. Just what you've always wanted, I'm sure," Jameson smirked.

"It's probably some new app or something. I can only imagine. Click on the app and just keep your phone in your pocket. It emits some kind of signal that interferes with security cameras so you're always blurry. And you just know it was invented by some middle-schooler with no girlfriend and too much time on his hands."

"Just what we need. But how would it interfere with light? This is all just visible spectrum light. How would any kind of wave signal do that?"

"No idea. I was just making that up. But look there," Malli tapped the screen with her pen. "The blurry person—Bigfoot who's not all that big—follows the victim into the Hot Gothic clothing store. The clerk said there was a woman who came in right after and spoke with the victim. He never saw them leave."

"Right. But he admitted being distracted by another customer."

"Distracted?"

"I assume staring at girls. Teenage guys don't take a job at a mall for the money," Detective Jameson explained.

"Fair enough. So what about the footage from inside that store? I assume you already watched that, right?"

"It was lost or never recorded apparently," Jameson sighed.

"Of course," Detective Malli rolled her eyes. "Regardless, not so big Bigfoot must be a woman."

"Are you going to use that name as her alias when you type up your report?"

"Maybe I will. I'm kind of tempted."

"I'll call her Unidentified Woman in my report. You do what you want. I've got a description of her that the clerk gave but it's not very much. White, blonde, long black coat. Also, she is a smoker, apparently."

"How did he know that? Was she smoking in the mall?"

"No. He said she had a cigarette behind her ear."

"Classy," Malli mumbled.

"Yeah. And that's about all. He couldn't recall if she was tall or short. No distinguishing marks that he could remember.

Couldn't really give an age estimate—older than a teenager was the best he could do when pressed on the matter."

"Was her hair long or short?"

"Long. Whatever that means."

"Why didn't we have him sit with a sketch artist?"

"We assumed the footage would be available."

"Well we need to call him down to the station to meet with a sketch artist, wouldn't you say?"

"Agreed. But I doubt he will remember well enough now to inform the artist."

CHAPTER 12

Turning tattered pages Zoe began:

> "Her charms can cure what souls she please,
> Rob other hearts of healthful ease,
> Turn rivers backward to their source,
> And make the stars forget their course,
> And call up ghosts from night:
> The ground shall bellow 'neath your feet:
> The mountain-ash shall quit its seat,
> And travel down the height"

Standing in the circle at the back of Greenwood cemetery, Zoe read from a small book—old with purple cloth covers—while three other girls held candles and watched. They worked a tremendous evil in that dismal hole. The meandering words of the incantation went on.

"Hence wild desires and groveling fears,
And human laughter, human tears;
Immured in dungeon-seeming night,
They look abroad, yet see no light,"

A sudden gust of wind blew out all of the candles. The girls scrambled to relight them as Zoe's eyes flashed disdainful looks at each of them.

On Zoe's right was Liz. She was tall, very pale, and had long, straight, dark hair. She wore tall boots, fishnet nylons, a long black skirt with a high slit, and a black tank top—far too little for the weather this night. She had a long transverse scar across her left upper arm that she never talked about. She was a shapely young lady who flaunted it, and Zoe was jealous of her, though she would never admit it. Liz was an empty person always searching for something.

On Zoe's left was Lady. No one knew her real name. Maybe it really was Lady. She was the oldest of the group by a year. She had long unkempt black hair, and wore punk rock attire. She was very plain looking and had too many piercings, had done a lot of drugs, lived on a lot of peoples' couches, and really hadn't had a true home in three years. Lady was one of those people who counts days by when she sleeps. 'Yesterday' was actually three days ago since she hadn't slept at all in the last seventy hours.

Directly across from Zoe was Becca. She was the youngest of the group by several years. A tiny creature with no direction, she didn't even fit in with a group of witches who fit in with no one. Becca was a nice young girl at heart. She had frizzy brown hair, freckles, and thin glasses. She wore pink and blue jeans. Easily dominated by others, she really had no grasp of the scope of Zoe's vision. She just wanted to be a part of something. And that was exactly what Zoe was looking for.

Having regained their composure, and relighted their candles, the transgression continued.

"Nay, when at last the life has fled,
And left the body cold and dead,
E'en then there passes not away
The painful heritage of clay;
Full many a long-contracted stain
Perforce must linger deep in grain.
So penal sufferings they endure
For ancient crime, to make them pure;
Some hang aloft in open view,
For winds to pierce them through and through,
While others purge their guilt deep-dyed
In burning fire or whelming tide."

At the conclusion of these lines the four girls spread out to the perimeter of the circle and faced one another. Zoe closed the book and continued with her own spell.

"Now four form the corners within this great circle. One within nine, it is ever expanding. Like stars the dead bend around us, and we bring the force of one within." Here, Zoe produced from a bag the bones of a child. "Those below and within the Earth look to our cause. Spread fear and adoration through this city and bring the people under our power. Deliver also our enemies into our hands." Zoe poured the bones into a heap in the center of the circle and the three girls advanced to the center to meet her and surround the bones. They inverted their candles and pushed them into the soft dirt—extinguishing the flames and concluding their ceremony. As they climbed up out of the circle a flash of lightning darted across the sky above them. Zoe almost smiled.

The night was cool and the occasional wind raised great commotion from the trees. Here and there a star shone brightly between high clouds. The girls climbed up out of the circle, leaving behind the bones and candles still in the ground, and walked south through the graveyard. They said nothing as they went.

Zoe was short, petite, pale and sickly. She had straight blonde hair which hung between her chin and shoulders. Despite a feeble consitution, she wore a façade of strength and control. Her clothes were worn blue jeans, a black shirt, a knee-length black trench coat, and boots—much more suited to nightly travails in a graveyard than Liz's attention-seeking attire. Zoe was the genuine article in this group, and that created a considerable amount of strain among the girls at times. It is doubtful that any of them truly understood what was brewing in Zoe's hellish mind.

After a long interval walking in silence, Zoe spoke up as they entered the southeast corner of the cemetery.

"Tonight it all begins. Gather the others we've already recruited, then spread out in small groups to cover the city. Go to malls, high schools, movie theaters, clubs—any place that you are likely to find teenage girls on a Friday night. Recruit wherever you can. Tell them where to meet and what is coming. Tell them just enough to get them interested. It will start small but it will grow rapidly. There must be no pattern though. It is crucial that we recruit from all ends of the city. Take your new recruits with you if you can and start to mark the city. Tag everything you can with our symbols. Graffiti buildings, dumpsters, mailboxes, anywhere you see fit. And be sure to mark over previous gang signs. Disrespect them. Few will be convinced initially, but wait and see. Once we make headlines, then newcomers will actively seek us. And the rest will fear us. We will be inexorable. We will be the unknown and the ever present—immanent yet transcendent. And the cops won't even know where to start."

"How do you know it will work?" Becca asked.

"Because you are here now," Zoe quipped. "And because it was prophesied. 'Stand fast in your enchantments and your many sorceries, with which you have labored from your youth; perhaps you may be able to succeed; perhaps you may inspire terror.' Besides, now is the perfect time. Did you see the news? Some guy just confessed to killing Ashley in the cemetery on Ragner Boulevard and ditching her body by the river. Ashley told him she was going to the cemetery to meet some friends and needed a ride. She didn't mention us specifically—and that's the beauty. This is better than if we had managed to recruit her that night anyway. We can use his crime to manipulate people. That's exactly the kind of thing to add to public confusion as we get started. Suggest to outsiders that it was us. But tell new recruits we could have saved her if she had joined us. Why that guy confessed though, I'll never know. He had the perfect alibi. All he had to do was say he dropped her off safely and the cops should be looking for whoever she was supposed to meet. But I'm not complaining. And I'm just glad no one came looking for her that night, otherwise we might have shown up to find a search party instead of an empty cemetery. Remember how pissed off I was at her for standing us up? That's really funny to me now."

As they passed out of the cemetery and snuck through the playground behind the school, Becca whispered to Lady, "Why would she care about a murder we didn't commit? Didn't you tell me Zoe actually killed some girl already?"

Lady motioned to her to lower her voice then tugged her arm a bit to slow her stride. As they fell back away from the group slightly she finally answered.

"Nobody knows for sure but some of us think she did," Lady whispered.

"Who was it? Did you know her?"

"Yeah, I knew her."

"Who was she?" Becca persisted.

"A girl named Cheryl. She was about your age but was the one that started our coven. She taught Zoe. It was all just private then. There wasn't any kind of plan like there is now."

"So why did she kill her?" Becca stumbled over a lip in the broken pavement. Lady glared and motioned again to be quieter.

"I don't know. But it's been really different ever since. Zoe has ambition that Cheryl never had. It's totally different now."

"How did she kill her?" Becca whispered.

"No one knows. Her body was found in a landfill. I heard she was all mutilated beyond recognition and they had to test her DNA to figure out who it even was. I heard her teeth were missing, and that she was burned and stuff. Rumor has it that Zoe still has Cheryl's eyes in a jar. Wouldn't surprise me. But right after Cheryl disappeared, Zoe stepped into her place. She didn't lose a moment. Liz thinks she had been scheming for a long time."

"But why do we care about Ashley's murder?"

"We can take credit for a murder we didn't commit. We get street credit but can't ever be convicted of it because we didn't do it. Once people think you are a murderer, it doesn't matter that you're not. Even if someone proves you didn't do it, everyone will still always think you did it. Because that's what they want to believe. That's just how rumors work."

Meanwhile, Ryan was crossing Byron Street into Greenwood by the hidden footpath amid the trees on the southwest side. He took an ambling path north through the graveyard in an attempt to quickly survey as much as possible. When he climbed to the top of the circle his heart sank in his chest. He saw the inverted candles and the bones which he recognized as those of the baby he had dug up recently, and he knew he was in this deeper than he would have previously suspected. He was now connected to it by physical evidence (hopefully no one knew that but him). He contemplated regathering the bones to eliminate the evidence, and maybe also to resell them, but as he stared down he was suddenly aware of light in the distant south. It was the police. They had been doing drive-throughs spotlighting the place much more frequently since those ghost hunters had reported their friend missing. No one took it too seriously though, it seemed. They still hadn't found the body because the cops never got out of their cars. They just took the reports, started doing drive-throughs, and figured the guy will show up soon enough.

But it was suddenly apparent that this time it was different. It must be that enough time had passed and the ghost hunters raised enough noise to get their attention. It had been quite some time since he went missing, after all. This time multiple police cars streamed in from both entrances and they were actually getting out of their vehicles to scour the cemetery, and the ghost hunters were with them repeating their story and pointing out where it happened.

"We'll find him," one officer assured them.

Detective Malli leaned over to her partner and whispered, "will we?"

Ryan knew he was in a hard spot if he didn't get out of there immediately. He abandoned the bones, ran north through the trees, past the garage, out the path by the dumpsters, and made his way over to Willard Street all the while thanking God that the police didn't bring dogs tonight. He took an ambling route up Willard, across Ragner, down Valley, through Mount Carmel, and back to his car.

As Ryan fled the police, Idelette stepped down from the mausoleum in Holy Cross cemetery. She was intolerably thirsty so she moved quickly through the graveyard searching for teenagers, but found the place empty. She could hear the police in the distance, and the thought of draining an adult man of his blood was extremely tempting. But she knew it was stupid and decided to avoid Greenwood all together. It would have to be downtown if she was going to feed tonight. She considered a home invasion but compassion usually persuaded her against that. Killing people sleeping in their beds always seemed far more evil than killing people out and about in the night. It just always seemed like there was a higher probability that those victims were bad people anyway. So she decided to go downtown.

By the time she reached the city, she was ravenous. Fortunately, it was late summer and the city was filled with pedestrians. Her night was very productive. One victim in Mounds Park, another in the booth on Pearl street near Division, another near the soup kitchen, then she walked into a club called Skeletunes.

The music was intolerable and the light show was as bad if not worse. There were stupid obnoxious kids everywhere, mostly in faux leather and chains. Idelette did her best to ignore it all and struck up a conversation with a girl at the bar. They all looked like easy prey, this particular girl just happened to have an empty seat next to her. She had a partially shaved head, faded green hair, and black lipstick. She babbled about how awesome the band was that night, but she missed the old days, like a year ago, when the old owners were more lax with the rules or something.

"Have you met, Ermil? He's an energy vampire!" The girl next to her continued the conversation that Idelette wasn't even really listening to.

"A what?" Idelette replied, suddenly paying attention.

"I'm an energy vampire!" apparently Ermil replied. He wore eye makeup and had glue in his hair.

"What is that?" she asked with derision.

"I feed off people's auras. I drain their life force."

A look of rage flashed across Idelette's face. She gripped the Bible in her pocket tighter, calmed herself, and asked with annoyance, "how does that work?"

"It works," the girl interrupted. "He's fed on me before," she boasted, not picking up on Idelette's disdain.

"Jade's right I have," Ermil interjected.

"Can you feed off my, um, whatever it was you said?" Idelette was quick to reply.

"Yeah I can," he smiled and nodded slightly like an idiot.

"Where?"

"Not here."

"Out back then?" she persisted.

"Sure!"

"Let's do it," she declared with flat affect.

The two followed her out the staff exit at the back of the dance floor into the alley. Moments later, as she tossed their drained bodies into a dumpster, she noticed something. An ancient symbol was written in black marker near the bottom corner of the dumpster. She recognized it immediately and knew it was drawn by the witches. They were already spreading out. And Idelette had just killed five people in the area on a single night. Their blood was all over her at that moment, and she was seen in the club by lots of people. It was time to disappear after so much carnage. If she laid low for a while, she could return when the investigation began to slow down. This night's feeding was sufficient for a long slumber.

The vampire moves quickly when necessary and, freshly strengthened from unrestrained feeding, can cover tremendous distance. So Idelette did exactly that. Near dawn she entered the old cemetery in Clearwater—about a hundred miles west of Grand Blanc. This graveyard, situated adjacent to a large lake, contains a peculiar vault built into the side of a man-made circular depression, nearly 50 yards in diameter, in the middle of the cemetery. The face of the vault was a large stone wall, with low stone steps, and a great rusty iron door. She had slept here before. So she forced the door open yet again. Once inside, she bent the barricade that she made years ago back into place to keep the door closed. Locked inside, she laid down in a compartment in the wall and decided it was time to settle in for a prolonged sleep. She could return to Grand Blanc in a month or so. But no sooner had she closed her eyes than the thought of her victims flashed through her mind. The pangs of self-loathing set in again as she fondly remembered the taste of their blood. She considered her situation in the tomb and continued the prayer she had begun on the roof of the abandoned slaughterhouse.

"You have walled me about so that I cannot escape, O God who inhabits eternity, and dwells in the high and holy place. Though I call and cry for help, you shut out my prayer," she whispered. But she had hardly begun the lamentation when she was interrupted by a strange sound outside. The door began to rattle. She sat up and stared at it for a moment. It went silent. Then came a loud bang and the door rattled against its stone frame.

"Are you kidding me?" she whispered to herself. Someone was trying to break in. Idelette arose and stepped up to the door. It banged again, then once more, then before it could happen a third time, she bent the iron latch and pushed the door open. A man on the otherside fell flat on his back. His crowbar tumbled from his hand. Idelette immediately recognized what was going on. Judging from the supplies he had with him, he was a grave robber.

He tried to scramble to his feet and back away from hers, but she seized him by the hair and held him up. He started to speak or scream but the vampire held his jaw closed. He was still screaming against his closed mouth as her left thumb dug in under his jaw and her middle and ring fingers dug in to his right lower eyelid. He clutched and pulled at her wrist with both his hands in a futile attempt to free himself but she was immovable. His pupils were enormous and searched about with the usual look of panic that Idelette had seen so many times. This wasn't what she had planned for tonight, but it seemed she had no choice either. Plus, judging from his attire, he looked to be a small-time operation. It was likely no one knew he was here and no one would miss him. All those considerations combined with the fact that the long journey to Clearwater from Grand Blanc had made her thirsty. One last feeding would help her sleep more comfortably and for longer, she justified her decision.

"Bad business, isn't it? Well, we can't have this, now can we?" she asked the man who could not answer anyway. With that she turned his head and sank her teeth deep into his neck. Her top incisors scraped the front of his vertebrae. His arms flailed at her in a wild attempt to fight back, but she took no notice. When the blood stopped flowing she tore open his abdomen and pulled out his bowels. Then she tossed his body into a back corner, dragged his other things inside, and walked back into the trees and dropped his guts into the bushes along the shore for critters to eat. This would hinder putrefaction of his corpse inside the tomb and expedite eradication of the other physical evidence. She walked back into her temporary resting place and closed the door. A brief shudder went down her spine. She bent the iron latch back into place to secure the door as it had been, then she returned to the place she had lain before.

She took one final look at the man's carcass laying strewn atop the bones which were already scattered about. His blood was still drying on her fingers as her right hand reached into her pocket and clutched the Bible therein. She longed to read it. But unable to do so with bloody hands, she sat down and continued her lament, now under the burden of another murder.

"My life is spent with sorrow, and my years with sighing. My strength fails because of my iniquity and my bones waste away. You have made me cower in ashes; my soul is bereft of peace; I have forgotten what happiness is. My endurance has perished and so has my hope from the Lord." She sighed at the thought and could not bring herself to say more, so she laid down in silence.

Despairing in darkness, and now in hiding, she considered how it must have felt to be the vampire, in the wake of so many murders, hunted by the villagers all those years ago.

Chapter 13

Months later, Ryan strolled in to work through the loading docks at the back of St. John's hospital. It was Christmas Day, and he was taking the shortcut to the morgue. Walking through the morgue door he punched the time clock by the cooler and got straight to work. The autopsy room was anachronistic—like stepping back in time. The floor was tiled with dark brown ceramic, and the walls were painted tan. A brown chalkboard, and a chart of normal organ weights, which was hand-calligraphed in the 1940s, and set in a massive frame, occupied much of one wall. The lighting was surprisingly good despite the dark complexion of the room. The autopsy table was old with slats of fenestrated sheet metal. Its plumbing and drains were noisy but still functioned well, for the most part (though, Ryan well remembered an incident in which blood leaked from the table's pipes through the ceiling of the clinical lab directly below).

"Thanks for coming," Phil said as Ryan entered the morgue. Having arrived first, he already had the body on the table and was gowned, gloved, and blading scalpels when Ryan walked in the door. "What time is it anyway?"

Ryan walked to the autopsy table and looked at the still-ticking watch on the dead man's wrist. "Two forty-three," he responded, briefly pondering the irony of the situation. "I do apologize for missing your call though. My phone was in the other room and I just didn't hear it ring," Ryan continued.

"That's OK. You weren't even on call, and this wasn't supposed to be done today anyway. But what do you do when your boss calls?"

Policy was that autopsies were not begun after noon. The clinician had to request the autopsy and the body had to be in the morgue by noon, or the case was rolled to the next day. The practice of pathology bears no resemblance to all the Hollywood nonsense that has obscured public understanding, which always shows autopsies being done late at night and in a dark room.

The people who populate the world of pathology do not resemble the Hollywood illusion either. At the top of the hierarchy are the pathologists. They are the physicians responsible for issuing diagnoses. Immediately below them are Pathologist's Assistants. PAs are not doctors but have a master's degree. They can't render diagnoses, but they cut frozen sections, gross surgical specimens, and perform the dissections at autopsies. Then there are the dieners. The lowest in the hierarchy, they are considered unskilled labor, trained on the job as an entry level position. The word itself is German for servant. It has largely been replaced by the more polite term "autopsy technician." Dieners do whatever the pathologists or PAs delegate to them. This may range from merely cleaning and sewing up bodies, to performing entire eviscerations, or more. It is largely an undefined job.

Ryan and Phil worked in the department of anatomic pathology, which includes autopsy pathology, cytopathology, and surgical pathology. The vast majority of their days were spent in surgical pathology, or, surg path. Autopsies were uncommon, which was good because they added hours of extra work to their usual busy day in surg path. Contrary to most PAs and dieners though, Phil and Ryan at least enjoyed doing posts, which is what people in the business call autopsies—short for post-mortem examination.

They only did hospital autopsies, however. Forensic autopsies were an entirely different animal. Those were done at a different facility under the jurisdiction of the medical examiner.

Phil slid the seldom-used footstool out from under the autopsy table to gain an advantage over the bulk of the man's torso, which rested high above the table, and supported by a body block. The stool grated across the old brown tile floor with an obnoxious noise. Ryan hated that stool. Phil was about 40, medium build, wore glasses, and had sort of a brush cut, but not exactly. He enjoyed Star Trek and basketball. The Star Trek bit made sense. The basketball part, however, didn't really match the rest of his image. He pushed the microphone, which dangled over the autopsy table, out of his way and began to remove the residual therapeutic devices from the man's body.

"How was your Christmas going?" Phil asked.

"Fine, thank you for asking. It's still going fine actually. I was getting bored and thinking to myself, 'I wish I were doing a post,' when I found the voicemail you left. I'm glad this happened. What about you—how is your Christmas so far?"

"It was a lot of fun until I came here. I guess it's still fun. It's a different kind of fun though. I'm supposed to be off today. This is Doctor Mac's post. I don't mind doing favors but I still would rather be at the sledding hill with my kids. What can you do when your boss calls though?" Phil reiterated.

"If you like autopsies so much, why not take a job some place that does more of them? We hardly do any. Maybe you should apply at the medical examiner's office." Ryan finished gowning up. Their conversation carried on as Phil worked.

"Well, I like the other stuff, too. If I worked at the ME, I would be giving up surgical pathology. And that is the more marketable skill set. I don't want to compromise that if ever I found myself searching for another job," Phil explained as he made the usual Y-shaped incision and reflected the skin of the chest up over the man's face. The remainder of the flesh on the chest and abdomen were reflected to either side. Then he cut through the ribs with an instrument called a costotome. With the chest plate removed he did a quick in situ inspection of all the organs.

Phil handed Ryan the pan, cut the duodenum, and began to cut the bowel free of the mesenteric fat. The man was septic. This was not the type of smell most people would associate with Christmas. With the bowel removed, Ryan moved up to the head to take the brain while Phil continued in the chest and abdomen.

Ryan made the coronal incision from behind one ear to the other and reflected the man's scalp down over his face.

"Did you go to mass today?" Ryan asked as they worked.

"Yes, I did."

"Was it in English or Latin?"

Phil laughed. "It was in English. You don't know much about Catholics do you?"

"No, not much," he confessed as he cut the temporalis muscles on either side of the skull and then turned on the saw. The talking ceased as he opened the skull because the oscillating saw was deafening. Phil had begun training Ryan to do the entire autopsy, but today was not the day for more teaching. He needed to get home to finish Christmas with his family.

The unique sound of cracking open the calvaria, then peeling it back and off the underlying dura mater is impossible to describe. It is also rewarding in a way that few people will ever know. It is the sound of victory. Ryan rocked the brain out of the skull and laid it in the scale for Phil. He jotted down the weight on the chalkboard behind them, then returned to the pan full of intestines. He inserted the enterotome into one end, and opened the entire bowel along its length—a process called running the gut.

"Any blood in the bowel?" Phil asked.

"Plenty. Plus a bunch in the pan still."

"It looked pretty dusky on the outside. What are you thinking?" Phil quizzed the diener.

"Well, it looks like there's a tiny perforation near the splenic flexure—mostly walled off and covered in exudate now though. Since his cerebral arteries were severely calcified, I say ischemic enterocolitis with perforation and resultant peritonitis."

"Yeah, exactly. I'm finding pretty significant atherosclerosis in the organ bloc—aorta, renals, mesenterics—his vessels are all pretty bad. I think this one is pretty straight forward. Merry Christmas."

"These shoe covers suck."

Phil laughed at Ryan's shoes, now soiled by some bowel content that had leaked through his shoe cover.

The man had eaten very well before he died (which is surprising since peritonitis is usually exquisitely painful). Unfortunately, he was unaware that not only did his diet consist partly of his own blood, but he was leaking intestinal contents into his abdomen. As Phil finished cutting the heart, Ryan called Dr. Mac to inform him that they were finished with the post and ready to show him what they had found (Dr. Mac wasn't even in the hospital; he was still at home with his family enjoying Christmas and waiting for the post to be finished). Phil's title may have been Pathologist's Assistant but sometimes that seemed to be an ambiguous phrase, and he had a tremendous amount of autonomy. Because Phil began his career as a diener, and because Ryan demonstrated aptitude, he trained him in things well beyond the scope of a diener's usual responsibilities. Phil also gave him considerable autonomy. It was not uncommon for them to do an autopsy entirely in the pathologist's absence. Phil or Ryan would merely inform the physician of the case, tell them the medical history, then not speak to them again until they were ready to show them the autopsy findings. Similarly, Phil did not watch Ryan work. He merely checked his work when he was done.

"OK! What have we got?" Dr. Mac thundered as he barged in the side door. He was a 70 year old man who, despite still being very energetic, was becoming senile. Nevertheless he was a partner in the practice and the other pathologists couldn't get rid of him.

"That was fast!" Phil noted. "Well there's not a lot to see. The heart looks hypertensive, the lungs are congested, there's severe atherosclerosis everywhere, ischemic bowel with a perforation at the splenic flexure, and peritonitis."

"How much fluid was in the chest?" Mac interrupted.

"About 60 milliliters bilaterally. Anyway, the lungs are nearly normal, a little firm in some areas but nothing to get excited about, just a little edema. The only thing of interest is the bowel."

"The bowel?" Mac repeated back in slight surprise because he wasn't listening to anything Phil had just said.

"Yeah, diffuse ischemia, perforation, and peritonitis, right?" He turned to Ryan and rolled his eyes.

"Agreed," Ryan nodded.

"Yeah," Phil added for needless emphasis.

"That's odd for us," Dr. Mac explained to Ryan, assuming that the diener would know nothing. "We're used to MIs, PEs, and breast cancer at this hospital. Am I right?" Mac insisted.

"No, the bowel hasn't been a major factor in many autopsies I've done," Phil lied for the sake of agreement and to save time. Truth be told this was not at all uncommon and he had autopsied dozens of similar cases over the years—some with Dr. Mac.

"Well let's see it."

"If you look here," Phil pointed out an area around the splenic flexure, "you can see pretty extensive exudate and a probable perforation."

"Good. What did his vessels look like?"

"Severely atherosclerotic." Phil was growing tired of repeating himself.

As Phil showed Dr. Mac the rest of the findings from the autopsy, Ryan readied a biohazard bag and a long string on a post-mortem needle. Phil would show Mac an organ then Ryan would take it from him and put it in the bag. It only took a few minutes to walk Mac through everything (three times) and he was out the door as quick as he came. Ryan sewed up the body and cleaned the dried blood off the exterior with a Brillo pad and a spray of water. While he moved the body onto the gurney, Phil clicked on the microphone, reviewed the notes on the chalkboard, and dictated the preliminary anatomic diagnoses. Then he called the morticians to tell them that he was done with the post and they could come pick up the body. Ryan wheeled the decedent back into the cooler and started some music before he began to clean the morgue.

"Thanks for your help today," Phil said as he put a fifty-dollar bill on the dictaphone.

"You know you don't have to do that," Ryan insisted.

"I want to do that," Phil persisted.

After a long pause and a minor staring contest Ryan submitted to the Christmas present. Phil left through the side door and Ryan turned up the music nearly as loud as the speakers could handle. It wasn't Christmas music by any stretch of the imagination, but Blue Öyster Cult was good morgue music. Only a few minutes passed before the door swung open and a man in a suit entered. The mortician, Larry, was—as all morticians are—a well-dressed individual with a perfect haircut and a freshly shaved face. These men never looked different. They were born in a suit, somewhere along the way they donned latex gloves, and they will die just as they live. Ryan found it interesting to think that the morticians always seem to dress the dead as they dress themselves—or was it the other way around?

"How ya doin'?" Larry shouted over the music as he wheeled a gurney in.

"Hangin' in there. You?" Ryan answered in a normal voice as though there were no music playing.

"I had a great Christmas. Now I'm here on a body call. What are ya gonna do, ya know?" He unzipped the velvet body bag all morticians seemed to favor.

"I've been here all afternoon so don't complain."

"Well, I'm glad you're here now. There's something I want to talk to you about." Larry said casually.

"Oh?"

"Yeah. We're alone, right?" He asked as he stepped through the door from the morgue into the autopsy room.

"Yep. This sounds a bit shady, Larry. I understood you to be a man of moral standing," Ryan said sarcastically.

"Oh, I wouldn't dream of doing anything misrepresentative of the funerary business." He closed the inner door to the autopsy room.

Ryan figured this conversation was going to take place.

There was a reason he always played music in the morgue, and kept the speakers right by the door. It was effective for covering the sounds of their voices.

"What do you need?" Ryan inquired as he walked with Larry to the back corner of the morgue furthest from the doors.

"Have you ever been to Greenwood cemetery?" Larry asked.

"Once, I think. Isn't that the one with the old spooky Victorian Gothic house for an office building?" Ryan remarked innocently. They both knew that this diener spent more time there than anyone—including the people in the graves. "What's the job and how much does it pay?" Ryan continued.

Larry pulled an unlabeled envelope from the inside left breast pocket of his suit coat and handed it to the diener as he told him the details about what grave he needed robbed. "This is cash advance. The rest will be paid upon completion of the work."

"I think I can handle this," Ryan muttered after briefly skimming through the contents of the envelope.

"I knew I could count on you." Larry began to walk away.

"Likewise. Pleasure doing business with you."

"This Spring. Right?" Larry replied as he began to wheel the gurney out of the morgue.

"The very first day after the snow melts!"

"That's what I like about you!" He called back as the door closed behind him.

"I do my best," Ryan murmured back unheard. He pocketed the envelope and returned to his task of cleaning. He sprayed the table and chalkboard with water and filled a pan with bleach water. He scrubbed the slats of the autopsy table and leaned them against the wall to dry. Then he scrubbed the instruments and dropped them in the pan. He scrubbed the table, cleaned the hair and chunks out of the drain trap, scrubbed the chalk board, and mopped the floor. He towel-dried the instruments, table, slats, and chalkboard. Not a drop of blood left. All clean and shinier than any other piece of 50 year old equipment.

Ryan donned his coat and strolled out the front door of the hospital into the snowy night. He had to traipse through slush and road salt to his car. The night was cold and dark. The sky was clear, though obscured by the glow of city lights. The final hours of Christmas dwindled, and the roads were mostly empty. The city smelled faintly of distant cigarettes. Winter would likely feel long, even if it wasn't. Larry had advanced Ryan a considerable amount of cash for this job. He was already eager to get it done and collect the balance of the pay, but he had to wait for the snow to melt.

Chapter 14

Spring came early that year, thankfully, and to everyone's pleasure, business could begin again. Traffic would be heavy this season and resurrectionists would have their hands full across the Midwest. Ryan had old business to finish too. He had thought about that envelope all through the winter. Now it was late March and the snow had already melted. He knew April would bring about two weeks of late snow—it always did—so he had to get working to finish the job before April delayed things more. The first order of business was Greenwood. Of all the city employees that worked in that cemetery, there was only one that Ryan genuinely trusted—someone who had been in the business far longer than himself. Mike was in his late fifties and had a voluminous mustache. He was a laid-back kind of guy with a deceptively honest look and a sense of humor—just right for this line of work. Monday morning Ryan found Mike in the office building of Greenwood.

"How's the ground?" Ryan called out from the doorway, startling Mike.

"Still a bit frozen." He spun around to see who was speaking.

"I don't believe we've met before. Have we? Did you want to inquire about available plots? Most of them are near the back of the cemetery," Mike improvised conversation as a coworker left the building.

"No, we've not met. I'm new in the area, and that's exactly what I've come to ask about," Ryan followed suit, watching the man leave.

"He's gone," Mike's tone changed entirely. "I was worried that I might see you soon. Listen, I know you've had it pretty easy here in the past, and I know you're not a novice, but since the Halloween murders, there's still no indication that the cops are going to slow down their patrols. It's been a year and a half and they're still at it. Anyway, you get my point."

"I do indeed. Nevertheless...."

"You have old business," Mike finished Ryan's sentence.

"Yep. Larry."

"That man needs to calm down. Has he been callin' you every day all winter long about this? I bet he has been calling."

"Not too much. Anyway, I need Lot 12 in section M."

"Potter's Field? Who wants something from there? There's probably nothing left to dig up! Well, maybe if that one vagrant who always passes through there falls off his bike and dies."

"Well some anthropologist seems to think that there's something worth seeing in that grave."

"I know I don't have to mention that there's an elementary school right there, and there are houses right by the school, and several street lights, and there are next to no trees, and nowhere to hide, and the cops can come around any of four different corners, and—"

"Yeah, I know. I'm not worried." Ryan interrupted, "So...."

"Thursday would be OK I guess," Mike consented. "It's college night at the bars so the cops will have their hands full in other neighborhoods."

"Thursday it is then. Try to soften the mools for me a bit by then would ya?"

"Soften the what?"

"The earth of the grave."

Mike merely raised an eyebrow.

"Um. It's a very old word. Just trust me," Ryan shrugged.

"Oh. So you want me to do what then?"

"Thaw the ground. It was an attempt at humor," Ryan shook his head.

"Ah, yes. Hilarious."

Not about to be hung up by misdirected humor, Ryan left still feeling enthusiastic to be working in graves again. Winter brings about a strange kind of seasonal depression for resurrectionists. The snow covers their revenue stream and the frozen ground is even less penetrable than the concrete vaults below. But to top it all off, because of the snow, you can't even really see the graves. There's no way to even just optimistically survey the graveyard for future prospects. You have to wait and trust that winter won't last forever. It's depressing. That was a thing of the past though, and there was work to be done now. The next order of business was Calvin.

In a past life Ryan had held a job cleaning the meat department at a local grocery store. Calvin worked in the produce department. They both moved on after a few years, when Ryan went to work at the hospital and Calvin went to work at a box factory. Though they now had little in common in their day jobs, as old friends it was easy for them to adapt to working with each other. In this business people had to be friends to work together as closely as he and Calvin did. But that didn't mean they fully trusted each other—Ryan actually trusted very few of his friends.

Calvin wouldn't be available until sometime that evening, so he had time to kill, and there was no better way than wandering through the graveyard. Moments later though his cell phone rang—It was Sarah.

"Hello?" Ryan answered the phone as if he didn't know who it was.

"Hey!" Sarah said eagerly. "Did you go see Mike today?"

"Yeah, everything has been arranged. Right now I'm wandering through Greenwood, but really I should also probably review some maps."

"When do we work?"

"Thursday. I think we'll start about 12:30." They both knew that 'Thursday at 12:30' meant Friday at 12:30 am. It was safer to be ambiguous about times and days though.

"I'm so excited! It's been a long winter," Sarah exclaimed.

"Tell me about it. I'm going to see Calvin tonight."

"Good! Do some real work in the meantime—it's not like you actually need the maps."

"The maps are to locate the exact plot. I still don't know the plot numbers very well. And it's not like they are marked in Potter's field."

"Well, as long as you're being productive. I've got to go. I promised my sister I'd go shopping with her. Wait! Potter's field? Are you serious?"

"Yep."

"Have you known that all these months?"

"Uh yeah. Why?"

"That's a hard spot. You didn't want to tell me?"

"I didn't figure it mattered. Would you turn down the job?"

"Well, no."

"So we're good. Enjoy shopping. I'll see you soon."

Ryan went back to his car, dug out some cemetery maps, and did a quick review. Then, tired of waiting, he drove to Calvin's house—which was only a few blocks away. Calvin currently worked first shift, though that changed all the time, and wouldn't be home for a couple more hours. So, Ryan figured he could stay busy by getting things organized in the garage.

Calvin maintained an extensive collection of tools. Power tools, hand tools, odds and ends, lumber in all sizes and shapes, rope, chains, pry bars, jacks, saw horses, and more filled the garage. When his van was pulled in, you could hardly open a door to get in or out of the vehicle. It took some time to rummage through it all and find everything they would need but Ryan managed to separate out the essentials. With that accomplished he sat down and started reviewing maps of other city cemeteries in anticipation of future jobs that might come along later in the season. About 5pm Calvin's van pulled slowly into the driveway. He drove a rusty old brown conversion van with a vinyl interior and no seats but the front two.

"You spoke with Mike this morning," Calvin declared as he got out of the vehicle. He was of medium build with long dark hair and he wore a hardware store ball cap.

"Yeah..." Ryan was surprised at being told what he thought he had come to tell Calvin. "When did you find out?"

"I get around. This is pretty extreme for so early in the season don't you think? Cops are still aggressively stalking Greenwood, and that grave is really out in the open and on the opposite side of the cemetery from the exit," Calvin noted.

"You can handle it."

"I'm not complaining, I'm just pointing out the facts."

"How's your van? Is it running good?"

"It's good now. I dumped $1500 into it over the winter—various problems—but it's good now."

"Are you going to be ready on Thursday by 11:30 or should I expect you closer to midnight?"

"Don't worry about it, man. I saw the first bat of the season yesterday. That's really early; I don't think he's going to make it. I know normal people look for the first robin of the season. Remember years ago when there used to be tons of bats in Greenwood? What happened?"

"Owls, I think," Ryan quipped, accustomed to totally random topics interjected in conversation with Calvin.

"Owls?"

"There's a great horned owl nesting in the pines in the southwest corner. And I've seen barn owls in there every now and again. That's my personal theory on the paucity of bats. Anyway, back on topic, I set aside some tools for your convenience."

Calvin scoffed. "Those are all duplicates—I've already got everything in here." He threw open the back of the van and pointed at the piles of tools. "But what we really need is a hearse. I know where one is for sale right now—you interested?"

"Oh yeah? Where?" Ryan was glad he was focused at least.

"Muskegon. Do you want to go see it with me?"

"Why do we need a hearse for this first job? It will just be random bones."

"I didn't mean 'we really need a hearse' for this job specifically. I meant we need a hearse for our whole operation. We would look much more legitimate driving a hearse in a cemetery than we do driving my van," Calvin explained.

"That's fair. Alright. Let's go to Muskegon."

"Are you ready to go right now?"

"Yeah, I can do that."

"Fantastic. Let's get some burgers on the way. I'm starving. Oh, and we need to make one other stop. I have to bring some groceries to my coworker's grandma. She lives in a retirement community and is laid up from a sprained ankle."

"How long will that take?"

"15 minutes tops. Besides," here Calvin stopped what he had

been doing and looked Ryan in the eye, "there's always time to help people. The corpses aren't going anywhere. We can worry about robbing graves once we make sure this old lady has food to eat. Charity is important."

While the two of them ate their burgers, Calvin called about the hearse he had seen advertised. The voice on the other end of the phone was not very reassuring. He sounded intoxicated and it wasn't his hearse. He said the owner wouldn't be available to show them the car until Thursday. They reluctantly agreed to meet him Thursday morning. Ryan wasn't particularly happy about doing this at the last minute, but Calvin was resolved to make it happen.

Chapter 15

Thursday came fast. Sarah was the limiting factor because she worked late. Calvin had the day off. Ryan managed to get the other diener to cover the afternoon for him. He was surprised she agreed, since she had put in her two weeks notice on Monday. And that meant Ryan would be twice as busy at work soon because finding and retaining dieners is not easy. It would likely take months to fill the position. But that was another matter. He spent all morning hoping that Mike was doing what needed to be done. Ryan needlessly reviewed his maps of Greenwood and the city. He had it all memorized, but he had to fill his time until the trip to Muskegon. He was nervous. The first job of the season is always indicative of how the rest of the year will be.

"I just gotta go down in the basement. I'll be right back," Mike said to a coworker as he climbed out of the yellow truck which all the Park's Department employees drove. "Then we'll call it quits in here for the day and head over to Fairplains cemetery to follow up on that work order. I think it is a leaky spigot."

Mike went into the office building as his fellow employee sat in the truck listening to the radio. Mike turned on the attic light, unlocked the basement door, and left extra digging tools in the basement. He pretended to lock the front door behind him, and climbed back into the truck.

"Just checking to make sure all the electrical was turned off," he lied, "and fill in my time sheet since we won't be back here today. I did yours, too."

It was early in the afternoon as they left. The cemetery would be cold and quiet for the rest of the day.

As Mike attended to the preparations in Greenwood, Ryan and Calvin finally attended to the matter of the hearse in Muskegon. The drive was boring, and the directions they were given vague, but at least Calvin remembered to bring cash. They found themselves parked behind a mobile home on an isolated stretch of road at the back of a partially wooded 20 acre lot. This land was turned into a car farm decades before. Fallow grass grew up through the hoods and doors of rusty old cars. Frames, portions of engines, and uncountable tires lay ensconced within the tall grass. Tarps draped over some newer cars flapped loudly in the breeze. Ryan could see spiders coming and going under the tarps. The owner claimed he actually owned several hearses—six that functioned, and three that were supposedly being rebuilt.

"There's not much left for you to do to this one," the owner bragged as he led them to a more encouraging spot, where the grass was cut and the cars were clean. He slapped his hand confidently on the hood of a black 1970 Cadillac Superior Three Way with power rollers and suicide doors. Calvin looked it over carefully for some time. It was in better condition than the man selling it. He was an anemic red-haired fellow in black jeans, a black t-shirt, and a black beret. There were copious amounts of grease caked under his fingernails. He looked malnourished.

Neither Ryan nor Calvin trusted him. But Ryan trusted Calvin's assessment of the hearse. Besides, it was Calvin's money. The two haggled a bit on the price, but eventually a deal was struck.

"I figure since this grave is old and the remains are just going to be in pieces, we can just toss 'em into a casket extended out on the rollers. When we're done, one person can tend the vehicle using the power features and get out of there while the other two stay to conceal the work done. Besides, most of the funeral homes in that area use similar looking hearses so we'll blend in."

"Sounds good. I hope Mike got everything prepared in case of an emergency," Ryan remarked. He decided not to point out that Calvin didn't actually have a casket.

"Don't worry about it. Do you want to drive it?"

"Not a chance. You bought it. When that thing breaks down 30 minutes down the road, I want you at the wheel, not me. I'll drive your van back to Grand Blanc while you register plates for that thing."

When Ryan arrived home, he immediately called Larry. There was no point in going to all this trouble if final arrangements were not made with his employer.

"Larry!" Ryan exclaimed in an artificially eager and friendly voice. "It's me. Tonight's the night. We'll hold onto everything until you are ready to collect tomorrow."

"Sounds good!" Larry responded. "I suppose you would like to know how much you are getting paid for this little operation, wouldn't you."

"That information would certainly help motivate me to do my best work."

"I'm getting paid well. I'll pay you double what I fronted you. Sound reasonable?"

"I can't complain. And considering how long this job has sat unfinished, I'll take what I can get."

"OK. I gotta go. I will meet you at Alan's at 8 p.m. tomorrow."

"See ya at eight then."

"See you at eight."

He wasn't about to let Larry know, but this was shaping up to be one of the highest paying gigs he'd ever had. Ryan was definitely motivated now. It felt like an eternity but finally 7:30 arrived. Sarah came to his door in her work clothes—she looked tired.

"Hey," they both said simultaneously.

"Are you ready?" Ryan asked.

"I will be as soon as I change my clothes," Sarah replied.

"I talked with Larry. I'm collecting double what he fronted me."

"Seriously?" Sarah nearly shouted.

"Yeah, but then it's minus expenses and divided among... five of us I think—you, Calvin, and me, and then smaller cuts for Alan and Mike... yeah, five of us."

"Have we ever made that much on one dig?"

"Nope."

"What's so special about this body?"

"No idea. If we weren't working for an established client I would be really suspicious," Ryan acknowledged.

"Suspicious?"

"Just that there might be hidden risks we aren't being told about and hence the higher pay out. But I don't have any reason to suspect Larry is withholding anything about this job."

"Fair enough. Does Alan know that we need to use his barn tonight and tomorrow?"

"No. I haven't been able to get a hold of him. But he won't mind the surprise."

"Good thing too," Sarah muttered. "I hate surprises."

The two of them changed into appropriate clothes and geared up for the night. Ryan noticed the slightest artifact in the wrinkle of Sarah's pant leg, confirming his suspicion that she had worn a knife there all day, as usual.

At last the two grave robbers drove a meandering route toward Greenwood, surveying the activity of the neighborhood. An inconveniently situated police car, or a block party they hadn't counted on could kill the plan before it even began. Fortunately, all was cold and quiet. At 11pm they parked on a residential street around the back of Mount Carmel Cemetery. From there they traipsed through Mount Carmel, across Leonard Street, and into Greenwood. Still early, they waited on the upper retaining wall. Gnarled branches swayed low above their heads, clattering in the gentle breeze.

At 11:20 Sarah spoke up. "How much longer?"

"Ten minutes. We don't have very long to wait. Calvin will be early, I'm sure of it. Which is why we were even earlier."

Sarah wasn't interested in waiting. She dragged him along and they descended into potter's field. On the way they noticed several tomstones painted with odd symbols. A few were on the trunks of the tall hardwood trees scattered here an there in Potter's field as well. Ryan wondered if they would have company tonight, but Sarah was not concerned. At 11:45 a black hearse came rolling silently into the swale. They were still ahead of schedule.

"I don't think we're alone here tonight!" Calvin exclaimed as he parked and approached his partners in crime. "I thought I saw lights over by the Byron Street entrance. You haven't seen it?"

Ryan gave a long sigh. "Well we should probably go investigate now shouldn't we? Sarah, do you wanna stay with the car while Calvin and I go give a look?"

"I always have to stay with the car," Sarah muttered.

"It's because you look the most innocent and patrollers are less apt to do anything more than just kick you out of here," Calvin replied.

"Fine." Sarah consented with a rather annoyed tone.

Calvin and Ryan ran over the hill, through the Jewish section, and peered out over the west half of the cemetery. Sure enough, there was another group of resurrectionists unloading equipment. It was immediately apparent that they were not professional material. They were working barely a hundred feet from the Byron Street entrance, and they were loud as could be. Ryan and Calvin approached.

"Nick!" Ryan snapped.

Nick was the diener that trained Ryan at the hospital. He was a worthless employee who did no actual work. Nobody liked him and they were thrilled to see him quit. If someone had hired him, that someone was desperate.

Ryan actually got into the resurrectionist business after figuring out what Nick was up to. He was not very good at maintaining a low profile, and blended this work with his diener responsibilities frequently. His conversations about grave robbing jobs were never as private as he seemed to think, and Ryan could hear much of what was going on. Once he figured out what Nick was involved in, and how it all worked, he started intercepting clients. Ryan rapidly proved he could be more discrete, more efficient, and more reliable. By the end of a very slow and selective first season, he had enough contacts within the business that his second season was already filling up. Like any other industry there are sellers and consumers for all pay grades. If one is looking for the lowest bidder, outfits like Nick's exist. If one is looking for lower risk and higher performance, then there are groups like Ryan's. It was actually convenient to be working the same night as Nick, because his group was more likely to draw the attention of the police. But that was only advantageous if they were working in a different cemetery, not a hundred yards away in the same one.

Nick did not reply to Ryan's less than cordial greeting, but merely scowled.

"What are you doing here?! Who are you working for?" Ryan insisted.

"Why would I tell you that? I'm busy. Get lost," Nick sneered.

"If you draw police attention to this place tonight, Nick, so help me I'll—"

"They'll behave," Calvin interrupted.

Ryan turned to see Calvin had one hand firmly clenched around the throat of one of Nick's coworkers, and was slowly forcing the man's pry bar toward his own eye. This situation had a good chance of escalating. Fortunately, few ressurectionists carried guns, because they are too loud, even with suppressors. Regardless, no one was attempting to intervene, but no work would get done this way either.

"What's your name?" Calvin asked his prisoner.

"Paul," he whispered.

"Nice to meet ya, Paul," Ryan chimed in, then turned to Calvin, "We're going to be late. You need to either just kill him or let him go."

"I remember these guys from last season. We put up with them then, and it created problems for us regularly. Some morticians even confused their shoddy work for ours. I'm not going to put up with it this year." Calvin withdrew his grip. "Just remember what we talked about here tonight, Paul."

Ryan and Calvin casually walked back toward potter's field. Nick and his clamjamfry shouted obscenities at them as they left but did not attempt to engage further. Once out of Nick's view Ryan and Calvin sprinted back toward the job site. Sarah was still waiting with the hearse. She had set up all the equipment and spread the tarp out beside the grave.

"Nick is over there," Ryan informed her.

"Did you kill him?" Sarah asked eagerly.

"I was ready to," Calvin said.

"Thanks for setting up! I'm sorry to make you wait here," Ryan changed the subject.

"I'll let you do the majority of the digging," she remarked. Then turning to Calvin, "when did you get the coffin?"

"It was a busy day today," Calvin remarked without further explanation.

Calvin opened the back of the hearse and, sure enough, a coffin slid part way out on the rollers. He opened half the lid.

"So much for being ahead of schedule," he noted. "We'd better start!"

They dug from 12:30 to 2:45, piling the dirt on the tarp beside them. As agreed upon, Sarah mostly kept watch while Calvin and Ryan dug—she had earned a break. The work was slow and exhausting because of the cold, hard ground. There were quite a few tree roots to put the mattock through as well. But at quarter to three they hit old wood fragments that were clearly not roots. Now they needed light to find the remains they were extracting. They dropped a few green glow sticks into the grave and began to pull up portions of skeletal remains—first a humerus, next a pelvis, then a skull, several teeth, a tibia and femur with the patella still hanging on by some ligament. One by one they extracted the fragments and tossed them from the hole into the coffin sticking out of the back of the hearse. The entire time they could hear Nick and his group creating a horrible din. It was is if they were deliberately trying to wake the dead—or at least the residents of the nearby houses.

Once they were confident that they had retrieved all there was to find, they loaded up all the supplies that were no longer necessary. Calvin shut the coffin and jumped into the hearse. He turned on the rollers, pulling the coffin into the car, and shut the doors so he could change into clean street clothes. Meanwhile Ryan and Sarah began to fill in the hole. Once that was done, they put the rest of the supplies in the hearse and Calvin pulled away. He would precede them to Alan's farm.

Ryan and Sarah replaced the sections of grass and sod they had cut—a fine job and well concealed. At 4:07 am they called it quits and went up to the office building. There was already dew on the grass as dawn drew nearer.

"Why are we here?" Sarah asked.

"Mike made some preparations for us in case of an emergency. We didn't need anything tonight, so now I have to undo what he did, so it will all look normal when the employees come to work."

They went inside and turned off the lights and buzzer, locked the doors, and put away the supplies Mike had left out. Afterwards, they changed into clean clothes and put their soiled garments in a backpack. Now they could leave. They locked the door to the office building and just as they were about to go, Nick and his gang showed up.

"Who was that punk?!" Paul yelled.

"Why would I tell you that?" Ryan quipped

"I'm gonna kill him! Where is he?!" Paul demanded.

"I dunno. He took off for the night." He maintained his unruffled demeanor.

"Where?!?"

"I don't know," he spoke more slowly and emphatically so Paul could understand.

Paul grabbed Ryan by the shirt, and screamed obscenities as he continued his demands to know where Calvin was. Sarah, who was kneeling down tying her boot, slid the knife out from under her pant leg, quickly rose, and swung it, drawing a long cut across Paul's forehead before he could release Ryan and dodge the blade.

Paul, who was not a small person, stumbled backward and shouted an expletive as he let go of Ryan.

"I don't know him, but I don't think I like him," Sarah commented.

"Well that just put his DNA on your knife. You will need to bleach it, or, maybe even ditch it," Ryan said to Sarah.

"I'm gonna kill all three of you! I'll see you again! You're so dead!" Paul screamed, temporarily blinded by the blood pouring down over his eyes.

Ignoring Paul, "it was not a pleasure to see you again Nick. Now if you'll excuse us, we're done here." Ryan pointed to the headlights of a police car turning in from Byron Street at the other end of the cemetery.

"Later," Nick muttered bitterly.

They jogged to the Leonard Street entrance. The street was empty for miles. They sprinted through Mount Carmel, across Willard and back to Ryan's car. The houses were still dark up and down the street. They broke the silence starting the car and then they were off to Alan's farm, which was located on a country road several miles north of the city.

Calvin had been there for some time now. He had stashed the remains in the old silo and was drinking hot chocolate in Alan's kitchen. Sarah paused in the barn. Ryan watched as she secured her knife in a vice and broke it in half with a hand sledge, then dumped the pieces and sheath into the fire pit behind the garage. She grabbed some logs off a pile nearby, tossed them in, poured on some gasoline, and set it ablaze.

"Alan is asleep," Calvin whispered and handed each of them a mug as they walked into the kitchen. "I woke him up and asked to use the place. Then I put the bones in the silo. He says he wants good money for this 'cause he wasn't informed ahead of time but otherwise, it's cool. And he's out of coffee."

"Did you bother to mention we tried calling him several times, starting, like, days ago?" Sarah whispered as she added some marshmallows to her hot chocolate. "I'm not sure he gets more money. He should have answered his phone."

They finished their drinks as Ryan told Calvin what had happened, loaded their equipment into the appropriate vehicles, and said good night. It was about six in the morning when Ryan finally collapsed into bed. The sky was already starting to brighten as he finally fell asleep.

Chapter 16

Idelette woke with a start, not knowing how long she had slept, and still gripping the pages she had borrowed from Dom Calmet. The candle at her bedside was burned down to an extinguished nub. Her memory immediately recalled the awkward conversation she had with Kurt last night. Why was he right outside her door anyway? He was so nice. She felt bad thinking ill thoughts of him. Then she remembered how kind Conrad was last night and how comforted she felt with him. She sat up, eager to start her day. Sunlight poured in through her window. But she heard something. There seemed to be a commotion in the distance. She leaped from her bed, got dressed, and rushed out into the street. Everyone was gathering near the city gate. Dom Calmet was at the front of the crowd but it was Conrad who stood atop the wall, ready to address the group. Idelette found a place at the back and listened closely. She saw Kurt on the other side of the crowd. He smiled at her. She politely but quickly smiled back and then looked again at Conrad. Finally, when everyone had arrived, he began.

"Friends, listen closely. Take heart. There has been much confusion and fear among us," he began, "but I know we can solve the mystery of these murders, and we can overcome this terror that now confronts us. Even now the evil spreads and a dark shadow from the forest steals across our lands and into our homes. I must tell you that I have seen this happen before." He paused. "Years ago, when I lived in another village, across the river, similar deaths occurred. It was a time of great trial. Horror pervaded the hearts of that village as it has here. The poor townsfolk there were certain that it was a werewolf. But now, having seen what you have seen, having heard the opinions of our beloved priest, I am convinced that these murders in our village—and those which took place before—were committed by a vampire! I am aware it has been rumored among you, but I stand here to tell you that I am now certain of it. Corpses without blood, no theft, fish near a body left uneaten—what more evidence do we need? Clearly, this is a vampire! It has declared itself!"

The crowd stirred and everyone began to speak at once. Fear and doubt dominated. People called out to Conrad, wanting to know what to do.

"Dear friends," Conrad continued, "we do not need to panic or succumb. We can fight back against this evil. Can there be any doubt that it will return? Have we reason to think it has moved on? No! So we are forearmed with that knowledge. We must prepare ourselves. Vigilance can save us, and we can destroy the monster! Let us fortify the wall. Let us arm ourselves. Let us search for the creature by day. Let us keep watch by night. And let us pray, as our cleric has so often reminded us!"

Again the crowd stirred but now with energy. Their enthusiasm grew as they shouted their affirmation of Conrad's speech. They would unite against the vampire to destroy the night terror. Conrad calmed them down though, so he could give further instructions.

"We will begin immediately, first by strengthening this dilapidated wall and the gate of our village. Everyone must help. Men, women, and children must all lend a hand as they are able. Let us begin immediately."

Small teams were formed to gather timber. Others brought buckets of mud and straw to make mortar. Rope and nails were scavenged from all over the village. They began repairing damaged areas. People swarmed like ants over and around the wall, passing wood and tools around, while Conrad tried to coordinate the efforts. Once the holes were patched and the collapsed areas rebuilt, a second wave of construction was begun to improve the entire circumference of the wall. Braces were added for additional support, sharpened timbers were set at odd angles along the top—increasing the height of the wall and making it far more formidable to climb.

The gate was next. The metal hinges were cleaned and oiled. New leather straps were added to help support the doors. Additional timber was added to make the gate more massive than it had been previously. A second, stronger bar was then placed across it to reinforce the lock. It had been merely adequate before. Now it was imposing.

The energetic day passed quickly with the hustle and bustle of the villagers. Conrad continued to encourage them and remind them of their dead friends so no one would lose focus or begin to think that this hard work was not necessary. Dom Calmet, despite his age, was not above physical labor, and joined in, working with his hands and reciting prayers for his parishioners all the while. Idelette worked alongside the priest making sure he did not overexert himself. They seemed to strengthen each other. Admittedly though, Idelette's thoughts were more often about Conrad. She admired him all the more for his heroic efforts today. If Conrad could help them all maintain this level of unity and focus, she thought, certainly he could lead them in the fight against the enemy.

"Hello again, Idelette," a familiar voice said from behind her. She noticed Dom Calmet smile as she turned to face Kurt.

"Hello," she acknowledged.

"I've noticed you hard at work alongside our esteemed priest all this busy day. You are such a kind woman."

"Thank you, Kurt. That is very nice of you to say," she looked at Dom Calmet.

"She is always very kind to me," the vicar added.

"And you take such good care of her, Dom Calmet. No doubt you are looking for a new suitor for her. She deserves a doting husband."

Idelette really didn't even hear this exchange because she had glanced passed Kurt and noticed Conrad walking in their direction.

"Yes. Yes, indeed. But for the time being I have had to move that consideration lower on my list of priorities—until this crisis is resolved. Doubtless you understand."

"Of course," he smiled at Idelette, who quickly looked back at the two of them and tried to hide the fact that she had not even been listening. She thought as fast as she could, looking for something generic to say.

"The evening star is dim in the sky," Dom Calmet interrupted her thoughts. "This day has passed fruitfully and God has sustained us. See what it is to be a community united in love and compassion—just as Christ taught and just as the Roman Church expects."

"Yes, Father," Conrad interrupted as he approached them. "The day has been admirable. But the night is drawing in on us."

Kurt stepped back and to the side slightly, and did not speak again, as Conrad joined the conversation.

"What do you mean?" Idelette interjected.

"Fear will again begin to sink into people's hearts. Courage will fail. Strength will falter. We must be prepared for whatever evil may come upon us in the misty night. Day has been our ally. We may fool ourselves in the light and think we are brave and safe, but our hearts are more honest in the dark. I fear that something terrible may happen even this very night."

Idelette's heart raced. "What do you think will happen?"

This time Dom Calmet interrupted. "We cannot know what is to come and we must not assume the worst. Stay focused on the cross and pray. God declares the end from the beginning. Do not give evil a chance to overcome your thoughts. Do not give the Devil a foothold. This night may pass just as any other, and the morning will rise in its course. Let us not begin to stumble prematurely. We have no reason to fear this night any more than any other night. Besides, it is not right to fear what may harm your body—as the Scriptures instruct—but we should fear only He who has dominion over our souls."

"All the same, I have a bad feeling about this night," Conrad muttered.

Those words lingered in her ears as Idelette returned home at last. She was exhausted from the day's work and tried to tell herself that it was merely the fatigue that made her so agitated by what Conrad said. She pondered it all evening, hoping and praying that he was wrong. Too many had died already. But they were alone and outside the gates when they died. Everyone was safe inside the walls tonight, so there should be little to fear, she thought. But what if Conrad was right? What if the vampire stole into the village tonight?

She wrestled with such thoughts through the entire evening. Darkness crept through the village as the sun sank below the western horizon. Night rose in the east. The evening star was pursued by half of a moon, waning in its course. Scattered clouds punctuated the heavens but no wind dared to speak in the darkness. Safe inside her home, Idelette extinguished the last candle of the evening and retired to bed. With much effort she eventually overcame her dreadful thoughts. Her restlessness gradually subsided and she settled into a deep dreamless sleep.

About the fourth watch of the night she woke—had she heard something? It sounded like a rustling or shuffling. Footsteps on the path perhaps? Lifting her head, she waited and listened for many minutes. But there was nothing. Calming herself she lay her head on the pillow again and closed her eyes. But mere seconds had passed when she heard it again. This time she was certain. There was someone, or something, outside—and close by. She tried to calm her nerves, but her heart quickened its pace. She forced herself to breathe slowly. Trying to remain calm, she listened closely, fearing the worst. Now she was sure of it. There was definitely someone walking out there, and the footsteps were approaching her door!

Idelette's house had only two rooms. There was a front room with the kitchen and table, and the back room where she slept. Whoever was outside was only steps away, and there was only the front door and the inner door between the two of them. Her mind raced. Should she call out? Perhaps it was Conrad, or even Kurt, here to check on her and make sure she was safe—but what if it were the vampire? Should she light a candle—but what if it tries to come in? How do you hide in candle light? How could she defend herself? If she screamed would anyone arrive quickly enough? How do you outrun the dead? Ten thousand such thoughts whirled in her brain in mere moments as she listened to the lurking steps come to a stop outside her door. She remained laying still in bed to avoid making any noise.

Suddenly the door slammed against its lock! Idelette sat upright, gasping in terror at the realization that it was trying to enter. Only a moment passed and it happened again! Slam! The door rocked against its frame. The lock was merely an old piece of board and would not hold for long. Slam! She heard the board crack. She began to panic—where could she run? The window! Out the window above her bed! Slam—the lock gave and she heard the door crash against the wall. Splinters tumbled across the floor. It was inside!

Idelette stood on the bed and fought to open the shutters. She could hear it walking across the room. It stopped at her bedroom door. For the moment, she was within and it was without, but how long could that possibly last? The inner door crashed open at that same moment. She flung open the shutters, pulled herself up, and let herself fall through, out onto the grass. She caught only a glimpse of the intruder, it was a tall and shadowy figure.

Immediately she was on her feet and running as far from her home as she could. She looked back to see if she was being followed, and saw her assailant come around the house—he must have gone back out the front door. He saw her immediately. Idelette gasped again and tried to run faster. She weaved in and out between houses, looking for a place to hide. She glanced back again and he was gaining ground—still in pursuit. Where to hide? Where to hide?

She threw open the gate to a stable and rushed inside—turning back she saw it was still approaching rapidly. Screaming in fear she frightened the animals. Startled from their slumber they ran out of the stable onto the path. Horses, cows, ducks, and pigs poured out that one door toward the vampire. They panicked and jostled about between it and the stable door. Idelette rushed behind a stack of hay bales and dove out a window on the side of the stable, behind the chicken coop. She had bought herself just a moment—what to do? Where to run?

The church! It was holy ground! And though it was on the far side of the village, she saw no other option. She took off like a soul sprung from purgatory. In abject terror she ran along the edge of the village, trying to take the most direct route she could among buildings while still staying out of sight. The final stretch was open ground—nearly 50 yards to the church door at the center of the graveyard. She hesitated before entering the open terrain. She strained her sight to peer through the darkness, but saw the creature advancing in the distant shadows! It had figured out her plan, and though still far from her, was approaching fast! Out of options, she had to chance it. She stumbled with her first step but then ran with all she had. The ground seemed to stretch beneath her feet as though the church were fleeing from her. Finally she reached the door. Screaming and banging on it, she looked back again. It had passed the houses and was headed toward the cemetery. Idelette could hardly believe how fast it moved! She screamed again when suddenly the door flung open and Dom Calmet stood there with a lighted candle. Idelette brushed him aside and slammed the door behind them. Crying she blew out his candle and peered through the cracks between the doors—there was only darkness.

"What has happened young lady?" Dom Calmet whispered.

"Shhhhh.... It's out there!"

As she continued to stare out through the gap, she saw lights begin to glow here and there in the houses. People were waking. They must have heard her screams or the animals loose in the village.

"Tell me what happened," Dom Calmet probed.

"I saw it!"

CHAPTER 17

Ryan drove to work and crammed a fistfull of vending machine cookies down his throat as he walked to the morgue. He was very lean but probably had some form of silent malnutrition, since he lived mostly on candy bars and donuts. He couldn't eat in the lab, and when not at work, he was so often on the move that he didn't bother with meals. Tossing the empty cookie bag in the trash, he waited by the punch clock next to the cooler for eleven o'clock to roll around, then wandered down to Surgical Pathology. A day with no autopsy meant his shift would be spent entirely in the lab. Ryan strolled into the grossing room and began to set up the specimens.

"You look tired!" Phil noted as the diener walked into the room. "Another late night doing, um, whatever it is you do in the cemeteries?"

"Yeah..." Ryan barely muttered.

"What do you do there anyway?" Phil asked. "You just hang out and pretend to be dead or what?"

"Yeah, pretty much. We play a lot of hacky sack."

"OK..." Phil replied in a confused and mocking tone.

"Yeah, most people don't understand, and I can't explain it. I just like it," the diener went on.

"Are you going back tonight? What time did you get to bed last night anyway?" Phil continued.

"About six."

"This morning?!?"

"Yeah, you know—"

"I had already gotten up for the day by the time you went to bed!" Phil interrupted. "Who do you find that will hang out with you in a graveyard until dawn anyway?"

"Well, last night I was there with Calvin."

"Who's Calvin?"

"A friend of mine. Does it matter?"

"No, not really. I probably won't remember his name in ten minutes anyway. Have you seen the news reports about Satan-worshipers or something like that? They might have been involved in a recent murder. The news said there is evidence of them meeting in cemeteries."

"Yeah, so I've heard."

"Are they friends of yours?"

"Heh. No."

"So you've met them but you're not friends," Phil joked.

"No. I've not met them either. But I have seen some of their graffiti," Ryan was getting slightly frustrated.

"So if you're not friends with them, but you're hanging around in cemeteries at all hours of the night, what if, you know, you're the next victim?"

"Yeah, what if," Ryan mused.

The conversation was interrupted by a frozen section. After that the day went on uneventfully. Phil left around five, after confirming with surgery that there would be no late frozens. Ryan was finishing up the paper work and the billing when the phone rang. It was an outside call. He knew who it was.

"Histology, Ryan speaking," he answered in a casual tone.

"Is Phil gone? How did everything go?" Larry asked.

"Yeah, he's gone. Everything went fine. Are you coming tonight?"

"Just like I told you before. Remind me how I get there though."

He gave Larry directions to Alan's farm, and instructions on how to introduce himself to Alan in case Ryan hadn't arrived. He finished his usual night work, grabbed some Hostess cupcakes from the vending machine, and proceeded to Alan's house. Larry wasn't there yet. Ryan met Alan by the fire pit and told him what was going on. He watched him stir the extinguished coals and could see tarnished portions of Sarah's knife within the ashes. As they spoke, a hearse pulled into the driveway.

"Evening," Larry said as he got out of the vehicle.

"Hey," Alan and Ryan replied simultaneously.

"Let's see what we've got," Larry insisted, brisk for business.

The two of them led Larry into the barn and to the door of the old silo. Alan opened the rusty old door and Ryan pulled out a body bag sparsely filled with human bones. He showed the contents to Larry and let him investigate them thoroughly. Satisfied with what he saw, Larry congratulated them on a job well-done.

"Anytime you want to pay me, Ryan...." Alan said casually.

"Anytime you want to pay me, Larry...." Ryan deflected.

Larry pulled another envelope out of his breast pocket and handed it to Ryan. He counted the money and shook Larry's hand. The mortician put the bag into a coffin in the back of the hearse.

"You do good work," Larry commented. "I look forward to working with you again in the near future. Did you encounter any witches on broomsticks doing black mass stuff while you were there?" he asked as an apparent last-minute thought.

"No. Do you happen to have any information on that?" Ryan redirected.

"Nope. I've just heard there are murders in cemeteries and witch-related gangs or something like that. Anyway, glad you aren't involved." With that, he turned and left.

Ryan paid Alan his percentage.

"You worried about whoever has been tagging the city and cemeteries?" Alan asked.

"Not worried. But I do want to find out who's behind it."

"It could affect business."

"Exactly why I want to know."

Chapter 18

On a cloudy evening, Ryan and Lydia stood on the upper retaining wall of Greenwood cemetery, looking across Leonard Street into Mount Carmel. They were old friends and he had contacted her to catch up, as it had been too long. But he also had an agenda. Unlike the rest of his friends, Lydia had no connection with body trafficking. He wondered if she had encountered any of the people who tagged the cemetery, and the rest of the city, with witch-related iconography. Maybe she would mention it.

"Why are you still coming here, anyway?" Lydia inquired as they sat down.

"Whenever I'm somewhere else, I wish I was here. I know no one else understands that, but it's pretty straightforward to me. I like cemeteries and cadavers. If I could combine those things I would. Greenwood comes close." He dodged the real answer because Lydia didn't know about the ressurection business. "I can walk through here all alone on a quiet night and enjoy seeing bats or owls. It's peaceful. I find it far more comfortable in here than out there with all those people." He motioned with his head to the left, toward the downtown cityscape. "If I could just do an autopsy here, well, that would be a dream come true. Maybe even the best day of my life, I dare say. Alright, why do you like baking?"

"It's interesting and I get to create new things. Baking is actually applied chemistry. Besides lots of people like baking and baked-goods. Not a lot of people like drifting around graveyards."

"Ok. So you like baking just because it is baking. But since you don't have the necessary funds to start up your own pastry shop yet, you settled for being a chef at a restaurant for the time being. And when you are preparing your exclusive over-priced entrees don't you wish you were baking pastries instead?"

"Yeah, pretty much. I'm always thinking of new pastry ideas."

"And so do you go home and bake even though you spent your whole work day in the kitchen cooking?"

"Not every day, but, most days, yeah," she conceded.

"Same idea. I get to do autopsies at work but I always want to get back here. I don't know why I like Greenwood any more than you know why you like baking. That's what you like and this is what I like."

"That's fair. You're still weird though."

"I know. And there's more to it than what I've said. I honestly can't tell you exactly what draws me back to Greenwood again and again." Ryan confessed in words that hid his true meaning. "And cloudy days like this just make it better. It's so dreary, so melancholy. How do you not love it?"

"Last time the weather was like this I was sitting with Zoe in a restaurant, sipping coffee," Lydia shifted gears. "Now that was dreary."

"Oh really? I saw her recently too."

"Yeah she mentioned that, in point of fact."

"Small world that all three of us old friends should happen

to see one another again. What's new with Zoe? What did you two catch up on?"

"She's got a whole new group of friends now and I think they're stupid. I don't have time for their drama."

As Lydia spoke, a pair of junior high girls passed by below them at the base of the wall. They bantered and laughed as they looked up. Ryan entertained the notion that those two could become future victims if they passed through at night.

"That's fair. We've all got our own lives to deal with now. Move on." Ryan was eager to change the subject, oblivious to the fact that she was already discussing the witches. "Have you heard about the murder in Tyler Memorial Gardens?"

"Yeah, I heard some gang tried to take credit for it, but another guy already confessed. Or something like that, I guess. I don't know. I don't follow the news."

"I heard they were Satanists."

"Really. I hadn't heard that. Like I said though, I don't follow the news."

"Has anything happened at your work? The hopsital has a lot of security so our buildings haven't been tagged yet."

"The alley behind the restaraunt was vandalized. No one has died or anything, if that's what you mean. Or if they did, I don't know about it. Like I said, I don't follow the news."

"That's probably to your advantage," Ryan nodded, disappointed that she hadn't had any closer encounters. It was a longshot anyway, but he was hopeful. He didn't know anyone else outside the graverobbing buisness to ask though. "Anyway, it's getting late. Didn't you say you have to work tonight? We should probably split. Thanks for meeting me to catch up a bit. It was good to see you again."

"I guess. It was nice to see you again too. Have fun cutting up dead bodies tomorrow."

Chapter 19

The Tick-Tock diner is exactly the sort of place you would expect somebody working the graveyard shift in the body trafficking business to eat. It is always loud, and the staff and patrons alike have all completely given up on life. Certainly, nobody cares what you talk about.

Paul palpated the suture scars on his forehead and sipped his coffee as Nick spoke to him about the incident in Greenwood. Paul had been pressing Nick for information for the past month.

"I know you've wanted to get revenge on them, but I couldn't do anything for you while we had work to do," Nick spoke in a matter-of-fact tone. "I know you're angry. And it works to my advantage too if something can be done to eliminate them as competition. Now that we are between jobs, I can clue you in on how to resolve your problem."

"Just tell me where and when," Paul grumbled angrily.

"I don't know where to find the other two, but I can definitely tell you how to find Ryan," Nick lowered his voice unnecessarily.

"I'll tell you how to get to the morgue, and I'll give you the code to unlock the door, but you have to wait until you know that he's there. It's the only place secluded enough that you can act without fear of getting caught. But I'm not going to do the spying for you. It's your vendetta," Nick elaborated.

"He's dead," Paul muttered as he felt his scar again. "And if I can find the other two...."

Nick gave him the information he needed, settled his bill, and left promptly. He was barely out the door when a young blonde woman rose from the booth behind Paul and sat down across from him.

"Um. Can I help you?" Paul muttered, still rubbing his scar.

"Yes. Yes, you can," Zoe replied. "Tonight, in fact."

"Oh?"

"Go to Greenwood cemetery tonight. Be there by 9pm. You will meet a nice brunette who can tell you about the people you are so angry with. Pay attention now!" She snapped at Paul as he tried to see his scar in his reflection on a spoon. "The brunette girl! She knows Ryan and his friends. She can tell you where they will be and also when. I'll arrange the meeting. She'll be there."

"Who are you and how do I know I can trust you?"

"I'll arrange the meeting. She'll be there."

"You said that already. And how do you know about all this anyway?"

Zoe rolled her eyes and sighed. "Listen. 9pm. Greenwood. She's a brunette. An attractive brunette. She'll be the only one there. I'll make sure of that. Get it right." And with that, Zoe rose and left the restaurant without looking back. Paul watched her go. When he turned back to his food his bill was sitting beside his plate. There were strange symbols drawn on it.

Chapter 20

"Cookies?" Ryan offered Mike a nutritious breakfast, fresh from a vending machine.

"No thanks," he laughed.

"What are we doing here anyway?" Ryan inquired through a mouthful of cookies as he cracked open a can of root beer.

The two of them were back at the office building of Greenwood on a beautiful April morning. It was a Sunday and the cemetery was empty. It would probably stay empty all day too. Mike walked around the building and unlocked the old wooden door. This was Ryan's first time seeing inside this part of the building. It was an extension of the basement that was about twelve feet square, with an eight foot high ceiling. In the center of the room was an old wood table that resembled an antique surgery table. Various instruments, equipment, and tools, of similar antiquity, lay scattered around the room. A few hooks on the north wall held some white frocks and aprons. In the southwest corner of the floor was a two by two foot square panel of sheet metal with a handle on it. The floor was concrete and the walls were the same. Wood with steel beams made up the ceiling. The open door provided better light than the couple bulbs which dangled from the low ceiling.

"I've always suspected…." Ryan muttered.

"More than a century ago, physicians and surgeons who did their own resurrections would sometimes perform their dissections right here after plundering graves. If they just had one clinical question to answer, they could do a hasty dissection then return the body to the grave that same night. Or, they could amputate limbs to package bodies for easier shipment. I called Sarah, by the way. She's on her way to help."

"Help with what exactly? I mean, I think I get the general idea but what are the specifics?"

"Well, it's Sunday. So we don't have to worry about visitors because you're the only one who ever comes on Sundays. And you're already here."

"Um. OK. Continue, please."

"I found a dead woman in the Jewish section yesterday. She looks like a loner. Probably a teenage runaway or something. I dunno maybe I'm wrong about that. Anyway, I decided that the law didn't need to get involved because that would draw even more attention to us and maybe even what goes on around here."

"If you've got a body stowed somewhere above ground, then I hope you're right about Sundays being poorly attended here. What are we doing with her?"

"We will dissect her, take what we can sell, and destroy the rest of her. Her body is in the floor below us—through that panel in the corner."

Sarah walked in the door at that moment. Mike filled her in on the details. The three of them pulled the dead girl up through the opening in the floor and put her on the table. They donned frocks, aprons, gloves, and rubber boots, and started working. The body was that of a healthy young brunette—she had been pretty while she was alive. She wore a gray coat and blue jeans. A quick external examination revealed conjunctival petechiae and a large bruise around her neck.

The whole thing proceeded like an 18th century French autopsy. It was hasty, deliberate, and somewhat unrefined. Because there would be no viewing of the body after dissection, the cuts were more liberal. Ryan opened her torso the old way, by an incision extending from the lower lip to the pubic region. He grabbed the skin on either side of the incision and pulled it to the right and left, cutting it free from the rib cage as he went. With a few quick strokes of the scalpel he was through the costal cartilages without needing a saw or costotome. With the sternum removed, he took out the chest and neck organs, including the tongue, as a single bloc. After that he took the organs out one by one, handing them to Sarah as he worked. The intestines were first, which he cut free from the spine by a few large strokes across the root of the mesentery. Then followed the liver and spleen. Next the stomach and pancreas together. Kidneys, adrenals, and pelvic organs completed the evisceration. There is an odd sucking and sloshing sound that happens when tearing the pelvic organs up and off the bone. It actually caused Mike to stop what he was doing for a moment.

She was young and slim so the dissection was fast and easy. Sarah and Mike bagged the organs and laid them out on the countertop. Mike and Sarah removed her limbs while Ryan took the brain. He made the scalp incision the old way too, along the midline from the bridge of the nose to the occiput. He had always wanted to try that. There was no oscillating saw though so he had to open the skull with a handsaw followed by some little effort with a hammer and chisel. It was by far the slowest part of the dissection, during which Mike and Sarah accomplished the amputations by large incisions circumscribing the hips and shoulders. A few additional deep cuts through musculotendineous components and the limbs were off.

Ryan opened the spinal column from the anterior approach and removed the spinal cord. Then, just to slow any chance of identification if found, he peeled her face and removed it entirely.

"Some of this we can probably sell but a bunch of it will just have to be incinerated. I can bag some things and sneak them into the hospital to add to the biohazard waste, but I can't do it today," Ryan said as he took a swig of root beer. Just then a tall, fair haired individual in khaki pants and a sweater walked in the door. It was Alan.

Mike glared at Ryan, who, in turn, shrugged and threw up his hands as if to say 'I didn't invite him! How should I know he was going to show up?'

"I figured I'd find you here. I just didn't expect you to be in, well, here," Alan continued.

"How did you know where we were? You didn't drive through the southeast part of the cemetery—we would have seen your car," Sarah replied.

"I saw your cars parked at the gas station across the street so I drove in. I parked my car by the crossroads and started walking toward the retaining wall. As I approached the office building I saw the back door propped open and a stream of blood was running down the hill. I immediately thought two things: 'I found Ryan' and 'the floor in that room isn't level.'"

Mike, Sarah, and Ryan all looked out the door. A stream of blood was in fact flowing out the door and down the hill.

"Well that's a little overly conspicuous, isn't it?" Sarah remarked.

"Put on some gloves and give us a hand," Ryan suggested.

"Eh. I dunno..." Alan replied. "Is that...?!"

"A dead girl found yesterday," Sarah interrupted.

Mike crammed the remaining pieces into bags. Ryan lifted the panel in the corner, and the began stuffing the girls remains back where they found them.

"How old is all this equipment?" Sarah asked.

"Some of it's well over a hundred years old. But some of it is only about fifty years old," Mike estimated. "The city once tried to monopolize the funerary industry. But ensuing legislation rendered it impossible. Private funeral homes have deep pockets and they weren't about to give up their revenue to the government. So they lobbied. This room used to have additional fixtures for embalming, and beneath that panel are fixtures for gas and electric. It was intended for a crematorium retort, but one was apparently never built. This room never gets used anymore, hasn't for decades, and most of the employees have no idea what is in here. We're the first to do this in many years. You don't have to scrub, by the way. Just use a lot of bleach," Mike added. "It's funny to me that I know that but the real employees don't."

"Real employees?" Ryan gave him a quizzical look.

"Oh yeah. Technically, I'm not actually a cemetery employee," Mike was quick to comment.

At this, everyone stopped what they were doing and just stared at him. It was a tense moment.

"I took this job illegitimately," Mike went on to explain. "I just showed up one day and started running things here in Greenwood, right from this building rather than downtown. The week prior, the mayor and governor were revealed to be involved in a scandal and their support staff was dragged through indictments with them. The whole ordeal involved employees in numerous city and county offices. There was also turnover to a new labor union at that same time. Mass layoffs and terminations quickly followed. So when things began to settle, and when people in the

Parks Department started to question who I was, I convinced the real new-hires in HR that I was a recent hire under the last administration. When they couldn't find my employee number, W4, or other paperwork, I blamed it on the group that had all just lost their jobs anyway. They believed my story that it must all just be clerical error due to lack of oversight. They all fully believed the corruption went all the way up and down in the previous organization anyway. So they issued me an employee number, and I started collecting a paycheck. It's been twenty years and I've been riding that wave ever since. No one has questioned it. Not even once. But don't any of you go blabbing about it!"

They all had a good laugh at that as they finished hiding the bags of the dead girl's pieces and parts under the floor.

Ryan poured bleach over everything and Sarah used a hose to spray all the blood and chunks out the door. The bloody stream became notably larger as it flowed down the slope and pooled at the bottom. The diluted bloody water seeped into the moist soil of Potter's field. So ended their illicit autopsy. Mike closed up the office as the other three left together.

"That was Lydia's coat laying on the floor! Was that her?" Alan interjected quietly as they walked to his car.

"Yep," Ryan confirmed.

"You didn't want Mike to know you knew her!"

"Correct. And I would very much like to know who killed her because I'm pretty ticked off about it."

Chapter 21

Several days after the clandestine dissection of Lydia in the graveyard, Sarah stood at the knife counter in a sporting goods store eyeing their fixed blades. She was lamenting the loss of the knife she cut Paul with. Everything around her was related to gun culture. There were floor safes behind her and reloading equipment to her left. The glass handgun case extended to her right. Shotguns and rifles densely lined the wall before her. They had a decent selection of knives too, but stores like this never had quite what she was looking for it seemed. Regardless, this was her best option because she could pay cash.

"Can I help you?" the man behind the counter eventually asked as he walked over to her.

"I'm looking for a new knife, and am trying to decide if I want a fixed blade or a folder. I've mostly used a fixed blade in the past."

"What do you use your knife for?" the incredulous man asked in a condescending tone.

"Hunting and camping mostly. I like a knife I can take apart a deer or pig with, but also trim branches for kindling. I don't do small game hunting so I tend to go for longer blades. A Bowie is a bit much because they're inconvenient to carry, and the bevel is never the angle I want," she mixed lies with truth.

"Well, what have you bought in the past?" The outmatched man looked perplexed.

"I carried a skinner for a while but then went for a longer blade. I wasn't happy with the edge retention though. Then I tried ceramics since those would pass through metal detectors, but they don't keep their edge. Now I'm wondering if I've been missing out with some of the new folders. The prices have risen dramatically, but I honestly think the quality probably has as well."

"Why would you care about the metal detectors if you are using it for camping?" The man tried to keep up with the conversation.

"What do your other customers say about the folders they buy? Do they like them? And do you know if that flipper is titanium?" She ignored his question.

"Ummmm...I'd have to pull the box from in the back and find out."

"Never mind. It looks like you have another customer. I'll get your attention if I need you over here."

The man seemed relieved to be free of the conversation. He didn't even glance back at Sarah who was now contemplating how difficult it would be to order a custom sheath for one of the smaller Bowie knives in the case. As she considered that, someone stepped up beside her. She was petite and blonde and wore a black trench coat. Sarah was several inches taller than her. She noticed some symbols scrawled on the back of her hand.

"Like knives do you?" Zoe asked.

"I like good knives. Most of these are garbage though."

"What's wrong with these folding knives over here? Those seem like good brands."

"Yeah the folders are pretty good but I'm trying to find a decent fixed blade. It's not easy to do."

"I only ever carry a little pocket knife. It was a gift from a friend years ago. Larger knives seem excessive for daily use. It's not like you can carry it into a restaurant or something. But I can carry my little pocket knife just about anywhere."

Sarah did not answer but knelt down to see some Ka-Bar knives and tantos at the back of the bottom shelf she had not noticed before. They had a kukri, interestingly enough. That could be fun. There were also some throwers. But she had throwers already. Then she noticed a Ka-Bar with a tanto blade. That might be a good compromise.

"You obviously take your work pretty seriously," Zoe interjected into the conspicuous silence. Here Sarah looked back up at Zoe and rose to her feet. She could not entirely conceal the suspicious expression on her face.

"Have we met before?"

"No. No, we have not." Zoe made very direct eye contact. "But, we've been watching you for some time." She relaxed her gaze slightly. "We are interested in you and we think you might be interested in our organization as well. You see, we are very goal-oriented people, like you. And we are aggressively pursuing that goal."

"Let me just stop you right there. Who is 'we' and what makes you think I'm so stupid that you can gaslight me? Thanks for the awkward sales pitch that doesn't actually provide any information though. It sounds like a pyramid scheme. I'm not even remotely interested, and I'm certainly not buying." With that she turned to the man down at the far end of the counter, "I'll take this tanto Ka-Bar."

Zoe stood next to her and silently watched Sarah buy her knife and leave. Neither said another word.

"Wow, a second pretty blonde at my knife counter in a matter of minutes. Is there something I can help you with?" the clerk asked Zoe.

"Drop dead," Zoe muttered without looking at him. She watched Sarah walk out of the store, then slowly began to follow after her.

Sarah looked about suspiciously as she traversed the parking lot. When she got to her car there was another young lady standing by it. Sarah paused and glared.

"Have you thought about what she had to say?" the stranger asked. "You should come see what we have to offer."

"Get away from my car. I don't want whatever it is you are selling," Sarah replied. Then she looked to her right. There was another girl.

"It's not what you think. We're not buying or selling anything. It's much bigger than anything like that," the second girl joined in. She had frizzy hair and glasses. She looked young and impressionable.

"We're changing the world," a third girl said from behind Sarah.

Sarah spun around to face the third girl. She was tall with long dark hair, a short skirt, and torn nylons. Sarah noticed a scar across one of her arms.

"You're going to change the world? You? I don't think so," Sarah replied and then spun back around to the other girls. But they were gone. She turned immediately back around. The third girl was gone too. Annoyed and admittedly confused, Sarah got in her car. There was an envelope on the dashboard with numerous symbols drawn on it. She opened it and found a note which read, 'Sibley Street tunnel tomorrow at 9pm. Come see for yourself.' Sarah cast it aside on her front passenger seat. She didnt have time for this nonsense. She had to prepare for tonight.

Chapter 22

Sarah paced impatiently atop a mausoleum in Oak Hill cemetery. She had thrown her backpack and shovel onto the roof before climbing up there herself. They were still laying where they had landed. Always early, she had sat waiting beside her gear for a while, but then grew restless and began pacing.

The full moon above, and the distant streetlights along the perimeter, illuminated every path, tombstone, tree, and sign. For eyes well-adjusted to night, it was uncomfortably bright. She could read the inscriptions on most of the nearby headstones. Feeling somewhat annoyed, she peered through her surroundings to the streets beyond, watching for Calvin's hearse. He was late.

Fortunately, tonight's job was a fresh grave, so digging should not take long. The body had been in the ground only ten hours. Ryan was unavailable, which meant the pay was split only between Sarah and Calvin. Easy money for easy digging. As she waited, Sarah thought on how it might be possible to grab some extras too. Once they were in the hole, perhaps they could dig sideways into the adjacent graves and pull out some skeletal remains. They had done it before to rob an old grave next to an open fresh one. It worked well.

As she ruminated on that idea, through the tall oaks and glowing marble stones, she caught a glimpse of the much-anticipated hearse. It was the only car on the empty street. Calvin turned into the north side of the cemetery and parked behind the office building. Sarah watched him hoist a backpack and two shovels over his shoulder, then walk south toward her. He confidently crossed the still-empty street with eyes fixed on the mausoleum he knew she would be atop. As he entered among the tombstones, Sarah made a final survey of their surroundings to ensure they were still alone, then jumped ten feet down to the leafy lawn below. The ground was soft and moist. It was an easy landing. She leaned against the wall and waited.

When he arrived, Calvin looked up at the cloudless sky, his face illuminated by the moon and stars. He looked back at Sarah in silence.

"I know it," Sarah lamented. "It's blinding."

"Well, let's get started while we hope for clouds to blow in," Calvin nodded and walked past her.

Sarah followed close behind. They each carried backpacks with equipment. It was not easy to be silent, but Oak Hill was empty. They were only steps beyond the front of the mausoleum when Calvin looked over his shoulder and stopped.

"That's a new development," he pointed.

Sarah turned to find that a large board had been secured across the entire doorway of the mausoleum. It was a hasty patch job, such that there was no operable door, only a sheet of particle board. She had climbed up the back side and had not seen this until now. Someone must have broken in recently. The city would probably brick it up later.

"Think we could get that off there when we're done with the grave? Might be an easy way to obtain skeletal remains if any are left," Calvin said.

"You read my mind."

The pair pressed on from among the trees, across open ground around a giant obelisk, and back into densely populated graves among tall oaks and maples. Reaching the targeted grave, they began immediately. Sarah laid a tarp down and the two began to dig. No sod had been placed yet so it was just loose dirt—an easy job.

"Ryan is missing out," Calvin noted. "This is fast digging and fast money."

"Meh. It's his own fault," Sarah shrugged as she threw more dirt on the tarp. "He thinks he's working on something big chasing vandals. It's a lost opportunity. If investigating who's defacing the cemeteries means more to him than the money he could be making while working in those same cemeteries, then that's his problem. Heck, there's some of that graffiti right over there," Sarah pointed with her shovel handle to a tall vandalized tombstone a few yards away. Strange symbols were spray-painted all over it.

"What do you think that stuff is all about?" Calvin kept digging without even looking at the graffiti. He saw no need to slow down for that. There were no roots or even any bugs in this dirt yet. It was the cleanest, easiest digging a grave robber could ever ask for.

"Who knows. I don't even care at this point, as long as they don't interfere with business. Well, ok. I guess I do care because they might interfere with business. So for that I'm glad Ryan is taking it so seriously."

"I mean, it does seem evil, though, right? And there have been killings. Shouldn't that matter?"

"I don't know if I believe in evil. And I certainly don't believe in whatever those stupid symbols mean. Looks like hocus pocus and nonsense. This shovel does more for me than whatever that magic does for them. Guaranteed."

"What about the opposite?" Calvin inquired.

"Opposite?" Sarah paused to look up and around the cemetery because she realized they had been talking much more than she cared for. All was still though.

"Yeah. So grave robbing, and making money doing it, clearly has meaning for you. But what about doing good things for others? If you don't believe in evil, even as you rob a grave, do you believe in good, or doing good?"

"I do good things for you and Ryan all the time."

"Sure, but we're your friends. I mean random acts of kindness. I think it's important to be a good person," Calvin replied.

"You think you are a good person?" Sarah quipped at the sound of Calvin's shovel striking the vault lid below.

"Well, I mean I do a lot of good things to make up for my bad behaviors. Being a good person is what's important. Sure I do this too, but I also do a lot of kind things. I think that's got to count for something."

"Count for something with who? God?"

"Maybe. I don't know. I think it just counts." Calvin grabbed a pair of pry bars and handed one to Sarah.

"I don't think I believe in a God. But if there is one, why doesn't he just stop us from robbing graves rather than requiring you to fetch groceries for little old ladies?"

"Well. I don't know. But I still think I am more good than bad. It's not like I rape or murder people. These people are already dead. What's the harm?"

"On that we agree," Sarah muttered as she raised her pry bar aloft.

The two of them struck the lid in a coordinated fashion, and watched a crack propagate across it. It was a technique that took time and practice to master. They flipped the bars around and pried up the corners. Then they leaned the broken piece of lid against the side of the hole. As Sarah thrust the hooked end of her pry bar under the lid of the coffin, Calvin climbed up out of the hole and sprinted back toward his car.

Sarah watched him go as she forced the coffin lid open. Looking around the cemetery—still empty—she thought on their conversation. It was hard not to get distracted by it, but this was a very dangerous point in the operation. If police showed up now, it would be a disaster. But she never got anxious.

Calvin quietly rolled up to the nearest point on the path and parked the hearse. He threw the back doors open and rushed back to their open grave.

He tossed the end of a rope down to Sarah. She grabbed the corpse by the hair, yanked its head up toward her, and looped the rope under its arms. Climbing out, she and Calvin hoisted the body up and out. It was dripping with embalming fluid, and the strong odor of alcohols and formaldehyde permeated the air. The two dragged it into a body bag, zipped it shut, and tossed it into the back of the hearse.

"What about Ryan? What do you think he believes?" Sarah asked.

"He used to go to church as a kid," Calvin replied as they cleaned up a bit of the mess. "I think he still believes in God. I think he even feels what we do is wrong, but does it anyway."

"That's weird," Sarah shook her head as she pulled some tangled strands of the dead person's hair from her fingers and flicked them to the ground.

Calvin jumped into the front seat and drove off, leaving Sarah to fill in the hole. It was best to get the hearse out of the graveyard as soon as possible, in case police showed up. He would drop off the body for their client then come back.

Meanwhile, Sarah continued to muddle over the idea that Ryan could think this was wrong but do it anyway. Why did he do it if he thought God would be angry with him for it? Were they all going to hell for this? She looked again at the graffiti on the nearby tombstone and noticed that there were a few used candles strewn about in the leaves near it. What about the witches who painted that? They were sorcerers and murderers, if the news was to be believed. Surely, they were worse people than she was.

The time passed quickly as she thought about this, and Calvin was back sooner than expected. He parked the now-empty hearse across the street and rushed back to Sarah to finish the job. There wasn't much left to do.

"Does he still go to church?" Sarah asked.

"I don't know. I don't think so." Calvin picked up his shovel. "I have seen a Bible on his book shelf though."

"What? Next to all those old poetry books he collects?"

"Yeah."

"I actually think some of the poetry books are neat. He's got a bunch of leather ones from the 1700s," Sarah admitted as the two poured dirt into the hole. "Old books are kind of cool."

"Yeah, I'm not a poetry kind of guy. I'll watch any Tolkien movie though, thank you very much."

Calvin grabbed the last of the gear, folded up the tarp, and the two turned toward the mausoleum in the distance.

"Well?" Calvin interrupted himself as he studied the particle board before them. "Should we try?"

"Might as well. You will have to mow your neighbor's lawn to make up for it though, so karma or God or whatever doesn't curse you."

"I will indeed. And that's fine by me. Maybe you should try making the world a better place sometime. I can give you a list to put us both square with the universe."

"So I'm not a good person?" Sarah quipped. "What about Ryan? Does just owning a Bible or going to church as a kid earn him points?"

Calvin sighed.

Sarah dropped it and pushed a bit against the door. She eyed the edges all around. Calvin tried to wedge his shovel blade between the wood and the stone, but it was too tight for the curved shovel blade, and the angle gave him no means to pry. If the shovel could not fit in, the thicker pry bar certainly could not. He rapped on the center of the wood with the shovel handle. A hollow reverberation answered back.

"Think we could just knock it down?" Calvin looked at Sarah.

She didn't say a word, but the two promptly threw their gear aside, and took four or five steps backward.

"Three. Two. One." Sarah said, and they took off running toward the door. Together they crashed against it with their shoulders. It shook a bit, but not much. Never known for quitting easily, they backed up and tried again. No greater success.

"Once more?" Calvin asked.

"Once more."

The two backed up and gave it all they had—which was not much at this point. It rattled a bit but didn't move or break.

"Forget it," Sarah rubbed her shoulder. "It's not going to happen and I'm exhausted."

"Bummer. Well, let's get out of here. I'm beat too."

The tired and sore grave robbers gathered up their things and walked around the back of the mausoleum. No sooner had they turned the corner, however, when they heard a loud crash which stopped them in their tracks. They spun around and stared back toward the sound.

After a tense moment of silence, they looked at each other a bit bewildered. Calvin noticed Sarah had, at some point, instinctively drawn a knife out of her sleeve. Calvin gripped his raised shovel. He motioned with a head nod to Sarah that he should go left and she should go right, back to the front of the mausoleum.

They stepped cautiously, avoiding crunchy leaves, and ready for combat. The night sky was so bright it worked for and against them. They cast shadows which preceded them, but saw no shadows around the other side of the building. The two resurrectionists met at the front of the mausoleum. No one was there, but the noise they heard was immediately clarified.

The particle board was shattered. Portions of it lay scattered everywhere. Fragments were on the floor inside, strewn about the grass, and on the stone pavers in front of the now-open doorway.

Something had broken out, not in.

The two looked all around but saw not a soul.

Calvin took a small flashlight from his pocket and illuminated the inside of the tomb. The witches had been inside at some point, evidenced by their symbols painted all over the interior. That was probably the reason for the board over the doorway. But over all the painted symbols there was something else. Latin words were freshly-carved into the stone. They read, "vanitas vanitatum, omnia vanitas." Over and over again, the phrase was carved on all the walls and the ceiling, obscuring the graffiti everywhere. Bits of rubble from the carving covered the slab floor.

"Do me a favor, will you?" Sarah broke the silence. "Don't mention this to Ryan."

"Why not? We both know he's going to find it."

"I know. I want to see if he mentions it to us."

Calvin looked at Sarah somewhat confused, but she only kept her gaze straight ahead into the tomb for several more seconds. Then turning without a word, she sheathed her knife, and continued on her way. Calvin followed.

Meanwhile, Idelette stood beside the grave those two had just robbed. Her eyes saw deeper into the darkness than any mortal could, and she watched the distant graverobbers leave. Her right hand gripped the Bible in her coat pocket as she then studied the refilled grave at her feet, as well as the vandalized tombstone nearby. Listening to the subterranean corpses around her stir in their coffins, she turned her gaze from the grave below to the silent deep far above her. A wispy cloud drifted off the brilliant moon. The excessive brightness caused her pupils to constrict. Just then, she heard new voices in the distance. Her ravenous thirst reclaimed all her attention, and she clutched the Bible in her pocket a little tighter as she tried to fight back the sanguinary cravings.

"The spirit is willing," she whispered. She turned and fled the cemetery to prevent herself from killing whoever was approaching.

Chapter 23

All the next day, Sarah perseverated about the note she had received. She wasn't one for being duped into a bad situation by a gimmick. And they seriously sounded like a cult. But she was sincerely growing curious. The daily routine seemed to drag on and she changed her mind several times before the afternoon. At 8:58 she looked at the clock one last time and shook her head. She wasn't going. After all, she didn't even know what she was missing, so she wouldn't regret it. At 9:05 she decided to go get a sandwich instead. Then at least she knew what she was getting for her money—a late supper, to be exact.

She walked outside and found there was another note tucked in the window of her car. She paused to consider the situation then looked around sharply to see if anyone was watching. She surveyed trees, bushes, other cars, windows, and doors. She saw nobody. She even knelt down and glanced under her car. Nobody there either. At last, she approached and took hold of the note. It read, 'Fine, have it your way, 10pm tomorrow instead.' Her eyes widened a little. She pocketed the little slip of paper and went to get her sandwich.

The girl at the sub shop made very direct eye contact with Sarah as she entered. She took Sarah's order, but then as she was making the sandwich Sarah noticed the young lady had a tattoo on the side of her neck which read, "so below." Sarah couldn't quite make sense of it, but wasn't going to give the sandwich girl the satisfaction of asking about it. When her food was ready Sarah got out her wallet to pay but the girl wouldn't accept it.

"For you, it's on the house," she said as she slid the sandwich across the counter top to Sarah. The paper wrapper had several symbols drawn on it. Had Sarah not just watched her make it, she probably would have refused to eat it and walked out. But she didn't see the girl tamper with the food at all and, besides, she was starving at this point. Deciding to roll the dice, she thanked the girl behind the counter and left with her food.

"Are you coming tomorrow?" a random girl asked her as she stepped out onto the sidewalk. Sarah looked up in surprise at her but she kept walking. "You should definitely come. You won't regret it," the girl shouted back to Sarah as she crossed the street.

It was all getting pretty weird, but admittedly intriguing. Sarah wondered why they were so interested in her. In fact, she wondered about it so much, she basically forgot that she didn't even know who they were or what they were up to. She just dwelled on the bizarre fact that they seemed to know her. And what's more, they were peculiarly interested in her for some reason. She had seen the symbols in the news and heard the reports about the crimes, but they all seemed speculative. Besides, she was a grave robber! She was no stranger to the underworld. What could these girls be involved in that could possibly surprise her? She had seen a lot of strange things with her own eyes before this group ever made the headlines. She decided to go.

The next night, she strapped her new knife under her coat and headed for the tunnel. She knew it well already. It was a concrete foot path through a hill under the expressway. The tunnel was the quickest way to get from the poor blue-collar neighborhoods in the valley, up the hill to the more wealthy white-collar neighborhoods on the upper west side. It was a pretty steep incline and water rushed down it during storms.

She drove into the valley, then parked a few blocks away, and walked the remainder of the distance. It might seem more strategic to approach from the high ground in case she was ambushed, but that would only mean that she would have to run up hill as well. Plus there were fewer places to flee to in the more affluent neighborhood. If cops came rolling in, she could disappear much more easily in the slums. Furthermore, the ground was flat down here so she could escape more quickly and cover greater distance if necessary.

The neighborhood was dark and only a few porch lights were on here and there. But a soft glow eminated from the tunnel entrance, faintly illuminating the middle of the darkened street. Dim fluorescent lights ran along the ceiling all the way up and down it. Sarah stood in the shadows directly across the street from the entrance and peered in as far as the incline would permit. She studied the trees on the hill above the entrance, but saw no one. Cautiously she approached the open gate at the entrance and looked up to the opposite aperture. The tunnel was empty.

As she considered her options, a black cat walked up behind her, brushing against her boot as it passed. She watched it stroll straight up the center of the path about thirty feet into the tunnel and turn around. Its penetrating yellow eyes stared straight at her as it sat down. The cat shifted its paws a little bit, the way cats do when they want attention and are hoping their owner will respond. Sarah shook her head slightly and stepped into the tunnel. The cat shifted its front paws a little more as she approached. When she reached it she bent down to rub its dark coat.

"We're glad you came," a voice behind and above her said.

Sarah immediately rose and spun around. There was a punk-rock girl looking at her. Sarah looked back down at the cat.

"Of course it's gone," she muttered under her breath.

"I'm Lady," the girl said, ignoring the previous statement. "And you are Sarah, of course. You made the right choice."

"So far I'm not convinced of that," Sarah insisted, deciding she was probably going to have to cut her way out of this infernal tunnel.

"Oh, we have so much we can show you," a new girl said behind her. This pretty much confirmed Sarah's suspicions that she would be murdering her way out before long.

Sarah stared at the new girl, uncertain of what to say. But as she did, more girls came in through both ends of the tunnel. There were dozens of them.

"Thanks for showing up to our ritual," Lady joined in again.

"Ritual?" Sarah raised an incredulous eyebrow ever so slightly.

"Oh yes."

"Where's the blonde girl I saw yesterday? The one who invited me?"

"I don't know. There are so many of us. If you don't see her here, she must be practicing somewhere else in the city."

"Practicing?"

"Our craft of course."

"Witchcraft," Sarah said blandly.

"Oh yes. We are powerful in the craft and can conjure, summon, hex, bewilder, and control. We have authority over life and death."

"Heh," Sarah scoffed.

Lady merely smiled, slightly. Then she pulled a little book from her pocket. It looked rather old, its brown cloth torn at the edges, and the spine cocked. With that all the other girls produced from their pockets and purses chalk, candles, lighters, incense, and spray paint. Working together they quickly filled the tunnel with all manner of bizarre texts and symbols. It was accomplished remarkably fast. Every surface was rapidly covered.

Several girls lit their candles. They dripped wax onto the concrete floor, and used it to hold their tapers upright in rows on either side of the group. This cast their commingled shadows toward the middle of the tunnel. They all sat down, except Sarah. Then Lady began to read. Some of her words were English, but others were not. Thick smoke filled the tunnel and Sarah watched as the girls passed something along from the high end of the tunnel down the slope to Lady. As it got close, Sarah recognized what they had. It was the cat she had followed in. It licked its lip and watched Sarah as they passed it toward her. Lady took hold of the cat and lay her book on the floor.

"Do you have a knife?" she asked Sarah.

"Yes," she plainly stated but did not move.

"May we borrow it?"

"No."

"Very well," Lady slightly smiled again. And with that, she twisted the cat's head around. Sarah heard the crack of its neck breaking. It fell to the floor in a lifeless heap and she muttered more words Sarah did not understand. The smoke grew increasingly thick and Sarah began to feel lightheaded. Lady's words began to slow and most of the girls became blurry and hard to focus on. She seemed to see movement between and among them, but could not identify what she saw. The candles seemed to flicker slightly in succession. It was as though the smoke were parting to allow something to pass through.

Sarah was having an increasingly difficult time trying to focus, and her concentration was strained to its limits. She continued to stand, but were the others still sitting? Or were they actually floating, as it appeared? Lady's incantation went on, and the other girls joined in. Sarah looked down at the dead cat. It lifted its head slightly and looked back up at her. Sarah's jaw dropped as the cat rose to its feet, and scurried out of the tunnel.

"Sarah," Lady caught her attention again. "We are powerful. You could be too. So very powerful. Is there something you desire? You can have it. Is there someone in your life who hasn't noticed you? He will be yours to command. Do you follow orders? You will give orders. Do you wait while others lead? You could already be leading them. Join us and we will teach you. I know it is a lot to take in. Think about it." Then she whispered, "we will be waiting."

As she spoke the other girls extinguished their candles and silently vacated the tunnel. Lastly, Lady turned and walked away down the slope, disappearing through the smoke that still filled the spinning and phantasmagoric tunnel. Completely disoriented, Sarah couldn't follow even if she wanted. But presently the smoke was clearing. As she looked at the graffiti which surrounded her she began to realize she was alone in this incriminating place. She was already beginning to sober and it was time to leave.

Driving home, a few blocks from where it had all happened, she noticed a cat in the gutter that appeared to have been hit by a car. It was large and black and its intestines were spilled from it's belly. She debated whether or not she should tell anybody about what happened tonight. That cat was probably the same cat. It was probably dead the whole time. It wasn't magic. No way. They probably just drugged her. But how? The smoke would have drugged them all, too. And if the cat didn't leave on its own, how did it vanish? It was dead, after all. She needed to take some time to process what had happened. When she arrived home she collapsed into bed, eager for some much needed sleep.

Chapter 24

Time never rests and neither do the dead. In fact, bodies move a lot. All through thespring and summer, morgues, cemeteries, hospitals, and funeral homes were hopping with work. Ryan, Sarah, and Calvin were robbing graves across the county and beyond. The work was risky, but the money was good, even for the difficult ones. Skeletons were the safest to traffic, especially if they were old, because they were hard to identify. But they could be difficult to extract due to of the fragmentary nature of the body. Foreign universities seemed to make up the majority of customers for the skeletal market. But it was also increasingly true for intact bodies. Embalmed bodies could be parted out for anatomic and research purposes. It wasn't like the black market for viable organs. That was a different business with different customers entirely. Notwithstanding, the resurrectionists seldom had knowledge of who was ultimately at the receiving end of their transactions. They were merely suppliers. Morticians (and others) were brokers. And apparently brokerage was good this year. Grave robbing had become increasingly lucrative over the last couple years. But it had also become increasingly competitive. Larry told them about a group in Pontiac, Michigan that stole thirty bodies in one night. He also informed them that the skeletal remains they had acquired for him were swapped for the bones of another individual in a museum near Detroit—not sure why though. Ryan heard rumor about a diener in Chicago who got caught trying to sell organs at a community college. Nick and his group were still doing low budget work that posed a constant threat to Ryan's team. But both groups had stayed busy this season. Resurrections were in demand after a long winter despite the fear caused a year before by the exposure of the crematorium in a neighboring state that was caught disposing of bodies in a nearby bog. And, more importantly, despite the unexplained homicides in Grand Blanc and the bizarre cult-like activity that had been spreading so rapidly.

"This started off as a great season, but the last few weeks have slowed way down. I don't like it," Sarah observed as she and Ryan helped Calvin change his oil and put new tires on his hearse.

"Tell me about it. I think the killings and witchcraft have made everyone nervous. My solo gigs have been sparse too. But I'll hear from Mark tomorrow. He'll have a request for me, I'm sure."

"I sure hope so. These were expensive tires," Calvin pointed out.

"How do you know Mark will have a job?" Sarah inquired.

"Call it a premonition. He'll call."

"Did he say he was going to call you? I mean just because you think work is coming, how do you know it will be Mark, and how do you know he will call tomorrow?"

"I just know, that's all. I've been doing this a while, and I have a sense of the rhythm this business has," Ryan defended his previous statement.

Sarah was unimpressed by that answer and glanced over at Calvin. But he only shrugged. She shook her head and continued to wipe grease off her hands with an old rag.

As predicted though, Mark called the next morning. He was interested in a body from Oak Hill cemetery. There was no rush—next Monday was good. Oak Hill was always an interesting challenge. It was urban. Lots of houses were densely packed on the streets bordering it, and their front doors practically opened right into the graveyard. That being said, there were two advantages to Oak Hill. First, it was vast (twice the size of Greenwood), and, second, it had elaborate architecture with huge monuments and lots of sepulchres to hide among.

Ryan immediately called his team. Calvin said he wouldn't be available, but Sarah said she would join him. He had hoped all three of them would be there, but two would work. The phone wasn't even out of Ryan's hand yet when Phil called. There was an autopsy to be done.

Chapter 25

"You killed somebody?!" Nick shouted, then looked quickly around to make sure no one heard him. They were in an empty parking lot behind an Episcopalian church, however. There was no risk of being heard.

"I'm sorry, man. I don't know what happened," Paul said sheepishly. "I tried to get her to tell me about Ryan but she refused. The next thing I knew...I had killed her."

"Are you insane?!?"

"I didn't mean it."

"Are you insane?!?"

"No...."

"Unbelievable! And in Greenwood of all places. Unreal. Ryan's gonna know who did this! You need to take care of him immediately."

"I will, man. I will."

"Unbelievable," Nick muttered as he walked back to his car and left Paul standing alone in the middle of the parking lot.

Chapter 26

"Phil," Ryan said excitedly, "I brought something new to try out on today's autopsy!"

"You can't play hacky sack while doing a post," Phil replied casually.

"Hmmmm.... I'll have to try that sometime. But seriously, I got a new bread knife for loaving organs. The company hasn't made them for years but I found one used. It's got an eighteen-inch blade! It's so nice!"

"How did you get that through the hospital without somebody seeing it?"

"Under my coat."

"I should have guessed," Phil shook his head.

The day was rather uneventful other than the autopsy. It was a stage four ovarian cancer case. She died of a pulmonary embolism. The rest of their work was minimal that day and Phil left about five o'clock. Ryan finished up his paperwork and cleaned the lab. After a late dinner from the vending machines he started cleaning the morgue. He stacked all the slats from the autopsy table in the middle and then put the hose through one of the holes in the top slat. When he turned it on, the water first forced all the blood out between the slats. For just one fleeting moment, he got to watch the table bleed. It was like a horror movie. He loved doing that.

About fifteen minutes into the cleaning process he heard the door swing open. It was Mark. He came in, got the body, and left without a word to Ryan—peculiar but not completely unheard of. Moments later the door opened again.

"I thought you'd be back," Ryan called out. "You must have something to say to me—about the job, or whatever."

"There's not much to say really," replied a voice that was not Mark's. "You know what you and your friends did to humiliate me. So you know what I have to do to you now—and as she breathed for the last time, that little brunette girl in the cemetery knew too."

"Paul."

Paul burst into the autopsy room, raising a tire iron as he ran, intent on putting it into Ryan's head. When Paul was just about on top of him, Ryan grabbed the bread knife from the autopsy table and swung with all his might. Paul fell to the floor with his legs parallel to his torso—he had been cut nearly in half and only remained together by his spinal ligaments. He started to utter what seemed to be a blood choked scream but Ryan plunged the knife into his neck before he could pass any air across his vocal cords. Ryan sighed, realizing he now had a long night ahead of him.

He shut the inner door that separates the autopsy room from the rest of the morgue. He quickly opened a new container of hydrochloric acid and put new blades on several scalpels. He had opened Paul's torso at about the middle of the lumbar spine. He passed through the stomach, intestine, both kidneys, as well as other less interesting portions of viscera. Bright pink blood from his abdominal aorta swirled about in the deep red blood of his inferior vena cava. Shades of thick, green fecal material were intermingled in the blood which pooled on the floor. Ryan mopped much of this to the drain under the autopsy table and began working on the solid components. He cut the remains of the viscera free of the two halves of the abdominal cavity and put them down the garbage disposal. He carved off huge chunks of skin, muscle, and fat from the torso and head. This also went in the garbage disposal. He opened the rib cage and removed the thoracic organs which he then loaved into manageable slices and put in the disposal. The head and axial skeleton he broke down into more manageable parts via the bone saw, hammer, and chisel, then put them into the hydrochloric acid. While those decalcified, Ryan put the legs and arms into separate biohazard bags and placed them in the freezer where they store the other amputated limbs. He could do more proper disposal of them later. Ryan cleaned the morgue as he normally would. Afterwards he changed into normal clothes, went to get some food, returned to the morgue and put Paul's skeletal components (now soft and rubbery) down the disposal. Exhausted he glanced at the clock. It was 12:30 in the morning—time to go home. He had a meeting with Alan in the morning, then the Oak Hill job that night.

Chapter 27

Alan and Ryan ambled through Oak Hill cemetery early in the morning. Ryan chose this spot for two reasons. Firstly, he wanted to further imprint the cemetery in his mind before the job that night. Secondly, he hoped the surroundings would work to his advantage. He was trying to recruit Alan to the resurrectionist business.

"Have you thought about my offer?" The diener asked his old friend.

"Some. I need to know more about it. Obviously, it requires late nights and sporadic work. And you tell me the money is good. But what does it actually entail? I mean, there are bodies in the ground and bodies in mausoleums. It can't all be the same. How does it work?" Alan asked.

"Do you want the whole spiel?" Ryan answered him with a question.

"Give it to me," Alan shrugged.

"OK," Ryan replied. "Here it goes. Resurrecting bones from

an old grave is pretty easy as long as the bones have not drifted around too much from erosion, soil settling, or roots growing through the grave. If the bones have spread out too much it can be a real hassle. But fortunately, that's generally not the case. Fresh bodies are a different story all together. But there are several tricks that can help an experienced grave robber work around the funeral industry standards.

"So, here's how a body is typically buried in the twenty-first century: The grave is usually only about four feet deep. Forget the 'six feet under' notion. A cement vault is placed inside the grave. It has a very heavy lid, which is also cement. This is to prevent the ground from sinking in after the body and casket have degraded away. For the purposes of mowing the grass, the city wants the ground flat. The casket is put inside the concrete vault, the lid is placed on top, and the earth is poured back over it using a backhoe.

"Now, to get a body out of a grave you don't have to dig up the entire hole—just the head end. This typically corresponds to the side with the tombstone. Hence the obvious name, headstone. If a marker has not been placed yet, you just look down the row at the other headstones to figure out which side is which. Once dug, the body can be threaded up and out of the hole by tying a rope around the torso under the arms. But you have to be able to open the top half of the casket lid which is usually separate from the bottom half of the lid that covers the legs. Obviously to open the casket lid, the vault lid has to be out of the way.

"Hang on, turn that way, toward the southern border," he interrupted himself, "I want to see how close the houses are, and if they have a lot of windows facing the graveyard. Where was I?"

"The vault," Alan replied.

"Oh yeah. Thanks. That stupid vault lid is by far the worst obstacle. There are a few ways to deal with it. The best is to have an ally at the cemetery. If the body has been selected beforehand,

and there is no way to obtain it prior to it going into the ground, then you need to pay a cemetery employee to prep the lid ahead of time. The lid is lowered onto the vault using a backhoe with cables. It's sort of an improvised crane. With a little technique you can drop the lid just right so it cracks across the middle as it lands—but it doesn't fall apart. That is a tremendous help. If you don't have prior help and you have to break the lid once you've dug up the grave, then the work is much harder. But it is not impossible. Prying it up a little bit near the mid portion with a pry bar, then putting weight on the partially suspended bit will cause tension forces across it, so when you hit a wedge hard against the middle, cracks will propagate quickly. This is loud and can be the riskiest part of the whole operation because you are vulnerable while doing it. Your attention is diverted away from your surroundings and the noise may be heard throughout, or beyond, the cemetery. Even once the lid is successfully broken, the pieces are extremely heavy and hard to work with. So, it's not necessarily smooth sailing even once you're inside.

"Some vaults are sealed. That's not usually too big of a problem since you have to break the lid anyway. But some caskets are sealed too. That's always frustrating. If it is sealed then sometimes you have to just break through the lid. It is slower and louder than you might think. And there is risk of damaging the body when you pull it up and out of the hole you just made. Then there is the body itself that can defeat you.

"Embalming is one obstacle. The fumes can be overpowering and the body is less flexible. But you would be amazed how well some common household items can absorb or neutralize the fumes. Development of a few simple techniques here and there can make an embalmed body easy to work with.

"Rigor mortis is similar. A body in full rigor can be hard to work with because it won't flex in the middle, but a body that has passed rigor can be even worse because it is not rigid enough to supply counter forces.

"Hang on. Let's cross the street over to the north side of the cemetery. I would like to mosey around in there a bit, as well. It's been a while and I'd like to refresh my memory as to where the paths go and what the layout is like." The two crossed over to the north half of Oak Hill and Ryan continued his sales pitch.

"Even simply retrieving body parts comes with its own challenges. Cutting off a head or arms down in the grave and smuggling them out is not too tricky once you know how, but legs are another story because you don't typically open that side of the grave. You have to pull the body part way up and out, cut off the legs, then return the rest of the corpse to the coffin. Alternatively you can just open the foot end of the grave, but it is usually larger than the head end because the casket lid is not usually divided in perfect halves. So you have even more vault lid to lift.

"And once the body parts are out of the grave, they are not as easy to conceal as you might think. Legs and arms are long and awkward. Heads are very round and rigid, and don't lay flat in anything. Plus, since you've cut into them, they leak. Blood and embalming fluid leaks everywhere, seemingly endlessly. So wrapping them properly is imperative.

"The whole process is labor-intensive and it requires a lot of foresight and preparation. There are lots of little surprises that can occur. If you are not ready to handle minor and major obstacles on the fly, then the job can go seriously wrong very quickly. That's how people end up in jail doing this stuff. Well, that's one way. The human factor is another. Everyone has to keep their mouths shut too. And I mean shut." Here he glared at Alan.

"Yeah, I'm not doing all that. Thanks though. You can keep it," Alan said dismissively.

"Seriously? I bet you already had your mind made up, but you still made me say all that anyway."

"Not completely. Pretty close though."

"And people think I'm weird."

CHAPTER 28

10:30 p.m. Not a cop in sight. Sarah and Ryan rolled into Oak Hill cemetery. It had been dark for a little while now, so the police had already made their rounds once and wouldn't be back until about midnight. The two of them drove to the darkest and most secluded spot they could find, then walked to the desired sepulchre. It had an inner door of solid steel and an outer door of steel bars. This outer door had no lock on it, but was permanently closed because the structure was no longer used. Over the two doors was a stone overhang which was high enough to permit a thin person, such as Ryan, to slide between it and the outer door. It was a tight squeeze but Ryan accomplished it by letting out all his breath. Even then his back and stomach scraped along stone and iron as he went over the bars. He would have to do it again to get out.

Ryan found the key that Mark had hidden between two of the large stones that made up the floor on which Ryan now stood. He opened the inner door, and lit a glow stick.

"Crap," the diener muttered.

"What?" Sarah called in to him.

"It's completely empty in here—not even parts."

"Are you sure this is the right one?"

"Yeah..." Ryan breathed as he stared at multiple familiar symbols recently painted inside the sepulchre. He debated on whether or not he should show them to Sarah. He didn't want to cause her undue apprehension about digging graves in the future. Good friends and good help were hard to find.

"Someone beat us to it, eh?"

"Yeah...."

"Well good! That makes our night easier."

"But we'll only get a small percentage of the money for our troubles."

The two of them replaced everything as they had found it. Sarah caught a glimpse of the symbols inside just before they closed the door. She debated on whether or not she would mention them to Ryan. But why didn't he mention them to her? She had suspected for a while that he wasn't always being fulsome with the information he gave to her and Calvin. Clearly she was right. They walked causally together through the moonlight back to the car. Neither mentioned what they saw.

"I need to call Mark and let him know what happened tonight. I was supposed to put the body in a cooler for him at the hospital, but obviously there's no body for him to pick up. Then I'm going to go home and catch up on some sleep. Do you want to join me in Greenwood two nights from now? Maybe after that we could meet Calvin and Alan for pizza to discuss future ressurections," Ryan chimed in at last.

"What are we going to Greenwood for?"

"I still have some remaining parts of Lydia there to pick up and dispose of."

"But what future jobs are we discussing?"

"No idea. I just want to get us coordinated for the rest of the season."

"Is there a reason you can't tell me? I feel like you're withholding something from me."

"I'm not withholding anything. I'm still figuring it out myself."

"Hm," Sarah's frustration continued to grow.

Chapter 29

"I sent photos of the symbols to several language professors at the University, and also to some, well, other, um, scholars," Detective Malli reclined back and tried to crack her sore neck.

"What other scholars?" Detective Jameson poured an obscene amount of sugar into his coffee.

"Just some magicians, witches, ghost hunters, and occultists I found online," she muttered sheepishly. "Don't judge me like that," she interjected as soon as she saw her partner's expression.

"Were they able to help?"

"Who? The professors or the weirdos?"

"Either."

"Yes and no. I got responses back from several of them, but even what they told me didn't really help much. Various respondents identified...hang on...I've got it on a sticky note here somewhere...ok: Scandinavian runes, Aramaic characters, astronomical and astrological symbols, pagan and wiccan magical symbols, something called Linear A which is apparently an old version of Greek, and characters from a book called the Voynich manuscript. But there are plenty that remain unidentified."

"So it's a hodgepodge of stuff," Detective Jameson keenly deduced.

"Yeah."

"But does that mean it's all unrelated?"

"See that's why I said yes and no. I mean, just because we don't know what it all means doesn't mean that it doesn't mean something, you know what I mean?"

"Um, oddly enough, yes. I think so."

"I mean it might mean something, we just don't know what yet."

"I got ya."

"Good, maybe you can explain what I just said to me because now I'm confused," Detective Malli continued to try to crack her neck.

"Well even if it's a hodgepodge, is this a known hodgepodge which is associated with any specific religious practice?"

"No," she tossed the pad of sticky notes back on her desk, then added, "apparently."

"Well if not a religion, what about non-religious practices or ideology?"

"No. Apparently."

"So there is no specific group we can say does this specific thing, using these sets of symbols, for a specific purpose."

"No. Apparently."

"And so we still really have no idea what exactly is going on."

"No—"

"Don't say it."

"—Apparently."

"I'm starting to really like the ones where people just shoot each other over a bag of weed or something. Those cases don't make sense either when you think about it, but at least you know what happened and why they did it."

"Tell me about it. Straight-forward gang violence would be a refreshing break right about now."

Chapter 30

Sarah sat in her car and watched as two gangs approached each other in a neighborhood near Straight street. She had received another invitation (or was it an appointment?) to come see the show. As she looked on, at least twenty people converged on the sidewalk in front of a duplex. Some came on foot, while others pulled up in cars and got out, as proverbial lines were drawn. They were well-known local gangs that had been dealing drugs in the area for decades. Both had reputations for violence and they often got into turf wars with one another. As they approached, several were already shouting over each other.

"Man I told you don't be coming into this neighborhood no more."

"Yeah you. I know you."

"Oh you think you know me."

"Back it up boy."

"Boy?!?"

"I ain't gonna say it again."

"And I told you we sell here. This is ours. Ain't no one takin' it. Walk away right now or there ain't gonna be nothin left of all ya'll."

"Oh you gonna threaten us now. How you gonna threaten us. We killed your man last week. We'll kill all you too."

With that, guns were drawn on all sides, but before shots could be fired something unexpected happened. Calmly into the frenzy strolled a short blonde girl in a black trench coat. She shuffled her feet and didn't even look up when she stopped in the middle of the mob. Everyone was caught off guard. Then many started to speak over each other again.

"What the—!"

"This hooker yours?"

"Don't be walking into this little girl—"

"Silence," Zoe interrupted them without even raising her voice. "Squabble over your drugs and your useless dead members somewhere else. We own this and all that you see. We own any place you go. There is no place for you because it is ours. And we are, at once, everywhere."

As she spoke, girls began to appear from apparently nowhere. It was as though they materialized within the crowd. The gang members slowly lowered their weapons as they saw that they were being outnumbered more than five to one. But looking around, they came to the bizarre realization that they were all the same girl! Eventually one man began to open his mouth to speak, but before he could, each of the girls pulled their hands from their pockets and blood flowed out of their sleeves and pooled at their feet.

"Nope," muttered one gang member, and he turned to leave. But as he did, he met one of the Zoe clones mere inches from his face.

"Leaving so soon?" they all asked in a single voice.

He looked around and they were all different girls now. He turned to look at Zoe again but she was behind him. And that was enough. The crowd began to disassemble and everyone went their separate ways.

"And to think, some women waste their lives hocking snake oil for pyramid schemes," Zoe said to herself before turning to the group. "Do not let them forget this or think it was a passing thing. I want our symbols on every square inch of this street—the houses, driveways, cars, trees, grass, pavement. All of it. If you find any gang graffiti cover it with ours."

"We should have made them give us their money before they went," one girl spoke up.

"Or their drugs and guns," said another.

"We have something far more valuable," Zoe interjected. "The power that we wield will accomplish more for us than street currency. And if getting high is what you want, then I dare any of you to approach me about it. I will bewitch you into a nightmare you can never escape. I will melt your useless brain inside your juvenile skull." She looked around with disdain. "Now here's that guy's cell phone. When you're done tagging this street, someone call the police to report a disturbance."

Zoe left the group to do her bidding and approached Sarah, who now recognized Zoe as the girl at the knife counter. "See how they fear us. See what power we work. Join us. We will share it all with you and won't hold back any secrets. Can you say the same of your current friends?"

"OK. You're starting to get my attention."

"Good. Go join the others then." And with that Zoe continued down the road.

She turned up and down a few streets, passed impoverished houses, a pizza place, and a funeral home. She crossed under the expressway, then stopped behind the library on Bridge street where she met a man who had been waiting for her.

"I have been doing all that you taught me and it is working. My power is growing, and their faith is too."

"Good. Soon you will have more," the man responded.

"Then will I have Ryan? I want him like a marionette."

"Yes, but there is another matter at hand. Watch for a woman who is not easily enchanted. If you see her or she approaches, have nothing to do with her. But tell me all she says or does."

"Who is she?"

"Never mind that. I will tend to the matter."

"Will I recognize her if I see her?"

"Without a doubt."

"What does she want? Why would she approach us?" Zoe pressed the subject a little further.

"She's been wandering for a long time. Consider it coincidence that she showed up here and now. You are merely in her path. In the meantime, just continue studying the conjuring and the necromancy I showed you. Your time is coming."

Chapter 31

In the back room behind the office building, where they had previously dissected Lydia, Ryan lifted parts of her corpse up from under the floor. He still had Lydia's brain and heart to dispose of, but before doing that, he had an idea. Sarah sat on a stool in a corner. She occupied herself with a Mad Lib book she had picked up as an impulse purchase at a gas station. Ryan placed a couple cutting boards on the dissection table.

"Verb," Sarah said as she looked at the first page of her book.

Ryan continued to set things up and locate the appropriate equipment for a little macabre experiment.

"Unlock."

She jotted that down while he continued working. He placed the heart on the cutting boards and made a careful incision into it in pursuit of the atrioventricular node. Once located, he inserted the exposed end of a copper wire into the node and then stripped and separated the other end into two exposed portions of wire.

"Do I even wanna see this? What are you doing anyway?" Sarah asked.

"I have no idea if this is even going to do anything," Ryan laughed.

"Good. Plural noun," Sarah continued.

"Shoes."

"I forgot to tell you that the last verb you gave me is past tense."

"I unlocked on somebody's shoes huh?"

"Yep."

Ryan disappeared out the door. Sarah felt vulnerable in there all alone. She couldn't watch her surroundings through that one door. She hated that feeling, so she slid the knife out from under her pant leg. Many minutes later Ryan came back into the room with a car battery.

"Where did you get that?"

"Out of one of the trucks—I forgot to grab it before we came in."

Ryan wrapped one end of the wire around the cathode. He donned a lab coat.

"You only put that on to look cool and you know it!"

"Correct," he responded. "So, the heart is an autorhythmic organ. If it weren't innervated by the central nervous system it would beat as fast as it could until it just gave out," the diener pontificated. "The parasympathetic nervous system slows it down. Because of this, if the heart is separated from the body instantaneously it will continue to beat at its own pace. Furthermore, the heart is in essence a fluid pump containing an electrical circuit within the myocardium. This circuitry, if you will, should be responsive to any electrical stimulus."

He completed the circuit by touching the remaining free end of wire to the anode of the battery—nothing happened.

"You were saying…" Sarah mocked.

"Crap," Ryan muttered.

"You were saying...."

"I told you I didn't actually know what I was doing."

"Sorry. But you looked cool doing it," Sarah consoled, then glanced at her Mad Lib. "Adjective."

"Thanks. 'Disappointing.'"

"What are you going to do with the brain?"

"Nothing, I guess. I'll just dispose of it all now."

"Give me one more adjective, and let's get out of here."

They walked out of the back of the office building and replaced the lock. The cemetery was dark, quiet, and ominous, yet peaceful, but that would not last. As they walked to the car a light suddenly shined on them from several yards away. Nick and all but one of his coworkers popped up from assorted hiding places.

"Interesting," Ryan muttered. Sarah jotted it down in her Mad Lib book.

"What did you do with Paul?" Nick demanded.

"I cut open his forehead. You were there," Sarah replied contemptuously.

"He was asking me," Ryan said to her. Now turning to Nick, "he attacked me in the morgue. I know of two people presently in this cemetery who know how to get into that morgue, and I don't recall telling Paul where to find it, nor the combination to the door."

"What did you do?" Sarah asked calmly.

"I narrowly escaped. I slipped out of the morgue and haven't seen him since."

"That's crap!" Nick shouted.

"Don't you have work to be doing?" Sarah ignored Nick's rage.

While all of this was transpiring, Calvin, unnoticed by anyone else, had snuck up behind one of Nick's diggers and slid the guy's cell phone out of his pocket. He crept away and made a quick call then casually moseyed up to the group.

"A party and I wasn't invited?" Calvin said. "Anyway, we all might want to clear out of here. I just called 911 from that guy's phone and told them that I was chased into Greenwood cemetery by," here he looked directly at Nick, "a tall, pale, spiky-haired Dutch kid dressed in a black shirt and khakis, and I need help immediately. Also, I think he's a satanist." As Calvin spoke he tossed the phone to its owner who immediately checked the last number dialed. His brow furrowed at the sight of the number—911. "So anyway, now the cops are gonna come looking for you and you need to invent a good story, like, quickly, I would think." Calvin pointed toward the Leonard Street entrance as he began to step away. They all looked and saw a police car turning into the cemetery. Everyone hid except Calvin, Sarah, and Ryan. They darted off toward the other side of the cemetery and walked casually to their cars. It was just barely Tuesday.

The three of them drove to a pizza place in Standale. Alan met them there to discuss current events. Ryan explained the failure of the Oak Hill job and that he needed to find more work, because Mark would only be paying a small fraction with no body produced. Alan listened intently and somewhat disapprovingly as Ryan and Calvin went on about business. Alan was interested even though he had already made it clear that he would never dirty his hands with such things. Even having been present in Greenwood for the dissection of Lydia, he behaved as though he disapproved yet wanted to be involved. Storing bodies on his farm for a bit of extra cash was one thing. But digging them up or dissecting them. Nope. In the meantime, the conversation turned to more interesting matters.

"I've been wanting to tell you guys that I followed Nick's car after a resurrection they did recently," Calvin said, "and I know who he's been working for. It's a funeral director we've turned away in the past. The guy is thoroughly unscrupulous, and exactly the sort of person who would be cheap enough, and desperate enough, to hire Nick. And since he's on the northwest side, that's why Nick seems to be everywhere we go lately. From what I could gather from their conversation—what little I could hear anyway—it seems that he's been moving a number of bodies between the three funeral homes he works for in the area. And though I couldn't be sure, I got the sense this funeral director was not the employer. It sounds to me like there is a woman involved who has been requesting the bodies," Calvin continued.

"I don't get it," Sarah spoke up. "What exactly are they doing to keep him so busy and why do they need to traffick the bodies around so much?"

"Maybe as stand-ins for funerals if they had already accidentally cremated the person," Ryan joked.

"Sure, just put on enough make up and you can make a total stranger look like your dead loved one."

"Or just tell the families that people look different when they are dead—it's the embalming that does it."

As they consumed their pizza and speculated on all that Nick had been up to, more was transpiring just outside that they were not yet aware of.

"Now listen. When you go in, you'll see a guy with brown hair, a blonde with him, and a guy with long black wavy hair seated in the back corner. Try to stay close to them without being noticed. Listen to their conversations and report back to me everything you hear." Nick slipped the young man some cash and sent him into the restaurant. When his new-hire spy was gone, he hid behind the building. And much to his surprise and annoyance, there was Zoe.

"You do mediocre work, Nick," she said, "but you're the pony I've picked. You've gotten the bodies we've requested and the money has come in as needed, but I'm getting sick of your half-measures and apathetic approach to getting things done."

"Well maybe I should stop working for you then," he muttered, still caught off guard by her presence.

"Unless you're tired of living, you'll finish what we started. And that guy you sent in better get the info I need."

"It will work."

She glared at him incredulously.

"It will. It will," Nick insisted.

"It better. Find out where they will be and finish off Ryan's team. You've lost members faster than he has. Fix that. I want them gone and I want him left all alone in the world."

Meanwhile the conversation continued inside.

"I'd like to get a job in Elmwood cemetery," Sarah said. "If we could work inside that area walled in by hedge, that would be so cool. Talk about easy!"

"So just do it for fun," Alan jumped in.

"We don't work for free," Ryan corrected.

"What's the bit about a hedge?" Alan pursued.

"Right in the middle of Elmwood there is a large square of tall hedge, basically forming a roof-less room, with a door cut through the hedge. It surrounds a group of several graves. Totally private. You can't see in from the outside at all. Like a penthouse for resurrectionists," Sarah explained as she sketched it on a napkin.

"With the minor caveat that you have to listen much more closely to your surroundings because from the inside you can't see anyone approaching," Ryan added.

"True. But no one would approach to look inside anyway," Sarah rejoined.

"I'll talk to a few people and see if that funeral home next to Elmwood—what's its name again?" Ryan mulled it over, "Buchholz, that's it. I'll see if anybody there is in need of our services."

"Can I get in on that conversation?" Sarah asked.

"Oh, don't worry about it. I'll take care of it."

"You killed Paul, didn't you?" Sarah was quick to respond.

Ryan was startled by the change in topic and hesitated to respond.

"I feel like you've been keeping Calvin and I out of the loop on some things and I don't know why. But I think I'm going to take a break, Sarah confessed her growing frustration. "If you can get us an Elmwood job I'll do it, but after that, well, I'm taking a break."

"I'm sorry you feel that way and if—what are you looking at?" Ryan realized she was looking past him. He turned to look behind him.

"Who's that guy?" Sarah demanded. "Hey! Yeah, you! Did you want to join this conversation or just listen to it? Get out of here!"

Alan, Calvin, and Ryan all glared as the young man fumbled for an explanation but failed to find any words.

"Leave!" Calvin insisted.

Nick's spy looked somewhat relieved to be leaving without a word.

"That was careless of us. I think it's time we all leave, don't you agree? Let's settle the bill and regroup at a later time," Calvin cautioned.

Chapter 32

"Grave robbing? Are you serious?" Detective Jameson exclaimed. He planted his forehead in his palm then ran his fingers though his hair along his scalp. His brain hurt and he was tired.

"Oh, I'm serious," Detective Malli affirmed.

"How do we know that?"

"Well, we don't yet, but we've got reports of potentially disturbed graves."

"Ugh. So where are we going?" Jameson sighed.

"Greenwood. Again."

"Well that's fortuitous because we've just been assigned another missing-person/probable-homicide."

"In Greenwood?" Malli looked up from what she was doing.

"In Greenwood."

"Are you serious?"

"Oh, I'm serious."

"What is going on?" She planted her forehead in both hands and massaged her own scalp. Her brain hurt now too, and she was just as tired as Jameson. "What is it about that place?"

"I don't know. Your guess is as good as mine. But it's business hours so let's go talk to the groundskeeper there."

"That's the parks department. They are unionized so we might have to talk to their union rep first."

"Well, let's just play ignorant on that for now."

Detectives Malli and Jameson rose reluctantly from their desks as Malli grabbed the car keys. They drove from downtown to the northwest side, back to Greenwood, yet again. Once at the cemetery, everything looked quiet and beautiful as ever as they turned in from Leonard Street.

"Hey, remember the pumpkins in here on Halloween? That was weird."

"I still think whoever did it was still in here with us."

"That makes it even weirder. That yellow truck parked by the office building looks promising. How do you want to handle this? I think we should start with the missing person bit because that's a lot less weird than the grave robbing bit. I don't want this guy to get defensive for no reason."

"I agree. I doubt anybody actually robbed any graves anyway. Imagine how difficult that would be. And if they did, I doubt any city employees were involved. But if we just question him as a possible bystander, who might have noticed something helpful in a missing persons investigation, he's likely to transition more easily to the other topic."

They parked and walked in through the open office door.

"Hi there. I'm Detective Malli, and this is my partner Detective Jameson."

"How can I help you today?" Mike asked.

"Well, we're investigating a missing person who may have last been seen in, or around, this cemetery."

"Interesting. We don't have any security cameras or anything, so I hope you weren't hoping to catch them on video."

"Well that would have been nice but we weren't counting on that. No, we were just hoping you could tell us a bit about who comes and goes, and what the procedure is if anybody finds something strange."

"Heh," Mike smirked a little. "Well, there is a whole host of full and part time employees that work somewhat random shifts here. Mostly it's mowing but occasional other odd jobs too. I'm in charge of this particular cemetery but honestly I'm not actually on the grounds more than a couple times each week. And the mowers only come once every week or so—typically in the afternoons because they also mow the city parks in the mornings."

"Would you be able to tell us if you or any employees were here working if we gave you a range of dates?"

"Maybe, though I would have to get that through payroll. They keep the logs for shifts worked. The union doesn't move very fast on that kind of stuff. Did you need it today?"

"No, not today. We'll get back to you soon with a range of dates."

"Who went missing?"

"A young lady. White. Brunette. Possibly wearing a grey coat, blue jeans, and a dark blue shirt at the time."

"Doesn't ring any bells for me," Mike lied. "We get lots of visitors. There are acres and acres of graves here."

"I understand. And circling back a bit, what would an employee be expected to do if they found anything weird while mowing?"

"I guess that depends on what kind of weird," Mike gave a puzzled look.

"Like clothing or personal effects among the headstones maybe."

"Well they might put them in the lost and found box here under the desk. Finding clothes isn't all that weird. People often remove layers as they get warm cleaning up a loved ones marker in the hot sun." Mike slyly tipped Lydia's clothes out of the box while it was still out of sight under the desktop, and then raised the now-empty box marked "lost and found" over the desk to show that it didn't contain any items like they were describing.

"What if somebody found blood?"

"Blood?" He paused. "Um, OK, well, I guess it would depend on how much and where. We get foxes and deer and other critters in here. I occasionally find a dead squirrel and such. If someone found a little blood in the grass I imagine they might not think much of it."

"I understand. And what if you found a grave that had been disturbed?"

"Oh we get vandals in here tipping headstones every now and again. We have to submit a work order to have a crew come out and replace or repair the stones. The mowers aren't authorized to do that. Union rules you know."

"Sure. But I mean like a grave that has been dug up."

Here Mike gave a long and incredulous stare. Then at last he slowly and calmly asked, "I beg your pardon?"

"You know, like if someone tried to rob a grave," Jameson asked as though it were a reasonable question.

"Well, I think first we'd all have to get ourselves a time machine and go back to the nineteenth century."

"Oh yeah? Why is that? I don't follow," Malli interjected.

"Well that kind of thing just doesn't happen anymore."

"Since when? Why not?"

"Well, city regulations. That's why."

"City regulations against grave robbing?" Detective Jameson spoke up.

"City regulations about burials. To be buried in a city cemetery you have to purchase a concrete vault for the coffin to go into. That's to keep the ground from sinking in as the coffin and body degrades. Most private cemeteries require them too. They are really big and really thick and really heavy. You need heavy equipment to move the lid. You can't just get through with a shovel. You'd have to be crazy or stupid to even try. It can't possibly be worth the trouble."

"Hm. Makes sense."

"Why do you ask?" Mike turned the tables a bit.

"Well, we had some concerned citizens report noise disturbances recently at night in here—"

"Teenagers getting high most likely," Mike interrupted.

"—Sure, but also folks reported some disturbed graves."

"Oh!" Mike laughed heartily. "That's just woodchucks! I told you there are plenty of critters milling around in here. Mostly they live in the woods at the northern end of the property, but they make their way into the cemetery too. I find woodchuck burrows all the time. Old ladies like to complain to me about the graves not being properly kept, but what am I supposed to do? Maybe the city can issue trapping permits for the cemeteries."

"I see your point. Forget I said anything about it. Do you mind if we look around in here?"

"Sure. I guess. There's not much to see. There are only three rooms on the main level. The basement is perpetually locked. And the attic is filled with old boxes and a floor covered in bat feces."

"Sure. Pretty vacant in here really." Malli and Jameson looked around and up and down.

"It's not very secure so we don't keep anything in here. We don't even lock the safe with the burial records. In fact, we only keep those in a safe to avoid fire damage."

"How long have you worked this job?"

"Nearly twenty years."

"Do you like it?"

"It's a living." Mike pointed to a sign in the window which read 'I work a dead end job on the graveyard shift with a skeleton crew.'

"What's in the basement?"

"Plumbing, electrical, and some odds and ends, like an old desk chair and stuff. And spiders. Lots of spiders."

"What about the other door on the back? The one that doesn't go into the regular basement. What's in that room?"

"That's just a storage room. It's got lawn maintenance equipment like weedwackers and edgers and stuff in it."

"Sure. Well we're going to do a quick drive around and let you get back to work. Thank you for your help today."

"My pleasure."

Detectives Malli and Jameson returned to their car and slowly rolled through Greenwood. There was nothing criminal to see and they knew it. Even if someone robbed graves somewhere in Grand Blanc, nothing here indicated that. And even if a girl went missing from here, there weren't any clues to her whereabouts in here now. Furthermore, if she was dead, well, the body wasn't here. As they looped around toward the Byron Street entrance, Ryan walked in. He cut across the grass to keep a bit of distance between the police and himself. They passed by him without incident and he walked straight to the office building.

"Those nice detectives were asking about a missing girl, and something else...what was it? Oh, right, they asked about grave robbing," Mike said as soon as Ryan walked in. He didn't even look up but stuffed Lydia's clothes back into the lost and found box.

"No kidding. Well, maybe we'll just keep that in mind for the near future."

"I agree. Also, remember three years ago when I told you I was catching woodchucks on my property and bringing them here? Well, you're welcome."

"I'm not sure I follow."

"Just that you're welcome. That's all. So, what brings you here today?"

"Well nothing now. Suddenly I'm changing my plans. I do need to call and cancel a job I just accepted though."

"Bummer."

"Yeah, well that's how it goes. We can let things quiet down in here for a bit. There is work to be found in other cemeteries."

Chapter 33

A few weeks later, Greenwood worked its usual sedating effect as Ryan approached the office building again after a long shift at the hospital. Just being there improved his attitude. Mike was not inside, but greeted Ryan at the door instead.

"I spend too much time inside there. Let's walk and talk," he suggested. They proceeded south onto the path which loops through the southeast corner of the graveyard.

"I borrowed a battery out of one of your trucks recently. I already returned it, but I needed it to see if I could get a heart to beat," Ryan confessed. Mike laughed aloud at this. "What's so funny?" Ryan insisted.

"I know which truck you must have taken it from. It was the only one accessible to you. That truck's battery is dead! Ha! Would that actually work anyway?" Mike mocked.

"In theory," Ryan sheepishly muttered, frustrated that he was defeated by a dead battery. He quickly changed the subject. "Joseph Albright M.D. 1837—1915," he read off a headstone as they walked.

"What about it?"

"Well, I was just thinking about the nineteenth century resurrectionists and their physician patrons. Reading that headstone makes me wonder, what kind of a man was Joseph Albright M.D.? Was he a reputable physician or a monster in society's eyes—or both? Was he the esteemed and beloved neighborhood physician during the day? But then was he a patron of the resurrectionists by night—or even a grave robber himself in his youth? I really do wonder if Dr. Albright back there participated in such things. And more than that, I wonder if his body is even there, or if there is anything to that eastern karma thing—you know, if he got his just desserts and his body was stolen and dissected."

"Why is everything so Jekyll-and-Hyde-like for you?" Mike pushed.

"Jekyll's own tastes were 'rather chemical than anatomical,'" Ryan refuted.

"Whatever. You're a strange guy. Anyway, you wanted to know about working in Elmwood, so I made some phone calls. It turns out that the guy who used to work there for the neighboring morticians left to work down here in Grand Blanc. He was apparently reported missing recently though—Paul I think was his name. Anyway, they've been in need of somebody for a while, so I imagine they would pay pretty well. I gave them your phone number."

"Thanks," Ryan replied, suppressing his thoughts about Paul.

Mike continued, "Do you ever feel remorse for what we do? I was just wondering. I mean, things have been pretty intense lately, you know?"

"How do you mean?"

"I don't know. It's just been lots of bodies, and that girl I found, and cops showing up, and investigations of occult stuff.

I don't know. I was raised Roman Catholic and I think about that sometimes. But it's been a while since I felt anything for the dead people. That's what got me thinking about it really. I don't feel bad about it. But I feel like I should, shouldn't I? But I don't. What about you? Do you feel bad about any of it?

"Only for deceiving the people who aren't aware of this. I feel nothing for the bodies though—they're just dead flesh. We aren't harming the dead in any way."

"Same here," Mike muttered.

"I know," Ryan paused. "All that said, I was raised going to church too. But I have wandered pretty far from the fold of God. And, admittedly that does weigh on my mind lately. I don't feel bad about the dead bodies, but I have started to think about all the falsehood in my life. Constantly pretending and hiding what I do from the rest of the world has been eating at me a bit."

"Yeah that's a good point. I still don't feel anything though."

"Maybe I should heed that as a warning and start reading my Bible or going to church again or something."

"But you're not going to stop robbing graves."

"No. I need the money."

"Of course. Priorities, after all. What do Calvin and Sarah think? Do they ever have moral dilemmas?"

"Sarah, no. As far as I can tell anyway. I don't think she ever gives that any thought," Ryan was quick to acknowledge. "And Calvin, heh. I think he honestly believes he is a good, moral, law-abiding citizen. He's always doing random acts of kindness and charity even for total strangers. I think there is just a total disconnect in his mind and he really thinks he is just a good guy with a clean slate."

"Hey, did you hear that the Ada Witch's headstone was vandalized?" Mike changed the subject, referring to a local folklore about a 19th century grave in a forested cemetery which was rumored to be the grave of a witch.

"Yeah, I heard about that. I doubt that poor woman was ever a witch anyway. It's just old wives' tales."

"I agree."

"I haven't been to that cemetery in years. If I find the time, I might go look at the damage."

"I wouldn't recommend trying to rob it right now."

"Yeah, too much attention. Lets focus on work in Elmood."

Two days later Ryan received a strange phone call from a quirky funeral director who refused to give her name. Even stranger than the mortician's behavior was her request. She wanted a body to be put back in its grave—or a grave anyway. This was not entirely unheard of but was pretty uncommon. She offered no explanation nor would she mention any names or grave plots over the phone. It was no wonder Paul quit working for these people, Ryan thought. Who would want to work for them if that is the type of treatment you receive? This may be a one-off for his group.

The two of them agreed that he and his team would meet her at the funeral home on Thursday, and they would be given all the details then. Ryan was not happy about it, but the money she offered was good.

Sarah and Calvin agreed it was inappropriate, but they were not scared off by weirdos. They firmly believed they could handle any job. Just to be cautious though, they agreed to take two vehicles, just in case something fishy happened and they needed to make a hasty exit in separate directions.

On Thursday they pulled into the parking lot at 7:01pm. There did not appear to be anyone there. It wasn't the way they wanted to start the evening.

At 7:04 a woman in a hearse pulled into the lot and parked in the employee parking space near the front door.

"Come inside," said the woman brashly. The three of them followed her into the funerarium and promptly demanded explanations.

"My name is Natalie and neither the name nor the history of the body you are re-interring for me tonight are any of your business. The corpse is to be buried in the first grave on the right when you enter into the hedge."

"It's a good thing you're paying us well for this," Sarah interrupted.

With a glare Natalie continued, "You may stay here until you are ready to begin. I trust you to shut off the lights and lock up as you leave." They walked as she spoke. "The body is in this cooler. He's tall and thin so it should be no trouble." She handed Ryan an envelope. "Here is your money. Good night."

"Um, bye," Ryan added quickly and contemptuously as she left.

The three of them hung around until quarter after nine and then lost patience waiting for the moon. Not a single person had come to the cemetery since they arrived, and only a handful of cars had driven past, so they all agreed to start early. They went into the cemetery and excavated the grave. Calvin pulled open the top half of the coffin lid. By then it was 10pm and time to bury a body.

They returned to the funeral home, pulled the gurney out of the cooler, and brought the body to the door. Ryan and Sarah lifted it upright, each with an arm under one of its shoulders. They walked the body, feet dragging behind, to the edge of the graveyard. Meanwhile, Calvin locked up the funeral home, ran across the parking lot, jumped the fence, and waited for Ryan and Sarah to pass the body over the fence to him. It was difficult, and they basically just controlled the corpses fall over the other side of the fence. Calvin facilitated it down and leaned it against a tree. The other two climbed over and they moved the corpse to the grave.

The next step was a strange and awkward task. The usual situation of dragging a body up out of a hole that only uncovered the top half of the coffin was reversed. They had the tedious job of threading the body down the hole, then sliding the feet into the grave, thus laying the body into the coffin in a reasonable fashion. Ryan went down into the grave. Sarah was backed into the corner of the hedge wall. Calvin, nearer the opening of the hedge, passed the body down to him so he could direct the feet into the coffin. While trying to snake the body into the coffin the shirt slid up the torso and Ryan saw numerous familiar symbols drawn in ink on the man's chest and abdomen.

He had hardly begun to recognize the significance of that when, suddenly, he heard a loud cracking noise. Calvin fell to the ground in a heap. Ryan looked up from the grave to see blood spouting out of a gaping skull fracture on the top of his friend's head. By the time he scrambled out of the hole and to his feet, Sarah was chasing a man across the graveyard. Ryan sprinted after them both.

As they raced through darkness and among headstones, with knives drawn, Ryan processed the situation. Obviously Calvin had been struck with a heavy object, such as an axe or something similar. The man Sarah was chasing would not be running if he were armed with such a weapon.

"Sarah! There must be a second person in here!" Ryan shouted.

Suddenly, a man with a metal pipe rushed at Ryan from behind a large tree on his left side. They tangled and fell to the ground. Ryan broke free of his grasp enough to run his knife along the inner part of the man's thigh. Crippled and bleeding he let go completely. Ryan stood and looked across the cemetery to see Sarah throw her knife as the pursued man turned to confront her. The knife entered under the right side of his mandible. Ryan could see the tip of the blade protruding from the back of his neck as he fell through the moonlight. Sarah put her foot on his forehead, reached down and extracted her knife from his hemorrhaging neck, wiped the blade in the grass, and walked to Ryan.

"Who are you?" Ryan asked the man he had cut. No response came. Ryan rolled him over and realized that in their struggle he must have hit the man's head against a grave stone. His skull was fractured and he was dead.

"Still no one with an axe or anything," Sarah commented.

"You noticed too, huh?" Ryan replied.

As they spoke, the sound of rapidly approaching footsteps caught their attention. Ryan and Sarah turned to see Nick, axe in hand and held aloft, rushing toward them. They stood their ground, ready to defend themselves, when suddenly Nick was swept sideways off his feet, and was dragged inhumanly fast into the shadows. His axe fell from his hand as he was dragged away. A terrible scream emminated from the darkness, but it was immediately silenced. The two grave robbers looked at each other, equally puzzled.

Moments later a blonde woman in a long coat stepped out from those same shadows. She carried Nick's corpse like a briefcase back to Sarah and Ryan. His neck gaped open and there was blood dripping down her chin.

"That was, um, unexpected," Ryan said as he recognized the woman he first met in Greenwood nearly a year ago.

"Who is she?" Sarah and Idelette asked simultaneously.

"Oh. Right. Sarah, Idelette. Idelette, Sarah." Ryan turned toward Sarah. "I met Idelette briefly in Greenwood last year." Then turning back toward Idelette, "I knew there was something interesting about you when we met. I always had this nagging feeling you would show up again, but I, uh, I gotta say I didn't expect this. Where have you been?"

"Clearwater for a while. Then elsewhere." Idelette replied matter-of-factly.

"What's in Clearwater?" A still-confused Sarah chimed in.

"Not much. And that's the point. But there's a large cemetery with an old vault that I occasionally sleep in."

"I know of that cemetery," Ryan replied.

"Hang on. You sometimes sleep in tombs?" Sarah interjected, recalling a certain shattered door on a mausoleum in Oak Hill.

"Yeah."

"So it's possible that if we, or some other group, got hired to rob a particular mausoleum, which you happened to be sleeping in—"

"That might not end well for you," Idelette interrupted. "But I rarely sleep in graves, so it's unlikely to happen anyway."

"Sleep in graves—" Sarah began to scoff.

"What would happen to somebody who found you though, um, if it ever did happen?" Ryan interrupted.

"Well that person would probably have to die, wouldn't they? I can't leave them alive to come looking for me." She glanced at Sarah. "Plus I get kind of irritable when I'm not well rested."

"Well hold up, does that mean we're going to die next, then?" Ryan brought the conversation back to the present situation.

"Die next?" Sarah interrupted. "I'll freaking cut your head off if you try anything, lady! And what's in your pocket that you've got your hand on?"

"Relax. I'm satiated now. And I have a Bible in my pocket, since you ask."

"Yeah right," Sarah rolled her eyes.

"How did you know we were here? And thanks, by the way,"

"I have my ways. You're welcome." Here she turned to Sarah, "Both of you."

"No. I want explanations," Sarah insisted.

"Let's just get these bodies disposed of. We'll talk more some other time," Idelette suggested.

"No! I want explanations! Who are you and how did you do that?"

Idelette sighed, then pulled her hand from her pocket. She showed them her fangs and pulled Nick's head back to reveal the gaping bite mark on his neck. Then she wiped his blood from her chin and licked it off her fingers. "But, as I said, I'm satiated. Let's get this done."

"We're just supposed to trust you? Apparently vampires are a thing, and we're talking to one, and we're just supposed to trust you?"

"No. You don't have to trust me at all. But daylight is coming. I'll carry the bodies. We need to dig that hole bigger."

"What about you?" Sarah turned to Ryan. "You're taking this all in stride. You're pals with a vampire and you weren't ever going to tell me? Or Calvin?"

"No. I'm not taking this in stride, and I didn't know she was a vampire. I've only met her once, a year ago. I'm just trying to temper my response because she just killed Nick, but didn't kill me when she could have. So she seems to be our ally. You'll notice I haven't let my guard down completely either." He turned his arm slightly to reveal he was gripping a knife but had been keeping it concealed behind his forearm.

"Actually, I think you're both taking it pretty well, all things considered," Idelette shook Nick's corpse to make her point.

"We've seen worse," Ryan and Sarah both rejoined.

"Well then, we're all pros at total depravity, it would seem. Let's get to work."

Ryan and Sarah returned to the square of hedge which encompassed the grave they had previously opened. They quietly stared down at Calvin's corpse. Rage welled up with sorrow for their friend, and when Idelette dropped Nick's body next to Calvin's, Sarah glared at her, then dragged it to the other side of the hole.

"Once we get this hole dug bigger we should quarter Nick and his coworkers. They will fit better in pieces and parts. Also, Calvin gets laid on top, not under their putrescence," Sarah insisted.

"Agreed. I gotta say, things aren't going to be the same without him."

"Things aren't going to be the same for more reasons than just that," Sarah sighed.

"Oh?"

"I told you before. I'm taking a break."

"That's right. In all this excitement I had forgotten you told me that."

"Let's just get this done," she replied without looking at him. She pushed a shovel into Ryan's hands then thrust her own shovel into the soil.

Working diligently, the three of them cleaned up the blood (some of which got licked up), chunks, and other evidence. They dug the already open grave much larger. Five bodies went into that mass grave—Calvin, Nick, his two coworkers, and the body from the funeral home.

"For dust thou art, and into dust thou shalt return," Idelette quoted in words barely surpassing a whisper as they stared down at the ground which covered Calvin's remains. Sarah and Ryan looked up and stared at her for just a moment but she only continued to look down. Having done and said all that could be though, it was time to leave the cemetery. The undead one vanished to the north, and the two remaining graverobbers traipsed back to the parking lot. They were exhausted.

"That's it, then. I'm officially done," Sarah said to Ryan when they returned to the cars. "It has been building for a while and now it has become too much. You've been keeping too much information from us. Calvin is dead, you killed Paul and didn't trust us to know about it, you have a vampire friend, and I don't know why you didn't mention the symbols in the Oak Hill sepulchre to me when you saw them. But I've got secrets of my own and I'm moving on. I'll see you around, maybe." And with that, she left without giving Ryan a chance to respond.

He stood alone in silence for a time, grieved and hurt. His thoughts consumed him in that empty parking lot. The funeral home was dark. The cemetery was desolate and apathetic to everything that had just happened within it. Ryan's close friend was now dead, and in an unmarked mass grave, no less. Another friend had just abandoned him. And could it all be his own fault? Maybe Sarah was right. Was there really something intrinsically wrong with him? Had he really been treating people so badly? He drew a long breath and looked about, feeling void, but realizing he shouldn't linger any longer.

Chapter 34

Dom Calmet urged his hyperventilating student down the steps below the sanctuary just as quickly as he could. The chase from her home to the church had taxed her drastically. He poured some wax off the top of his candle to heighten the flame, recited a quick prayer, and hurried back to the door. He peered out through a crack in the wood. Darkness. He held the lock tight and watched for a moment or two. One more prayer. He undid the latch and threw open the door.

His candle extinguished immediately. His eyes took a moment to adjust but he advanced out into the churchyard anyway. There was no one nearby—only folks just starting to leave their houses. He cast his eyes this way and that, but saw nothing suspicious. The animals were wandering about everywhere. Then he saw something being pulled over the wall. He gasped then sighed with relief. It was a sheep and not a person. Shaking his head, he returned into the church. There in a pew was Conrad.

"Was I wrong, Father?" Conrad asked without turning around.

"When did you get here?" the still-startled priest answered with a question.

"I told you something would happen tonight."

"Yes, I suppose you did. How long have you been in here?" He re-lit his candle.

"Is she safe downstairs?"

"She is safe. You have not answered my question."

"Only moments. What say you, Father? What shall we do next? Return to our prayers? Or shall we find the creature where it hides?"

"Perhaps both? It will be dawn soon. I shall give a morning Mass and then we shall set out afterwards."

"I suppose you're right. No sense in leaving now. We'd never find it in the dark anyway. No doubt the night is its ally. In fact, I'm not sure it can move about at all by day. But that puts us at a decided disadvantage. How can we pursue it at night? How can we find where it hides during the day? We need light to keep it subdued. But in darkness, it overpowers us in every way."

"Remember the words of the apostle whom Jesus loved. The light shines in the darkness, and the darkness has not overcome it. We will prevail if we are fixed on Christ."

"But how, exactly, should we proceed if we are ever to prevail, Father? That is my question. We need a plan of action. We need to formulate some kind of strategy and—"

"We need to kill it," Idelette interrupted from the top of the stairs.

Both men turned toward her, surprised to hear her voice.

"You should be resting," Conrad muttered as he turned away again.

"I will not live through another night like this one. I will not suffer it to have another opportunity. We need to search the forest. Today. We need to find it and we need to kill it by any means."

"I agree completely," Conrad nodded.

"So that is our plan and that is our goal. Find it. Kill it. Today." Idelette paused. "But, how do we kill it?"

"I am not sure what means will actually accomplish that goal," the cleric rejoined.

"Have you no books on these matters, Father?" Conrad asked.

"No. I have useful tomes on handling witches and their familiars, as well as exorcising demons, but I have no books nor tracts to consult on the matter of vampires. This is an entirely different manner of Godlessness, and I know of no authority on the matter in the scope of Christendom. There are some among the Jews who claim special knowledge of such things—their traditions having been handed down through obscure texts—but I would not stray from the Church on matters of such deep import. Nor do we have time to seek such counsel anyway. Perhaps I could send a letter to the archbishop for guidance."

Chapter 35

"What do you make of it?" Detective Jameson asked his partner as he got back in the car and handed her cup of coffee to her.

"They all have to be connected, right? I mean there's just no way these aren't all related."

"Oh, yeah, definitely." He set his cup down and unwrapped his bagel.

"But I still don't see how yet." Detective Malli paused to sip her coffee. "Let's run through it again."

Detective Jameson proceeded, "Okay, here we go. Two boys killed in Greenwood on Halloween night. Blood everywhere in the basement of the office building. No signs of forced entry. No suggestion of employee involvement based on subsequent investigation. Boys' bodies found in a dumpster at the back of the cemetery. No obvious evidence left between the murder location and the dumpster. No apparent reason for why the kids were in the graveyard that night other than the fact that it was Halloween. Chalk symbols were found in the cemetery across the street.

That's all for those two. The following summer a girl goes missing from the mall and her body is discovered days later in the landfill. Next is a missing person who was 'ghost hunting' in Greenwood." He made air quotes with his fingers as he spoke. "His friends who were with him couldn't provide any useful information but their stories seemed credible. We find his body later in the trees along the edge of the cemetery. We also find old baby bones and tons of occult-type symbols in that empty circular reservoir at the back of the graveyard. That same night, a young girl—Ashley—killed in Tyler Memorial Gardens just a few blocks away. She was supposedly meeting 'friends' in the graveyard." (More air quotes). "Her body is found decomposing days later in the woods by the stream several hundred yards from the cemetery. Her cell phone was found in the graveyard. We still don't know who these friends are, but a guy later confesses, which is great and all, but there's no other evidence to connect him to the murder. And then there were the two bodies in the dumpster outside Skeletunes—"

Suddenly a voice came in over the radio. "Possible person of interest identified in the Tyler Memorial Gardens killing. Details coming by text message to Detective Malli's phone."

"Here it is. Let's go pay a visit."

Chapter 36

"I found a genuine real life Scooby-Doo style clue, Phil," Ryan boasted.

"You did, did you?" Phil barely acknowledged as he typed with two fingers.

"Yeah. I haven't seen this one reported in the news. Seems like maybe the police don't know about it yet. I was walking the trail behind Ragner Park—"

"Oh, back in college I dated a girl that lived in the apartments near there."

"Yeah, I think you told me that before, Phil—"

"Oh did I?"

"Pretty sure. Maybe several times."

"Well, I must have thought you should know since I keep bringing it up."

"Regardless, there's an old railroad bridge back there and some concrete frames of buildings that are supposedly old slaughter houses. And that's where I saw it. They're always covered in graffiti but now it's new graffiti. It's all satanic, pagan, and witch craft stuff. Some of them are easy to recognize. They are ancient. But some of them, I really have no idea what they are."

"Well, speak of the devil, here you go." Phil had been checking his email as they spoke, and when he signed out his home page brought up a news article. "It says here that someone defaced one of the big mausoleums in Oak Hill cemetery. There's an interview with some guy on the Historical Society."

"What else does it say?"

"Just that they are incomprehensible symbols, um, they weren't there yesterday," he skimmed, "and that everyone basically thinks it's unacceptable behavior to vandalize the graves."

"Yeah, but we knew they were tagging cemeteries already. My point was that I found a secluded spot that is also tagged. Maybe it's significant since it's hidden. Maybe they meet there."

"Well, it looks like they've already moved on," Phil tapped the picture of the vandalized mausoleum on his monitor. "These are brand new."

"Hm. I see your point."

"So. Are you going to examine them yourself?"

"Absolutely. Tonight. I'll go straight there after work," he confirmed as he poured formalin on a placenta.

"You know, you could just look at the pictures in this article instead. Why do you need to see them in person? It'll be dark anyway."

"You never know what you will find that is not in those photos. Maybe whoever did it will return to do more."

"Aren't these people linked with murders around the city?"

"Yeah. So? Oh, I see. Well, I'm sure the cops will also be there tonight," Ryan shrugged off Phil's concern.

"Won't that be a problem for you too then?" Phil rejoined.

"Won't what be a problem?"

"The police."

"Heh. We'll see," Ryan smiled ever so slightly.

"Look at this," Phil tapped the monitor. "Here's a totally unrelated news clip filmed downtown and you can see several more examples of that graffiti in the background. Crazy."

"Next we'll be seeing crop circles," Ryan replied with flat affect.

"What are these people trying to accomplish anyway? I don't get it."

"Who knows. But eventually they will have to declare themselves. People are afraid. Bodies were found in dumpsters right near here with that same graffiti on it. No suspects, if the news is to be believed. What's the point of causing people to fear you if they don't know that you're the one they fear? Like I said, they will eventually declare themselves. I'm just wondering how many of them there are."

Chapter 37

The detectives were back in Ashley's neighborhood, looking for the address that had been provided. It was an older, blue collar neighborhood with houses built in the 1920s. Given the low socioeconomic area, many had been converted to duplexes. The lots were small and the houses stood close together. Few had garages. Some didn't even have driveways.

"OK. So like I was saying, neighbors had seen Ashley getting into a car with a man they recognized. He is now in custody. But who were these so-called friends she was supposed to meet?"

"And how do we prove they were or were not there when the murder happened?" Detective Malli interjected.

"We've already gathered statements from others in the neighborhood. We tried this address several times before, and no one was ever home. It's going to be empty now, too. You know it is. And it wouldn't matter if anyone answers the door anyway. So far no one could tell us who the friends were that she was supposed to meet in the cemetery that night. Nor would they tell us why she was meeting people in a cemetery of all places."

They parked along the curb in front of the house. It was dark. Reluctantly they got out of their car and went up to the porch. The boards bent slightly under their weight. The doorbell didn't work, of course. So they knocked. And they waited. Growing impatient, they knocked again and waited some more.

"What'd I tell ya'?" Detective Jameson sighed.

As the two fatigued detectives were returning to their car, a call came in requesting police response to an address three blocks away. There was a report of a noise disturbance and a lot of teenagers coming and going—apparently a party.

"We should get uniformed officer pay on top of our detective pay for this."

"I agree."

"Any more ideas yet about the symbols? I still don't know where to begin."

"Maybe we need to call some more departments at the University. Did we try comparative religions? Maybe we can find a prof there who can help us."

"Or a sociologist who studies occult practice—or gangs?"

They both glanced back at the house they were leaving, with vain hope that someone would come to the door before they drove off, but they knew that was wishful thinking.

"Let's go," Malli sighed and took a sip of her coffee. Detective Jameson grabbed her hand. He had a disturbed look on his face. He took the coffee cup from her hand and held it up for her to look underneath. There were familiar symbols drawn on the bottom. She stared at her partner in silence for a moment.

"Um, I guess we'll have to go back to that coffee shop when we're done here, won't we?"

"The noise disturbance is on our way there anyway. Maybe we can just roll right past." Jameson put the car in gear and they moved on.

The report of a party was not quite accurate. When they arrived on scene there were people coming and going from several neighboring houses, on the street, between cars, and in yards. Most appeared to be teenage girls. If this was a party it was a peculiar one. There was no loud music. There were no obvious signs of alcohol use. There were no decorations. When the detectives parked their car, all the people outside rapidly and conspicuously disappeared inside. The detectives had to pick which house to approach first.

"So much for just rolling past. What do you think? That one?" Malli pointed to a house.

"Sure," Jameson sighed as he got out of the car.

They continued to assess the situation, and looked around each way as they approached the porch and climbed the stone steps. They knocked on the door, but all was silent. They knew the house was occupied, but it went black. Suddenly all the houses did the same.

"Ooookay."

"That was weird."

"Let's check the back doors."

"Yeah. Sure."

The detectives split up and did a quick walk all the way around each of the suspicious houses. Neither of them noted any activity. Jameson stopped at the car and requested additional support. They returned to the front door of the first house and knocked again. Nothing.

Then from the house across the street there burst out a scream accompanied by other strange noises. The detectives ran to the front door and kicked it open. There were candles burning and a horror movie playing on the television, but no one to be seen. Jameson decided they should check the status of their backup. He looked back at the car and his jaw dropped. It was covered in graffiti! Symbols, most of which he recognized, were scrawled all over it.

Without even checking the rest of the house he and his partner approached the car. No one was around. Then suddenly the door of the house they had just left slammed shut. They could see several girls inside through the windows. They ran back and kicked the door open again. The living room walls now had similar graffiti! It had not been there a moment ago. Spreading out they searched the house. Detective Malli caught sight of someone.

"They're over here!" Malli called out to her partner. "They're running!"

"I saw two over here!" he shouted back. "Behind you!"

Malli turned but there was no one.

They worked their way from room to room, clearing each as they went. Before long they had been through the entire house, and though they had previously seen girls in many rooms, somehow, they now found it to be entirely empty.

"What is going on?" Jameson said.

"Let's go back out to the street, there must be another exit we're not seeing."

They walked back out into the streetlights, then split up and went around the house again from opposite sides. As Detective Malli was reaching the back side she saw one of the girls running up the back porch and into a neighboring house. She yelled to Jameson and they rushed after her. Malli went back to the front door and Jameson kicked the back door in. They worked their way through this house as they had done the previous one.

"Room clear!"

"Room clear!"

"Clear!"

"Clear!"

"Clear!"

"Basement!...Clear!"

"Upstairs."

"Hallway clear!"

"Clear!"

"Clear!"

"Clear!"

"This house is empty," Malli stated but in a way that resembled a question as she holstered her gun and turned to face her partner.

Detective Jameson had no response. Through the thin curtains, blue and red lights flashed upon them from the approaching police cruisers as they stared at each other in silence, completely perplexed.

Chapter 38

Dom Calmet slouched over his desk with a stylus in hand and a blank sheet before him. Idelette sat beside him. He thought long and hard about what he could write. He was hesitant.

"Why do you stall, father?" she asked at last.

He sighed and looked up at her.

"The villagers look to me to be their protector. I confess a touch of sinful pride compels me to put off writing the letter, and finish this without the Cardinal's help."

"Father, no one will think ill of you for requesting help. You must write."

"I do not want to trouble the Cardinal when there is so much unrest besieging the Church elsewhere."

"The existence of other problems doesn't nullify this one. We are perishing."

"So my student presumes to preach to me," he sighed as he reclined back in his seat. "And she is right. Please leave me be for a short while to pray and think how to pen the words we need."

Idelette arose and ascended the steps. She looked back to see him take up his stylus once more, and slouch over the paper again. Then she left the office and found a seat in the sanctuary to pray as well. As she eagerly petitioned Heaven, the priest reluctantly petitioned Rome:

Most holy and esteemed Cardinal Cajetan,

I write to you in earnest, seeking your righteous counsel. We have been beset on all sides by grievous evil which defies my studies and abilities. Multiple parishioners have died by violence done to them in the wilderness surrounding our village. Their deaths have presented a great mystery to our parish and, as priest, the burden for shepherding this flock through this valley of death has exceeded the bounds of my little wisdom. After careful inquiry into the matter, and witnessing phenomenon of an extraordinary character, I have come to the opinion that we may be besieged by no less than a vampire, or some other, but equally demoniacal, creature. This conclusion was not reached in haste nor was it reached without substantial evidence. I humbly seek an audience with your holiness, but regret to say that I cannot, in good conscience, abandon my flock for even a moment during this dark era to come to you. If you would graciously extend all unmerited sympathy to me and to all the worthy loyal Catholics here in our little parish, I boldly and insufferably plead that you come to us at once, to exorcise the demon that taunts us. Or, if such is not possible, please do us the kindness of sending an agent on your behalf who is experienced and wise in such matters. Finally, if no such person is available, please write to me with your true and helpful counsel so that I may, by the acquired merits of Christ and his martyred saints, defeat the evil which oppresses us daily.

Hail to our most righteous Pope, vicar of Christ and light of Rome.

Your obedient servant,

Dom Augustine Calmet

Post Script,

I have included the particulars of the events and the location of our parish in a separate document, which I have been compiling for some time now. You shall find it included with this letter.

Grace, Peace, and Salutations

Having reached the bottom of the paper, the priest set his pen down and reclined back in his chair once more. He reflected on the bold step he was daring to take, but knew it must be done. His parishioners expected it. Idelette demanded it. He also knew that it would take many days or even weeks to reach the Cardinal, and that it may be much longer before help could become available. He held a stick of wax over the candle for a moment, then dripped it on the envelope. He set his ring to the wax then placed the letter in a drawer. Though he had written it, he had not yet acquiesced to send it.

Chapter 39

Ryan lamented his situation as he traipsed through the mall to shop for books on witchcraft. He had struck out at the public library. Maybe Nobility Books would be more productive. Perhaps he would catch a break and cross paths with a witch while in the mall. Maybe they like smoothies and escalators. It was Friday afternoon and the place was busy. But he wasn't seeing any obvious witches. At least, no pointy hats rose above the crowds, and no black cats were scurrying between people's feet.

It took a moment to find the right section in the bookstore, but once he did, Ryan immediately felt out of place among the new age and occult authors. The random amalgamation of ideas, evidenced by the titles, was difficult to take seriously. The shelves behind him held political science and philosophy. He kept wanting to turn around and browse those books instead. But Alexis de Tocqueville wasn't going to help him get answers to the occult.

He was leafing through a book on spells, when a man walked up beside him and started thumbing through similar books.

"I'm a little out of my league here," he interrupted Ryan. "Do you know much about this stuff?"

"What stuff exactly?" Ryan asked the obvious plain clothes police officer.

"Witchcraft and stuff. You're reading about it. Can you help me?" Detective Jameson asked.

"I never read this stuff either. I've just seen the newspapers lately and saw the pictures of graffiti around the city. So I was doing a little speculative investigation."

"No kidding. Me too," Jameson said. "Just doing some investigating. Have you found anything?"

"Not much. Nor would I probably even realize it if I did." He returned the book to the shelf and selected another to glance through.

"So you don't know anything about this stuff at all?"

"Nope," the diener shook his head.

"And you've never read up on it before?"

"Nope."

"You were just curious."

"Same as you, detective." He reshelved the book and grabbed another.

"Now what makes you think I'm a detective?"

"You said you were investigating."

"Ah. Gotcha. Have you ever tried any of this magic stuff before?"

"Like I said, I've never read about it and I've never tried it."

"So you don't know what these symbols here mean?" He pointed to some in a book. Ryan recognized a couple of them.

"No idea," Ryan lied as he looked the detective in the eyes.

"I think you might," Jameson furrowed his brow slightly.

"Could you be any more transparent, officer?"

"What book is that you're holding?" he pointed down at the book Ryan had been leafing through.

"He's not holding a book," Idelette interrupted as she appeared behind Ryan, seemingly out of thin air.

Detective Jameson did a double take when he looked at her. Blonde, long black coat. This could be the woman who was blurry on the security footage.

"He's holding a book in his right hand. Are you with him?"

"He's not holding a book, and, no, I'm not with him."

"OK, so he's not holding a book and you're not with him," he quipped, not knowing that he was nearly mesmerized, "but I think I've seen you before."

"No, you haven't."

"No, I haven't."

"You did not see him or me here today. You came and looked at some books about witchcraft, but didn't have any success, then you left the mall uneventfully."

"That's exactly what I did."

Idelette took a book off a shelf and handed it to Detective Jameson. "Look at this book for a few minutes and then leave." With that she took Ryan by the arm and lead him out the exit and into the parking lot.

"That was quite the experience," Ryan observed. "Have you ever done that to me?"

"You're welcome." She ignored his question. "Did you find anything before the cop showed up?"

"No. I recognized a few symbols but didn't gain any further understanding. Will he recognize us in the future or will he forget all of what just happened?"

"If he sees us, he might think he remembers us from somewhere, but he won't be able to piece it together. It will just be a strange feeling like deja vu or something."

"Poe once commented on the odd phenomenon of being on the verge of remembering something but in the end unable to remember it."

"That's exactly what it will be like for the cop if he sees one of us again. More importantly, did you notice the symbols?"

"Where?" Ryan looked about.

"Not here." She rolled her eyes. "There were symbols drawn on the bookcases behind the wiccan books. You could see them when I pulled one of the volumes off the shelf and handed it to the detective. So if these people acquired their books from this store, maybe that's why you couldn't find any that were helpful. They already bought, or stole, the ones they are using and marked the shelves. The books that remain are just the ones they left behind."

"Interesting observation, but it doesn't help. I'm not sure any of this helps. Even if we figure out what they're doing, we still don't know who is doing it, or why. It might just be a rabbit hole. But," he bobbed his head about slightly, "it's the only trail I've got. So I still plan on checking some antiquarian book stores too, when I find the time. Maybe old books have what new ones lack."

"They often do. Let me know what you uncover." Idelette turned to leave but Ryan grabbed her wrist. It was cold.

"Hang on," he said.

She glared down at his hand and then at him. It was intimidating.

"Please," he entreated as he let go.

She lowered her eyes slightly as she loosened the death grip she had on the Bible in her pocket.

"What is it?" she allowed.

"That was Genesis you quoted over Calvin's grave the other night. Wasn't it?"

"And?" she asked with some annoyance.

"I looked it up."

"And?" she asked again, even more annoyed.

"I—," Ryan cast about for the right words but didn't have them. "I don't know."

Idelette sighed and softened her tone. "Well you think on it, and maybe we can discuss it further the next time we meet. Maybe."

With that, she turned and vanished between the rows of cars which populated the parking lot. But Ryan was encouraged. Her parting words were the most encouraging thing he had heard since Sarah abandoned him. He was strangely comforted by the thought that at least he would see Idelette again.

Chapter 40

There are only two rare and antiquarian bookshops in the greater Grand Blanc area. They happen to be almost next door to each other in Old Town, which was a trendy part of town with brick roads and little shops intermingled with chain establishments. Ryan knew that if the witches obtained any antiquarian books in town, their options were limited. It had been two weeks since his run-in with the detective in the shopping mall, and he still hadn't made any progress finding who was behind the witchcraft. He had trafficked bodies they had marked, and yet had no idea who they were. He was growing frustrated.

The first bookshop Ryan entered was stocked primarily with literature and comic books. But there were also Bibles, nonfiction, reference, local history, and other general stock. There was slim chance of finding any information about the witchcraft symbols here, but Ryan poked around anyway. The employee running the shop that day was not aware of any such subject matter in their antiquarian stock, but thought they might have something in the religious books. Ryan thumbed through a few books but quickly struck out.

He hoped the second bookstore held better prospects. Like the books it contained, this shop was older and darker. It also had a basement full of dusty books below the main floor. Ryan stepped in off the street and gave a brief nod to William, one of the two shopkeepers who owned the store. He was a scruffy man in his sixties with a long scar under one eye and knuckes deformed by arthritis. Ryan only knew the owners' names because he had purchased copies of some of the eighteenth century graveyard poets from them a year before. Otherwise, they never exchanged a word. Ryan gave little attention to William's nod back, but immediately turned to the stacks. One after another, he pulled leather volumes off the shelves, and flipped through them quickly, scanning for anything resembling the symbols he had seen, or topics related to witchcraft. He perused an enormous 1732 Dictionary of the Bible written by Antoine Augustine Something-or-other which looked promising for Greek and Hebrew symbols. Even though it was three folio volumes, dense with fold-out maps, and charts of semitic alphabets, it turned out to be a dead end as well.

Having exhausted the main floor holdings, he descended the narrow steps into the basement. The ceiling was low and the shelves narrowly spaced. He pulled a string on the light dangling above, doubting it would even work. Humming a bit as it sputtered on, the bulb cast a dim light which barely served half the basement. As he turned to his task, the other shopkeeper, also named William, brushed past him without a word. The floor space was minimal between the already too-close shelves—cluttered all the more by stacks of Dutch and German theology and hymns, piled everywhere. The grave robber had to get down on his knees regularly just to see many of the books on the lower shelves.

Eventually he happened upon a few twentieth century books of some use. There was a dictionary on the occult and a grimoire of some sort. Ryan found a small area of available floor space to sit down and started paging through the few items he had found.

Soon he recognized several symbols, all unrelated to each other. The more pages he turned the more he recognized, though it was still only a fraction of what he had seen in the graffiti. Some of the symbols were of established antiquity, others were dubious. Some had prior meanings unrelated to their later occult usage. Others seemed to be invented specifically for demonology. But even trying to read the text associated with the symbols, Ryan could not find any real commonality. There was no overlying theme other than the fact that the symbols he found were indeed used for witchcraft and demonology purposes.

As Ryan sat engrossed in the books, a familiar icy hand fell upon his shoulder. He glanced up and who should be looking over his shoulder but Idelette.

"You should give that up," he said, pointing at the cigarette behind her ear.

"Oh, I don't smoke. It's just part of blending in with mortals. Do have any cash? I generally don't carry any money," she said.

"A little. Are you buying something?"

"I'm considering it."

"What did you find?"

"It's a three-volume treatise on anatomy by Alexander Monro Tertius from the 1790s."

"Sounds cool. I didn't know you were interested in anatomy."

"I knew Alexander Monro." She seemed to look right through Ryan, back through centuries. "He, his son, and his grandson all held the same professorial chair of anatomy at Edinburgh University Medical School. One after the other. But here's the secret. It was all the same Alexander Monro. There was only one.

He just kept coming back. First posing as his own son, then as his son's son. For three generations he held the same position at the university. I never did figure out what he was exactly, or how he did it. I would kind of like the book just for the memories, though," here her voice softened, "not really of him." She stared at nothing in silence, then suddenly looked back at the diener. "But maybe another time. I'll think about it."

"Well that's an interesting story. Did you know Victor Frankenstein too?"

"Fiction," Idelette shook her head.

"Ah. Well, so what other creatures exist? Are there werewolves and zombies and leprechauns too?"

"I don't know. I don't think so. I've never encountered anything else that I could identify. I'm the only vampire that I know of right now. It's been centuries since I've seen another. Like I said, I never figured out what Alexander Monro was or how he did his little rejuvenation act. It seems there are still mysteries which elude me, even after all these years."

"The obvious question still remains, then. What about witches? Have you seen witches before?"

"I've seen some weird stuff and I've seen people tried and executed as witches, but I've never watched someone succesfully perform any type of spell or hex."

"Do you think it can work? I mean, like really work?"

"I don't know. The Bible commands not to do it. So I guess that implies that it is possible. Or maybe it's not, but the moral principle violated when attempting it might be the reason it is prohibited."

"That makes sense."

"Then again, the magicians in the book of Exodus were able to perform miraculous signs. But maybe they were just as surprised when it actually worked as the other people in the room.

Maybe God merely allowed it to work just those couple of times but never again for them. Maybe the same was true for the witch at Endor that Saul consulted."

"Don't forget Simon the magus in Acts."

Idelette gave a look of surprise.

"Oh, yeah, by the way, I've been reading the Bible furiously since your one-line eulogy over Calvin's grave. I'm not totally sure why, but it caught my attention."

"I suppose that's good."

"In any event, maybe God is actually letting this current crop of witches perform magic. Maybe it's merely a function of loosening Satan's chain just a little?"

"Your guess is as good as mine." Idelette seemed to stare off into the distance. Then she quickly glanced back to Ryan. "Well, you're already doing the research I came to do, so I'll leave you to it. Let me know what you find."

"How and when will I do that?"

"You seem to know how to find me. Keep doing what you've been doing."

"What, you mean go about my life and wait for you to show up?"

"Exactly," and with that she left.

Ryan's eyes and brain gradually fatigued from scouring the books in that claustrophobic basement. He reshelved the books and went upstairs, passing a large clock on the stairway wall as he ascended. It was almost time to go to work. As he walked toward the counter he passed the Christianity section and thought maybe he would buy a book for himself. While he looked up at the commentaries on the top shelf, Detective Malli walked in and inquired about occult books at the cash register. William directed her downstairs. Ryan quickly passed around a large group of bookcases in the middle of the room and slipped out the front door as the detective turned to go down the stairs.

Ryan needed to get to work anyway, and didn't really want to be repeatedly associated with searching occult books when witchcraft-style murders were going on around the city. The last time was a narrow enough escape. He returned to his car and drove to work.

When he entered the morgue, there was Idelette sitting on the edge of the autopsy table. Ryan turned on the radio (quite loudly) by the outer door then walked to the back of the room. He sat down beside her. The stainless steel was cold and not particularly comfortable.

"I've become pretty adept at staying in shadows and going unnoticed, but I think you have me beat. In fact, I'm confident that you have been close by for some time now. I just never noticed. Am I correct? Is that the case?"

"How long have you been in the resurrectionist business?" Idelette changed the topic.

"A few years."

"Always in the Grand Blanc area?"

"Yes. How old are you?" Ryan was equally abrupt.

She paused. "About 35."

"About?"

"Yeah."

"And what sins have you committed in all those 35 years?" Ryan asked, not about to be outdone asking uninvited probative questions. He suspected his time with her would be fleeting, and he did not want to waste even one minute of it on small talk. He had too many questions swirling in his mind since she entered his life.

She paused even longer, seemingly unfazed by the question. "Most, I think. How about you?"

Ryan sighed. "Many." He paused as well. "Redeemed by the blood of the Lamb though, right?"

"So you have been reading your Bible. But have you not read what is written about those who go on sinning?"

"I have. And I repent many times an hour now. And you? Do your countless sins weigh upon you as mine do me?"

"Like a millstone," she lowered her head a little more.

"Is it really a Bible in your pocket, like you told Sarah?" It hurt to mention her.

"Yes," she glanced back up momentarily.

"And you believe it, don't you?"

"Yes."

"But you go on sinning too."

Idelette gave no answers but only looked down at her feet.

Not wanting that situation to continue, Ryan forged ahead. "Random thought. Have you ever read the Pilgrim's Progress?"

"Yes. I probably should again, it's been centuries—"

"Centuries," Ryan interrupted. "Remind me. How old are you?"

She made no reply.

"I'm pleased to know you," Ryan abruptly changed the course of the conversation one more time, and extended his hand.

Idelette looked up but hesitated.

"It's nice to have a friend," she eventually conceded, and shook his hand.

"So I gotta know. What is your interest in this whole occult situation that has been developing? Why do you even care?"

Once again, the vampire looked through him, as though to some distant memory. Even someone as guarded as her could not disguise the fact that she was remembering something or someone deeply painful.

"It's evil and I abhor it," she said at last. "But it's more than that," she trailed off. Then she shook her head, furrowed her brow and looked at Ryan with suspicion. "It seems to be following you."

"You seem to be following me."

"Because they are following you." She looked down again.

"No, I feel like you have something bigger on your mind."

"Why would I tell you even if I do?" she glanced at him out of the corner of her eye.

"Because you can. And I haven't got another friend in the world either, remember? So what's on your mind?"

She gave no response. Ryan stared a hole through the side of her head as the vampire stared down at her feet once again. Her pocketed right hand compulsively probed the corners of her Bible. Ryan was just about to give up.

"I'll answer you with a question," she spoke up at last. "Have you ever thought 'what if the promises of God don't apply to me?' I know the promises of God. The Scriptures are clear. But, what if they just don't apply to me? What if they are for everyone else?"

"How do you mean?"

"My very existence testifies against me. I cannot stop sinning. Anyone who goes on sinning does not have the love of Christ in him. But the only mechanism by which I can stay alive is a sin. And I cannot die apparently, except suicide. Which is a sin. If I stop the sinning that keeps me alive, I am committing the sin of suicide. Am I therefore outside salvation? What am I? What hope is there for me?"

"Are you not already dead?"

"Do I look dead?" Idelette sounded somewhat exacerbated. "Do I act dead? Have you seen another dead body do what I do? Have you seen a corpse walk and talk and have emotions?"

"No. But are you alive?"

"Aren't I? Don't I do what living things do? I move, think, speak, sleep, and feed."

"It seems to me that there is a third option," Ryan attempted to reason. "You commit sin if you keep yourself alive. You commit sin if you let yourself die. But what if you are killed? Would you not then know that it was God's will that you die there, then, and by that means, and the guilt is not on you?"

"But I went on sinning up to that point. So I'm not guiltless at the point of death. Have I been given over to a depraved mind and iterative sin? Am I already condemned to death and Hell, but also a protracted existence as a slave to this compulsion?"

"Can you be killed?"

"Do you honestly think I'm going to answer that?" she was quick to ask in a stern tone entirely unlike her prior exacerbation.

"Well, backing up a little, it seems to me that your focus is on yourself. I mean I'm no counselor and I'm no theologian, but I was raised as a Protestant and I still remember a pretty big chunk of that. You sound like a Roman Catholic." (Idelette actually almost laughed a little at that comment). "You're operating on a theory of works righteousness, or, some sort of inversion of it. You say, to die and to be saved, you have to stop sinning. But where is your faith? Isn't it in yourself? I'm still playing catch up, and I'm as much a sinner as you," (the vampire rolled her eyes), "but isn't the whole point of the Bible that Christ atoned for all our sins on the cross and that you don't have to fear death if your life is hidden in him?"

"And that's exactly why I converted from Roman Catholicism and became a Puritan centuries ago. Or, at least, I think I did. But where is the spiritual fruit in my life now? Despite all my prayers, I'm trapped in a cycle of sin. So much so, in fact, that presently I'm fighting the urge to kill you!"

"Well, you're talking to me instead of killing me, which I sincerely thank you for. And it may be that you are helping my own soul merely by having this conversation."

"Maybe that's why I'm following you then, instead of the witches. Or maybe that's why they are following you too—for your spiritual well being."

"Funny. Well, I have work to do tonight, so we'll see if they follow me further."

"Where will you be tonight?" Idelette asked.

"Heh. You'll find me, I assume."

"So be it," Idelette nodded slightly. "You really love these cemeteries, don't you?"

"I do. I really really do. Thank you for this conversation. It's given me a lot to think about. But I have to get downstairs to work."

"Thank you, as well. We could have talked more at the book store, but I heard the police approaching, so I left."

"And you decided not to warn me?"

"I can't bail you out of everything," she reasoned as she hopped down off the autopsy table. "So long."

Ryan returned to the gross pathology department for the time being. He was still pondering how Idelette came and went as he entered the grossing room.

"Oh, good. You're here. I wanted to tell you we finally got an applicant for the diener position," Phil said.

"Oh really? That's good. It's only been posted for four months."

"And even if she interviews tomorrow, which she won't, it will take the HR department another four months to process the paperwork and get her working."

"So it's a she this time."

"She is a she. That's correct."

"Does she have any prior experience?"

"No. No one ever does. You didn't, and I didn't either."

"What's her name?"

"I think it was Zoe."

"I know a Zoe. We were good friends years ago. I actually saw her for the first time in a long time just reeently."

"Did she mention applying for the diener position when you saw her?"

"I doubt it's the same Zoe."

"So she didn't mention it."

"No," Ryan said absentmindedly as he wondered if Idelette was still up in the autopsy room.

"And you didn't bother to mention it to her."

"No."

"See this is why the position has gone unfilled for so long. You need to be more proactive to recruit people."

"Your mom needs to be more proactive."

"My mom? Did you just turn that into a your mom joke?"

"I did indeed, sir."

"It didn't even make sense."

"Your mom doesn't make sense."

"OK. I'm done with that. What day should we invite Zoe for an interview?"

"Same day we interview your mom I suppose."

Phil groaned in exacerbation. "What cemetery will you be in tonight," he finally asked.

"Oak Hill again. How about you?"

"Very funny."

Chapter 41

Idelette returned to Jamestown mall, yet again. It was abysmal but it was the place to hunt. She knew to look for young female subjects because that is who she saw last year doing the deal by the old slaughter house. And the pervading sense of evil she felt at that time was pretty compelling evidence that they were satanic. Young, satanic, and female adds up to shopping mall. So that's where she kept going. Even though she hadn't seen the same witches on her previous searches, they had to show up eventually. She had no fear of being recognized in the murder of that girl—what was her name?—whatever—because she knew that her image was always blurry on camera.

After a quick sweep through Nobility Books and Classy Lingerie, she made her way into the Hot Gothic. And there, on the corner of a back wall was a marker-drawn symbol which wasn't there on her previous visits. Encouraged, now she merely needed to kill time and wait for her prey. She shopped around the store casually and even occasionally brought something back to the dressing room as if trying things on, but no one she suspected of being a witch ever came. Plenty of people ripe for killing came and went, but no witches. Not even a hint of one. Clearly, she needed to move on before her behavior was called into question. She followed some emo kids into Cali Sun Wear. And that's where she saw her. A young girl wandered in, and on her backpack was a familiar marker drawn symbol. It matched the one in the other store perfectly. Idelette listened closely from across the store. The girl was alone though, and said nothing to anyone nearby. Idelette followed her out of the store and to the food court. She was met by friends who all bought tickets to the latest horror movie: The Fourth Autopsy of J. Doe: Michael's Revenge. Reluctantly, Idelette mesmerized her way into the theater too.

Following at a distance, she kept a close eye on the group. The movie was about to start when they darted from the concessions into the theater. They found seats in the third row from the back. Idelette approached the people who were already seated behind her prey, looked them in the eye, and whispered, "you're in my seat. You need to move closer to the front now." Without a moment's hesitation they got up and moved up to the front of the theater. The vampire sat down in the middle seat situated behind the teenagers, listened to their conversations, and read their text messages.

Most of it was gossip. But then the girl she had been following took a selfie and sent it to a friend with a message "as above." Moments later a familiar reply came back: "so below." The selfie that accompanied it was of a frizzy-haired girl with glasses. Then came another message. This one was more useful: "Fuller Street 11:30." The girl hastily texted back, "C U soon."

Idelette did not watch any of the movie. She just stared at the backs of their heads and waited patiently. She debated whether she should follow them afterward or take a chance and get to the graveyard beforehand. It seemed best to be there in advance. Perhaps she could intercept the frizzy haired girl. She seemed important. The moment the credits began to roll, Idelette was out the door, invisibly fast. The lights had not even turned on yet. She maintained that pace all the way across town and was in Fuller Street Cemetery well before 11:30.

There are only a couple ways in and out of this graveyard. Furthermore, it's surrounded by neighborhoods and not particularly big. So this meeting must be small and short lived, or the risk of being caught would be too great. Idelette watched carefully from a well-concealed position near the back. 11:15. No one. 11:22. No one. 11:28. No one. 11:31. No one. Furious, at 11:45 Idelette walked out of the cemetery, onto the sidewalk, and immediately saw the girl from the mall walking out the front door of a house just down the road! The meeting was not in the cemetery at all! The girl turned onto the sidewalk toward Idelette, took a few steps, and paused. She looked straight at the vampire with a slightly perplexed expression, and then turned around and began to walk the opposite direction. Of course Idelette followed.

The girl's pace quickened. She turned a corner and began to run. Idelette was around that same corner in an instant. When the girl looked back, Idelette was still just walking toward her. The witch ran now. She was young and leggy and fast. The vampire began to jog slightly. Might as well make it a real chase. It was just as easy to run her prey to exhaustion so there would be no fight at the end. Sprinting as fast as she could, the girl took several side streets, this way and that, doubled back through some yards, jumped a fence, and was headed back to the house where she had come from. The vampire cleared the fences with a graceful glide and continued to walk as her victim ran ever more slowly toward the back deck of the house. The girl was nearly stumbling now as her stride was becoming less coordinated. This was the time to strike.

Idelette passed her prey, and stood waiting on the steps. The girl shrieked, faltered, and began to run back the way she came. By the time she turned around though, the vampire was there behind her. She grabbed the girl by the neck, hauled her up the stairs, kicked the door in, and dragged her inside. It was time for the old face-to-face with these little girls.

But the house was empty. In the living room there were candles and spell books here and there among household items, but no people. They must have already left. But they had definitely been there. Idelette threw the girl onto the couch.

"How many were here tonight?"

No answer.

In an instant Idelette was holding her up against the ceiling. "How many?"

"Five," the girl coughed.

"How many of you are there total?"

The girl hesitated and Idelette began to slowly crumble the plaster ceiling with the girls body.

"Hundreds. We are legion," the girl strained to speak.

Infuriated by the cliché abuse of that Bible verse, Idelette dropped her to the floor. She put a boot on her stomach and stood firmly in place.

"Legion?! You are Legion? What is this some stupid exorcism movie?" Idelette yelled and pushed down with her boot. "What are you people doing in Greenwood cemetery?"

"I've never been in Greenwood cemetery," she squirmed under the pressure of the vampire's foot.

Idelette dug her boot in harder.

"I swear it! I've never been! Zoe—" she stopped herself.

"The blonde?" Idelette seized on the opportunity.

Wide-eyed silence.

"Yeah, the blonde. Got it." Idelette continued, "What is she up to?"

"She'll show you. You should join us."

Idelette kicked the girl across the room. "What does this have to do with Ryan?"

"Who?" The girl groaned as she writhed on the floor, holding her stomach.

Idelette threw her back across the room. She crashed hard against the wall and bent the baseboard heater.

"I don't know a Ryan—I swear I don't!" she sputtered.

"You have no clue what you don't know. Now, talk. What exactly do you know?"

Silence.

Idelette, keeping a boot on the witch's stomach, reached down and began to pull steadily up on the girl's hair.

"Power!" the girl shrieked. "That's what I know. Zoe showed us how." Her expression changed from fear to resolve. "She taught us to stand fast in our magic—to inspire terror. We will not be dominated. 'We have made a covenant with death.' Now we are insidious. Soon we will be inescapable!"

"You're brainwashed, you moron. 'In spite of your many sorceries, evil has come upon you which you do not know how to charm away, and ruin shall come upon you suddenly, of which you know nothing.'" And with that the vampire stepped off from the witch's stomach, lifted her off the floor, and sank her teeth into her neck. She drank voraciously for nearly a minute then dropped her. She shuddered at what she had done yet again, then licked the rich iron-tasting hemorrhage from her lips. She picked the corpse up, put it on her shoulder, and went south to Oak Hill cemetery.

It wasn't long before she found Ryan. She could hear him inside one of the sepulchres before she even crossed the threshold into the graveyard. She waited outside the tomb and thought about what deep and inappropriately personal question to interrogate him with this time.

• "Why do you 'long for death, and dig for it more than for hidden treasures, and rejoice exceedingly and are glad when you find the grave?'"

He gave no reply as he stepped out.

"What are you doing?" she shifted gears.

"Working, of course. And you?"

"But where's the body? Isn't that what you do? Dig up bodies?"

"Not always. This time, I was asked to put something back in a grave. I see you brought a body though. I can take care of that if you'd like, for my usual rate."

"No, thank you. She's a friend actually. We just met at a party earlier this evening and had a good talk. Though we didn't agree on everything."

"I can see that. And this seems like the kind of place she would hang out while alive, and be found dead the next morning. Did you learn anything interesting during your little meet and greet?" Ryan leaned against the door frame of the mausoleum.

"She mostly withheld. But I got us started. It's big. She claimed there are hundreds of them. Hundreds."

"That's a lot. What's their goal?" His brow furrowed slightly.

"We didn't get into details but it's a rise to power. I think these girls are mostly peer-pressured into this. Herd mentality, right? These people can't even go to the bathroom alone."

• "Heh. 'Mere puppets they who come and go....'"

"Is that Poe?"

"Of course."

"Anyway, the blonde in Greenwood—Zoe—she holds the strings. And you know her."

"Zoe! The Zoe I know?"

"As I told you. That Zoe. You do know who I'm talking about, yes?"

"I do," Ryan nodded slightly. "It's been years, but we used to be fairly close friends."

"Used to be? But you saw her in Greenwood recently. When you first found the symbols. You two walked arm in arm."

"Yeah. You saw all of that, huh? That's kind of embarrassing—it was all right in front of me while she played ignorant."

"This girl says she's never heard of you and she's never been in Greenwood. So, no, apparently it wasn't all right in front of you. This is much bigger than what you saw there. I think Greenwood and you are just cogs."

"For just cogs, we seem to be important cogs—otherwise why would they keep showing up there, and why would they keep crossing my path?"

"Coincidence," she shook her head. "You just happen to be there. It doesn't matter though."

"Do I detect a witch hunt in your near future?" the diener asked somewhat optimistically.

"I've been in witch hunts. I plan to root them out and scatter them. I'll kill who I find and break their coven into fragments. If even ten of them are left in a house, they will die."

"Very Old Testament of you. Will you 'not suffer a witch to live?'"

"'In spite of their many sorceries and the great power of their enchantments.' I will not, again, watch Lucifer gain such a close foothold. He already has gained too much in me." With that remark, she turned and walked away.

"So should I just take care of this rotting corpse for you, then? And free of charge?" he called after her.

"Leave it, for all I care," she called back without turning around or even slowing her pace.

"And people think I'm jaded," he murmured to himself as he took a seat on a nearby headstone.

Ryan sat for a time staring at the body and contemplating these things. As he did, two girls approached from deeper in the cemetery, and stopped suddenly when they saw him with the corpse. One of the girls had a book of spells under her arm. Ryan leaped off the headstone and was confronting them in an instant. One girl fled while he held the other tight by the arm. He glared at her for several moments in silence, letting her get a good look at him, then, to her surprise, forced her away. Confused, she stumbled and ran after her friend. Letting them make the mental association between his face and the sight of the dead girl seemed like a more powerful statement than anything he could speak. Rather than hunting the witches, now maybe they would hunt him. After the girls were out of sight he stared down at the corpse again.

While that was transpiring, the vampire had climbed on top of the Clark mausoleum at the opposite end of the graveyard.

"Jaded," she whispered as she climbed. Reaching the top she noticed the dried blood on her hands. It was the sticky residue from her most recent failure to resist her sinful nature. All at once the reality of her depravity rushed upon her as it had done countless times before. Yet again the sin which clings so close, and the burden of what she was, and had so-often done, preoccupied her thoughts. This time, she could not overcome the attendant despair. Idelette did not stand or even sit on the stone roof of the sepulchre, but fell on her face and began to sob as contrition overtook her. She grabbed and ripped at her clothes as she dwelled on the sins she accumulated over the centuries. Then with a broken whisper that was suffocated by her own hair and the dismal shroud of night, she began:

"From the end of the earth I call to you. Lead me to the rock that is higher than I, Christ Jesus, my Lord and my God. I have committed great sins against you, then come and stand before you and say,'I am delivered!'—only to go on doing these abominations. Save me from the sin which clings so closely. You have cast me into the mire and I have become like dust and ashes."

She turned her head, scraping her cheek and tearing it open along the mossy stone, then pressed her forehead hard against her palms. "I cry to you for help and you do not answer me; I stand, and you only look at me. For I know that you will bring me to death and to the house appointed for all living. For my transgressions are multiplied before you and my sins testify against me. My transgressions are with me and I know my iniquities—denying the Lord, and turning back from following my God."

Even as she prayed the sanguinary thirst came upon her again and she fought hard to suppress her addiction. She reached out her hands and grabbed hold of the edge of the slab roof. She clutched it as she continued her petition. "My voice comes from the ground like the voice of a ghost. And from the dust my speech is a whisper. I am allotted months of emptiness, and nights of misery are apportioned to me. My flesh is clothed with worms and dirt; my skin hardens, then breaks out afresh. My days come to their end without hope. For now I shall lie in the earth; Does it seem good to you to oppress, to despise the work of your hands? My spirit is broken; my days are extinct; the graveyard is ready for me."

The edge of the massive stone she had previously clutched now crumbled under her tightening grip as she sobbed harder still. Her feeble voice gathered some strength. "Annul my covenant with death and my agreement with Sheol. Save me, O God of my Salvation, that I may give thanks to your holy name, and glory in your praise. Blessed be the Lord, the God of Israel, from everlasting to everlasting. For I know that my Redeemer lives, and at the last he will stand upon the earth." She only then noticed the stone rubble cutting into her hands. She continued. "All my days pass away under your wrath and to dust I return. And after my skin has been thus destroyed, yet in my flesh I shall see God. My heart faints within me! For you are the Christ, Son of the Living God. Have mercy on me Lord, a sinner. Amen."

She loosened her fists and let fall the rubble of tomb she was still gripping. Her pale cold hands were bleeding. At last she rolled over onto her back and stared silently up at the night sky. The abrasion on her cheek and the lacerations on her hands gradually closed without scars.

From part way across the cemetery, while contemplating the dead witch at his feet, Ryan thought he had heard Idelette's voice. He wondered who she could possibly be talking to. Leaving the dead girl, he silently followed the sound to where she was, and though he only heard a portion of what she prayed, it impacted him deeply. He thought about saying something, but felt it was best to leave her alone. Feeling despondent himself, he returned to the corpse and hastily dumped it inside the opened mausoleum. That done, he wrestled with the idea of approaching Idelette again. He took one step in her direction, but then thought better of it. He left the graveyard, but, with great and somber wonder, he pondered all he had heard for the rest of the sleepless night.

Chapter 42

Idelette returned to her little home to fix the damage her assailant had caused. The hinges to the outer and inner door were both partially torn and the locks were shattered. It needed more work than she could do, so she merely improvised a secure closure, then attempted to get a little rest while Conrad and her beloved priest bravely formulated a plan.

At first light the next day, everyone gathered together at the church. Kurt stepped up next to Idelette.

"Good morning," he greeted her, polite as usual yet still sounding awkward and ill-adjusted to conversation.

"Hello again, Kurt." Idelette cast about in her own mind looking for a way to avoid another awkward interaction. She felt so guilty about trying to avoid him, but it was always such a trial to keep the interaction casual and not forced.

"Today shall be a day to remember, I suspect," he said, sounding much more bold than usual.

"Why do you say that?"

"I believe the time for action is upon us. I am eager to see what plan Dom Calmet and Conrad have devised—for no doubt they have devised one—and I think it will be a worth-while endeavor. I also believe I have guessed their intentions."

Before Idelette could respond, Dom Calmet opened the meeting with a prayer and then elaborated on the events of the previous night to the crowd.

"As you have all heard or deduced, our village was attacked by the vampire last night. It chased a woman from her home right up to the church. But it did not enter the holy ground, I should like to also point out. Regardless, in light of this heinous event, Conrad and I have decided on a course of action. We will divide the labor and improve our defenses. But we will not only be defensive. A hunting party shall be formed. Conrad has bravely volunteered to lead it. This group will go into the forest to search for the minion of Satan that plagues us. They will find it and kill it. We cannot wait for it to return. The risk is too great to the entire village. I need brave volunteers to take this risk on all our behalves."

There was a long pause as people looked around at each other. Dom Calmet was just about to chastise them when some of the men, including Kurt, stepped forward to volunteer. The few men who formed the hunting party were mostly those who had been present at the earlier death scenes. It was a small group, but the men who joined were reliable. Dom Calmet gave the crowd a last stern look for its reluctance, but did not rebuke them. He pulled the men aside and gave them instructions.

"Move swiftly. Cover as much ground as you can. The daylight will not last and you must return before sunset. The vampire cannot tolerate the sun. It may be in a building, in a cave, or even a grave. Keep your eyes open and your minds focused. You are doing God's work by driving the evil out of the land. Do not neglect your prayers as you go. I will give you each a rosary and crucifix to carry. These are even more important than the weapons you will bring to kill it. When you find it and the opportunity is at hand to rescue us from its grip, strike hard and fast. Deliver lethal blows to the heart and to the head. Separate its head and limbs from its trunk. Pour salt between the severed pieces. Wedge a large rock in its mouth. Leave a pike of iron in its heart."

The men looked about with some concern over these dramatic instructions. Idelette had attempted to listen from a distance but could not hear. But she saw the group's looks of concern when the priest stopped speaking. Conrad then took over the conversation before any of the others could speak.

"I will guide us through the forest. We know it cannot be close because we have often been in the nearby trees, and to the river. It must be in deeper forest, but we don't know which direction. We will sweep in a counterclockwise fashion around the village until evening and then return directly before the sun has set. If we do not find it today, we can pick up the hunt where we left off the next day."

Idelette watched the men leave, and she watched the gate latch behind them. Then she joined the priest and the others in strengthening the defenses. In addition to the physical work, assignments were given to post guards throughout the night in the event that the hunting party returned unsuccessful. No one volunteered for the first shift. So lots were cast.

The day was long and it was nearly sunset when the hunting party returned. They looked tired and defeated. The men dragged their feet and some dragged their weapons. Conrad was in front, Kurt in the rear. All eyes were on them as they progressed through the gate. It was immediately apparent that a man was missing.

"We lost one," Conrad muttered as Dom Calmet approached them.

"Tell me everything," he replied with urgency while gripping Conrad's shoulders.

"We set out to the east and circled through the forest toward the north. We were deep in tangled wood, and the terrain was difficult. Not long into our quest the forest began to defeat us, and we had to divide and spread out to pass through the craggy wood. As the landscape began to ease again, we grouped back together but it quickly became obvious that not everyone was present. Heinrich was missing. He had worked the cover furthest north and so he was deepest into the forest. We were forced to sweep back through the ground we had already covered. We lost all hope of searching more for the vampire and instead spent the rest of the daylight searching in vain for Heinrich. We never found even a trace of him. Finally, to prevent further losses, and though the men valiantly protested, I ordered them to return. Night was coming."

The town listened in terror and many prayers were made for Heinrich. Dom Calmet ordered everyone to the church for a mass. Afterward, he dispersed everyone to their homes for food and rest. The first guards were ordered to their posts.

The sun was on the western tree tops when a posted guard perked up and called to a companion below.

"Get up here quick. I think I see something."

The other man rushed up onto the wall. The two looked out among the darkening trees.

"I don't see anything. Where?"

"It was over there. To the north. Just a minute ago. It was something moving fast."

"Well what was it? Do you think it's still there?"

"I don't know. But it was right over there in those trees."

"I don't see anything."

The two watched for several more minutes but only saw the gentle swaying of branches in the breeze.

"There! Over there now!"

"I saw it too!"

"Do we alert the town?"

"Probably bett—"

The first man was struck in the head by a flying log and down he toppled. The second man was taken completely off guard by this. He tried to grab his injured colleague but was pulled over the side of the wall before he could be of any help. The first man lay unconscious and bleeding. The other was gone.

Two passersby saw what happened and rushed to help their friend. But as they were attempting to revive him suddenly there was a crash against a more distant part of the wall. They saw some planks break as that entire side of the wall shook. Then it was silent. Men started calling out for assistance and passing torches and weapons around. People rushed about frantically when they heard the commotion. Some ran to hide and some to help. But no one really knew what to do. Many minutes passed with no activity from outside the wall. The sun dropped below the tree tops, and long shadows darkened the village. Then it happened. A sheep was bleating frantically near the south side of the village. It was suddenly silenced. Only moments later another blow crashed against the same point in the west wall. The structure failed. Logs and splinters went flying. The top crumpled and there was now a large gaping hole and a pile of debris.

Conrad came running to the west wall. He quickly rallied several men and sent them to fix the breach. They lit torches and tossed them out through the gap hoping it would intimidate the creature. But even as they were tossing out the torches a second attack came against the southern wall this time.

"It killed a sheep over there!" one man said. "We heard it! That means it was already inside. Why is it doing this if it was already over our walls?"

"It doesn't matter," Conrad snapped. "As long as it does this we know, at least for a moment, where it is and where it isn't."

With that remark there was another crash against the north wall. It cracked but did not fall. Dom Calmet came running from the church to help. Idelette was surveying the south wall with others.

Silence. Many long minutes of mysterious silence. Half an hour of silence. The sun was now completely below the hill tops and the eastern sky was dark.

"What do you think will happen next?" the priest asked Conrad. Just then something dark and fast passed over them. It was heading south, quickly. The men shouted at the villagers by the south wall, trying to alert them to the approaching danger.

The thing ran among houses and seemed to tarry there. It began bursting into doors, kicking them off their hinges. The creature was searching for something. Villagers came with torches and weapons prepared to die defending themselves. Their courage was admirable.

When the monster rushed out of a house and suddenly saw itself surrounded by several advancing groups of people, it stopped in its tracks. For the first time the villagers all saw what had plagued them. It had the appearance of an elderly man. And there was blood about its mouth. Their suspicions were confirmed. They rushed toward the vampire, screaming all sorts of curses upon it. In one swift motion the vampire grabbed a man, pulled the pitchfork from his hand, and threw him against the advancing horde. Several men were struck and fell.

He leaped over the cluster of villagers and stole one of their torches. He ran into the barn near the north wall and set it ablaze.

Men came running to open the gate so the animals could flee. Others ran for buckets and water. Idelette, however, ran for the church. The undead creature ran after her.

Idelette did not look back to see if she was being pursued. She forced her stride to the point of incoordination, incapable of running any faster. But she expended such energy needlessly. Just a few steps from the churchyard the creature was upon her. He grabbed her ankle and dragged her, with speed she could hardly believe, toward the south wall. She screamed and screamed for help as she was purloined away, though she knew it was futile.

Conrad, Dom Calmet, and many others were already running after her, but they were hopelessly behind. She dragged her fingers in the dirt and screamed all the more when she saw Dom Calmet stumble and fall. Neither would help the other. The vampire tossed Idelette over the wall and then leaped over after her. Dom Calmet managed to partially get back up, but she was gone.

"No!" screamed the priest and he collapsed back to the ground sobbing.

"Everybody, gather to me!" Conrad shouted above the commotion. "Come quickly. I need everyone who is able to follow me into the woods. We will pursue the monster. We will find where it hides, and we will kill it. Perhaps it is not too late for our friend."

Kurt replied, "We cannot all go. Some must stay behind to try to defend the village. It may be that this was all a trick to get us to empty the village. Then it can glut itself on the blood of our women and children while we wander the wilderness on a fool's errand."

"Well stated," Conrad rejoined. "Thirty men, come with me. I don't care who. I'm going right this instant. Some of you come and some of you stay." And with that remark he turned and climbed through the debris in the nearest hole gaping in their too-feeble defense. Many men gathered up their courage and followed. Others set to work trying to contain the blaze which had already consumed much of the barn.

The torches of the hunting party could be seen spreading out rapidly among the forest trees. Gradually they disappeared over the hills to the north.

The priest still sat on the ground where he had fallen, and, looking defeated, muttered, "Mighty Lord, have pity on us."

Chapter 43

Detective Malli and Jameson surveyed the house on Fuller Street. There were symbols scrawled in every room but it was otherwise just an ordinary house. The only room disturbed had a dent in the ceiling and a broken coffee table. The back-door frame was broken as well.

"The dent in the ceiling has to be recent, right?" Detective Malli asked one of the crime scene analysts.

"There's not much plaster dust on the floor and broken glass below, but there is definitely some," the analyst replied.

"Somebody threw the table against the ceiling?" Detective Jameson suggested as he walked into the room.

"Maybe."

"I found this book." With gloved hands Jameson handed Malli a small and worn cloth-bound book of spells. "Maybe we can get fingerprints or DNA off it. Looks well used though. Might be from a used book store."

"Or the internet. Who knows how many people have handled it before it ended up here."

"Might be some writing in it too—maybe we'll score with a current owner's name and phone number somewhere in it."

"Wouldn't that be nice. Nothing in the front cover," she noted as she opened it. "Well, you can thumb through it more thoroughly tonight and let me know what you find." Detective Malli dropped it into an evidence bag.

A uniformed officer stepped in. He informed them that the property owner said the ceiling was not dented two weeks prior when he was last in the house. But he couldn't say anything specific about the last renters. Detective Jameson went out to his car and thumbed through the book while he waited for Malli. But after a few moments the uniformed officer called to him from the front door. He replaced the book in the evidence bag and set it on the driver's seat as he walked a few feet away so he could hear the other officer.

Having watched things unfold, Idelette saw her opportunity. She rushed behind the detective, grabbed the book, and escaped back the way she came without making a sound. Detective Jameson had only taken his eyes off it for a second but when he turned back it was gone. He looked inside the car, on the floor boards, and under the car. It was definitely gone. He scanned his surroundings, looking for anyone on the sidewalks or between the houses, but there was no one in sight.

Chapter 44

Ryan was back in the morgue, having just punched the time clock, when who should walk in, but Idelette.

"Do you live here? Are you my guardian angel?" he joked.

"There are no guardian angels mentioned in the Bible."

"So, about that. Do you read the Bible a lot? Like regularly?" Ryan was eager for a truly meaningful conversation.

"Yes. Do you? Regularly?"

"Regularly as of very recently. And yet what evidence of that is there in the life I live?" he threw back at her the question she asked of him previously as he took a seat on the edge of the autopsy table.

"I understand the phenomenon." She sat down beside him.

"I know you do. And now I do too."

The two sat in silence for a moment.

"Oh," Idelette broke the pregnant pause. "The reason I came here today, by the way, since I thought you would be interested to know, I stole one of their books."

She slid a small cloth volume out of her left coat pocket, and handed the venefical thing over to Ryan. "Here, take it. I'm relieved to be rid of it."

"Have you read it?" he asked as he studied the cover.

"Some of it. It's stupid. Look at this," she took it back from him and found a page:

"'Her charms can cure what souls she please,
Rob other hearts of healthful ease,
Turn rivers backward to their source,
And make the stars forget their course,
And call up ghosts from night:
The ground shall bellow 'neath your feet:
The mountain-ash shall quit its seat,
And travel down the height'"

She turned the page and continued.

"There is more of the same and then there are hand-written spells: 'Now four form the corners within this great circle. One within nine it is ever expanding. Like stars the dead bend around us and we bring the force of one within.' All of that poetry was just a block quote stolen from Virgil's Aeneid then apparently blended with some original nonsense."

"So you read Latin classics too. Fascinating. But are they any more or less charlatans whether they plagiarize their spells or not?" Ryan asked as he took back the book and paged through it a bit.

"It speaks to the caliber of people we are dealing with. It sounds impressive, I'm sure, to immature and uneducated girls. But you just know they don't have any clue it's stolen from classic literature. Stupid." As she spoke, Ryan walked over to a corner cabinet and ensconced the book behind a bunch of old autopsy stock jars that should have been disposed of 20 years ago.

"I'm getting hints of your past," he observed as he walked back over to continue the conversation. "Who are you exactly and where have you been before you came here? I can't even identify your accent."

"It's a long and tiresome story."

"Well give me some highlights," the diener insisted as the vampire stared back at him somewhat annoyed for several seconds.

"Very well. You asked. I left my home in Germany for Rome after I was turned. I thought I could seek sanctification there, if it was anywhere to be found on the dim earth, that is. But, it didn't take long for me to realize that there was no salvation for me in that obscene city. So I boarded a Venetian ship headed for the Holy Land. We made fast passage to the Aegean but we were detoured by weather. So we sailed up the Hellespont. It was heavily populated along Marmara. I, um, dined, on the Constantinopolitan cuisine while there, but I recoiled from the bleak religion of the Turks. After a time we sailed up the Bosporus and wandered the even more densely populated coast of the Black Sea. Their version of Christianity was almost unrecognizable to me, by the way. So I made pilgrimage to the Holy Land and Egypt as I had previously intended. I attempted to find the grave of my brother in Nubia but it was hopeless. And the sun was intolerable anyway. I returned to Europe by way of Carthage, passed through France, and then on to Britannia. I wandered about that island and elsewhere, then eventually made the voyage to the New World. I didn't stay long, however. The population was too sparse, so victims did not remain unnoticed for long. With mixed emotion I crossed the Atlantic back to England. From there I traversed Ireland, Scotland, Holland, and Scandinavia. Not long after, I sailed back to the Americas and have been here for quite some time."

"Wow. That's a foreboding itinerary—and it has been you against the world all that time?"

"Well, I'm not so sure that describes it."

"Fair enough. How long have you been reading the Bible, by the way?" Ryan brought the conversation back to the topic that had been plaguing him so much lately.

"All my life."

"Are you really a Christian? You said you were Catholic and then a Puritan. But are you truly a Christian?"

"I hope so. But it's just like I said before. Do the promises of salvation extend to someone who is undead? I'm trapped. I cannot survive except by continuing to sin. I have to feed to live in this constant death. Is there hope for a sin unto death? How do I stop sinning? If I do, it is suicide. Or, then again, is it?"

"Do you attend church?"

"Not in years."

"What denomination?"

"Originally Roman Catholic, as you could have guessed. But then I drifted toward Protestantism centuries ago and floated between Puritan congregations."

"Sure. That was a dumb question. So what changed?"

"I used to get so enraged and ravenous when I would attend mass because the priests would withhold the cup. I wanted the blood so badly. Jesus commanded us to eat his flesh and drink his blood. He said if we don't we will not inherit eternal life. And he said that anyone who comes to him would receive living water and never thirst again. I wanted the true blood of Christ so I would never thirst for blood again. I wanted so badly to be free of this thirst. I wanted to be a new creature. Well it happened one day that at a special annual mass in a particular town the priest offered the cup to the congregants. Can you imagine my disgust and disappointment when I tasted it for the first time and immediately understood that transubstantiation is a fallacy? I was appalled and felt hopeless. I of all people can tell you the elements of the Lord's supper are symbolic. And that's when I began my conversion to Protestantism."

"But what about the bread? Didn't you already know from the bread that it isn't literally his body?"

"I'm a vampire. The bread tasted like bread, just like it always had before, and just like any bread does now. But blood is like a sixth sense for me. It is more than taste, smell, and feeling. I know it on a primal yet conscious and intimate level. It's something you can't understand because you've never experienced it from an undead perspective." She paused, staring off through time, then mused, "There was a time when I only killed and fed on priests and nuns."

"Oh?"

"Yeah, I'm rambling now and I don't know why I'm telling you all of this," Idelette confessed, completely out of character and surprised she was confiding in this diener instead of feeding on him.

"That's OK. Continue, please."

"I figured since priests were under vows to the Church of Rome then they must be true Catholics, and therefore true Christians."

"I still don't follow."

"Well if I only killed true Christians then I could at least know that the people I killed ended up in Heaven instead of Hell."

"I see. That actually makes some sense."

"The problem is, over time, the more I studied the doctrines of grace and the more I watched matters unfold in the Catholic church, the less confident I was that it's a true and saving Christian faith. I also grew less certain that you can ever know from outward appearances who is or is not among God's elect."

"So now you don't even bother trying to sort it out?"

"Not really. The thirst overtakes me and I have to feed. Addiction is destructive and not just to the addict."

"That also makes sense. Unfortunately, I have to get back down to surgical pathology. Thanks for telling me all of that. I suspect few people have gotten to hear your story." He stopped and thought before he left. "One last question. What is it like?"

"What? Being le revenant?"

"L'revnahn? What is that?"

"Oh, sorry. Forgive my dialectical French. Revenant. A vampire."

"Yeah. That. What is it like to be, um, le revenohn?—the undead?"

Idelette's expression became very serious and sober as she stared at the floor and thought. She hesitated for a long time trying to answer but struggled to find the words. More than that she was still wrestling with the idea of confiding in someone. After all, she barely knew him. What possible relationship could she have with this diener? And how could he understand her anyway? This wasn't her first experience like this, and it ended poorly before. She ran her fingers along the fore edge of the Bible in her pocket. Finally, the vampire gave a long sigh and then just said what seemed to be the most true.

"It's mostly endless self-loathing. I'm so tired of being ashamed all the time."

The diener silently nodded for a moment and then ventured to reply.

"I can understand that, actually. And I bet a lot of other people can too."

Idelette gave an incredulous look.

"No, really. You are describing habitual sin. The magnitude of your situation might be more extreme, but lots of people are ashamed of who they are and what they do. Habitual sin is like that. Unfortunately, we will need to continue this conversation at a later date, because I have work to do downstairs. But, let me just say, I heard you praying recently. I think you are a true believer. I wish I knew how to pray like that."

The diener vacated the autopsy room, and left the undead woman staring down at the floor. With his final glance, he observed her eyes, which seemed to be looking back through time to painful memories he could only guess at.

Chapter 45

On a Saturday afternoon in 1609, decades after the events in her village, Idelette passed through southern England. She had spent years in aimless wandering, both on the continent and in the United Kingdom. Today she stopped into a Catholic church where the priest was waiting to hear confessions from his parishioners. Other than the priest, however, the place was empty. The wood floor creaked loudly in the vacant sanctuary as she entered. The stone pillars and stained glass seemed to amplify the noise. She took a seat in a pew at the back and wrestled internally with her motives for being there that day. She gripped the Bible in her pocket, prayed a quick psalm, then rose and entered the little booth in the back corner.

"Bless me father for I have sinned," the vampire sighed as she sat down.

"What sins have you committed young lady?'

"I have not kept the commandments," she responded in rote.

"Take heart. Forgiveness is nigh. Which commandment have you broken?"

Idelette gripped her Bible a little tighter as she whispered, "Thou shalt not murder."

The priest was not expecting that answer. He paused for a moment. The wooden bench creaked as he shifted a bit in his seat. Finally, he cleared his throat, and continued.

"You have committed this sin in your heart by despising your neighbor?"

"No," she was quick to reply.

"You have taken another's life—perhaps an undesired pregnancy?" the vicar was quicker to respond this time.

"No. I've never been pregnant. Nor have I procured an abortion for another. I have killed, father. Their bloods cry out to God from the fields." Idelette wiped a tear from her cheek.

"You make yourself a daughter of Cain. Then you certainly know your guilt. You must not hide the matter from earthly judges, as it is already known to your heavenly judge. Absolution can be had and the church can restore you to a right relationship with God but you must turn yourself in for your crime."

"I cannot," she snapped.

"You must. Tell me what happened, young lady."

"I was just so thirsty, father."

"And someone withheld water when you were in need, so you turned upon them?"

"No. They made no offense. My thirst was different. And I am so thirsty now. Can you absolve me before I sin again?" she sobbed.

"I must know the sins for which you seek absolution."

"Please father, before I sin again!" she shouted.

"I cannot without knowing more," he insisted.

"So be it," she sighed again as another tear rolled down her cheek. Idelette rose, stepped out of the confession box, walked around the other side, and tore the door off. She threw it across the sanctuary and it broke against the opposite wall.

The priest shrieked but there was no time for anything more. She was upon him in an instant. Idelette drank the warm viscous blood as he struggled less and less. The hemorrhaging slowed and her victim breathed his last after only a minute or two. She wiped the blood off her face on his robe, walked to the altar at the front of the sanctuary, genuflected as she passed a statue of a saint, then kneeled before the table. She prayed her Our Father, then rose and walked out the front door. She had not been seen, but it was time to move on to another town. Her right hand returned to the Bible in her pocket as her left hand wiped a final tear from her cheek.

Chapter 46

Detectives Malli and Jameson sat at their desks and continued to labor over the cases they were so hopelessly involved in.

"OK. From the beginning," Detective Jameson put his elbows on his desk and dropped his head into his hands.

"Again?'

"Again," he murmured without raising his head.

"Two boys in Greenwood on Halloween. Blood everywhere. Lots of nonspecific lacerations of their necks and other parts of their bodies. The bodies concealed in a dumpster. Witchcraft symbols in the cemetery across the street."

"Right. And then a lull until the following summer."

"Yup. Girl in the mall. Exsanguinated probably through neck injury. Body was also in a dumpster."

"But the body was damaged while being transported to the dump, so that the ME couldn't say for sure which were antemortem wounds and which were postmortem artifact," Jameson interrupted. "Then what?"

"Guy goes missing in Greenwood while ghost hunting at night. We later find his decomposing corpse at the same time we find skeletal remains of a child in Greenwood."

"Right near each other and there are witchcraft symbols everywhere. But the child's bones are likely a century old, as confirmed by forensic anthropology." Here he slightly waved the anthropologist's report in the air, still not lifting his head from his other hand.

"Young lady found decomposing near the river behind Ragner Park."

"I wouldn't include her because the perp confessed," Jameson interjected, finally looking up at Detective Malli.

"But she was in a cemetery when last known alive," she looked at him with a puzzled expression.

"Coincidence, I think."

"You agreed they were related before," Malli challenged.

"I know but I'm rethinking that. It makes our lives easier if that case is closed."

"Fine. For now. What else?" Malli conceded, since she didn't want to be doing this mental exercise again anyway.

"Several killings downtown on the same night. Symbols near one of the bodies. One pair of victims had been in a club with known vampire themes. Bodies in dumpsters, again. We have a serial dumpster killer."

"Lastly, girl thought to have been killed in house filled with occult stuff on Fuller Street, but later found in a vandalized mausoleum in Oak Hill cemetery. But that's just the murders. The context is that of the other crimes. Satanic or witch-related gang activity escalating with no apparent turf. Missing brunette with investigative link to Greenwood cemetery. Possible grave robbing going on too, which might be the source for the child's bones. Also several other missing persons—mostly males—with tentative links to being in local cemeteries."

"And none of the more senior members in our unit or any of the other nearby police departments can ever recall anything like this in Grand Blanc before."

"So what does this all point to? Other than the confession case, they all have to be related. If not the same perp, then associates or at least copy cats."

"The only other explanation is supernatural," Detective Jameson dropped his head onto his keyboard.

"What? Like people are actually getting killed by witches, or vampires, or mummies, or something?"

"Well, I suppose not really supernatural. But a mimic of it. Maybe somebody really is drinking blood like a horror movie vampire. Hence the neck injuries. And it sure seems like we've got actual witchcraft going on. We found some of the symbols in books. Maybe these are part of their rites or something."

"But do we have any evidence—circumstantial or otherwise—to link an individual to the murders?"

"None."

"Maybe the blurry woman on the mall security cameras."

"But that's not usable because even if we had a suspect we couldn't prove it is her on the video, nor could we link her to the death directly."

"This is getting old. Why can't we get a normal case like a domestic violence call or something? This is making early retirement look really nice."

"Maybe we need to hire that medium that says we were wrong on the Ragner Park case. Remember that woman putting a bunch of stuff on the internet?"

"Yeah, maybe she can solve it for us."

"Honestly, I'm ready for this to actually all be the work of some night-crawling, blood-drinking, undead vampire. Then I wouldn't feel so much like a failure for not being able to solve it," Detective Jameson confessed.

"Heh. What would you do if that happened?"

"I don't know. Show up to confession maybe."

"I'd sign a lucrative book and movie deal, staring as myself, with a bumbling partner, solving these notorious cases."

Chapter 47

Still hearing the screams of her friends from inside the village, Idelette tried to scramble to her feet. It was a hard landing from the top of the wall and she was sore. But before she could rise, she felt a strong, cold hand seize her by the shoulder and lift her from the ground. Through trees and brush it dragged her backward at an incomprehensible pace. It pulled her right into the dark interior of a hut deep within the forest. As the door slammed shut, the poor woman knew her life was at its end and swooned at that terrible thought.

She woke on the floor of the hut, apparently unharmed, however, and wondered how much time had passed. The light was soft. A single candle was near her. As she raised herself up, praying a psalm under her breath, she suddenly remembered Dom Calmet and how he had fallen. He was old and such a tumble might be more than he could withstand. She reasoned that he was likely now confined to his bed with what may very well be mortal injuries. She began to cry. But only a moment elapsed when she suddenly realized she was not alone. Her captor was seated nearby and very obviously watching her.

"Be not afraid," the creature stated. "Rise. Take food and water."

Idelette trembled and rose slowly to a nearby chair. But, somehow, she was comforted by the voice she heard. It was not sinister. It was not unholy. It was entirely...unremarkable. She turned and looked at the devil. He was just a man.

"Please don't hurt me," she whispered.

"Shall I plead the same from you? Did you not previously come to kill me—each and all of you? An entire village, even."

"Yes."

"And now that you have found your prey, you are suddenly not so brave."

"No." She lowered her gaze.

"But you are still resolved to kill me."

"Have you not killed many of my neighbors? Have you not plagued our village and haunted the forests and fields nearby? Are you not a demon?"

"I am no demon."

"What then? I know you are evil. You are in league with Satan and you kill innocent people to drink their blood!"

"You know nothing."

"You are the evil that has assailed us—that is enough. And yet, you look to be a man. I sense treachery." She stared it in the eyes.

"Treachery indeed! And an insidious evil! But not I. It is true that I have killed many, but not in your village."

"Liar."

"I never lie."

"Another lie. You are the son of your father the Devil."

"As surely as the Lord lives, I am not."

Idelette was momentarily startled to hear words borrowed from Holy Scripture. Then she remembered that even Satan can quote scripture to suit his purpose.

"Have you no reply? Or are you merely still wrestling with my reference to the written word of God?"

Idelette thought a moment longer. "In the beginning—"

"—God created the heavens and the earth. Genesis 1:1."

She paused again. "In the beginning—"

"—was the Word, and the Word was with God, and the Word was God. John 1:1."

"Where have you come from?"

"From roaming the earth and going back and forth in it. Job 1:7 and 2:2."

"What is this? What do you want from me?" A bewildered expression overcame her previous expressions of fear and repugnance.

"I want to speak with you, and you must hear me. We haven't much time. Your friends will find us before long. I must get you back to your village before that happens."

"Back to my village? You would use me as your agent? I think not!"

"Stay a bit, stay a bit. Listen and think clearly on what we shall now discuss," he soothed.

She looked back at him slightly askew. "I am listening."

"There is a great evil walking amongst us that you know nothing about. And it is not me. You have seen it and you know it. There is much danger and you are near to it. Apart from the killings, have you seen anything strange recently?"

"No."

"Think, young lady."

"Wait. There was the owl."

"Ah ha. Did it glow?"

"Yes! How did you do—"

"Not I. The dhampir."

"Dhampir...?"

"Yes. The son of a vampire. My son. He was conceived after I was bitten. I lay with my wife before I knew what I was becoming. She died during parturition. And by his nature he is incapable of any filial regard for me."

"And the owl? It is the familiar of the dhampir?"

"No. It was an illusion. Sorcery. He can conjure many things. He conjures up a will-o'-the-wisp in the form of a glowing owl. It is a favorite of the dhampir—used as a distraction, or to cause fear. It shifts the focus off from himself while still inspiring terror."

"What does it want?"

"Please, my son is a he, not an 'it.' He wants to torture me and he wants to create mischief. Not to stir up whimsy but to bring sorrow—do you hear that? The villagers are near. They come for me now at the break of dawn. The mob is all around us, fast approaching. We haven't much time."

"And where is it—he—where is he now? The dhampir. You said we are near to it?"

"You most of all. He is in your village. You must get close to him. The priest—"

"No!" she interrupted.

All at once the door broke down and smoke and flame rushed in. Torches landed on the floor around them and they heard some landing on the roof above as well. A great mass of people quickly rushed in. The vampire grabbed Idelette, turned his back on the villagers, and bit her wrist before flinging her aside. Just then a pitchfork stabbed through his back. Then another. A torch ignited his clothes. He whipped around to face his attackers, as the final blow, a scythe in Conrad's hand, separated the vampire's head from his body. It rolled partially across the room. While this gory spectacle unfolded Idelette attempted to get back up but was arrested by the sight of her own wrist. Examining the bite mark, she watched with amazement as the wound closed itself in only a moment—healed without a scar! Suddenly she was dragged by her feet from the burning hut and forced upright against a nearby tree trunk. Weapons and torches were pointed at her from all around.

"Has she been bitten?" one man cried.

"Why was she with the creature?" asked another.

"She is its consort."

"No, she was to be his next victim!"

"Examine her!"

The crowd was in chaos. There was little hope until Conrad again stepped forward and shouted over the horde.

"Silence!" Then turning to Idelette, "have you been bitten woman?"

"No! I am no vampire!"

"He looked to have bitten you as I entered the room."

"No, the first blow struck him before he could." Here she exposed her arms, neck, and even her thighs to the crowd.

"But what happened while she was with it for so long?" a voice from the mob sang out.

Idelette quickly replied, "Nothing. I was unconscious the entire time. I woke to the tumult of your assault on the hut. I think seeing me wake, he grabbed me believing he could make a meal of me before you entered. Why he didn't kill me as I lay swooned I do not know—perhaps he wanted me to be awake for my horrible death?"

"I am satisfied with her answers," Conrad declared, letting the poor woman free. All redirected their attention to the burning hut. Though many eventually returned to the village, including Idelette, many others, including Conrad, kept watch all morning until the flames were finally gone. They sifted through the rubble and found the charred skeletal remains of the vampire. As they lifted them out, each bone crumbled to mere ash.

Chapter 48

It was a slow day in surgical pathology and Phil was scrolling through the news when Ryan walked in.

"Did you see they found another body in Oak Hill?" Phil asked.

"Oh really."

"Is that the big cemetery on the southeast side?"

"Sure is," the diener affirmed.

"This article says the caretaker noticed one of the mausoleums was tampered with. I guess he went to examine it and found a dead woman inside."

"Why does finding a dead person in a cemetery at all, much less a mausoleum, make the news?" Ryan was only partially listening. He was busy wrestling with the idea of whether or not he should call Zoe to try to confront her directly, or let this play out. Idelette was in this for blood, after all.

"Hm. That's a valid point actually. I infer this one was fresh and wasn't supposed to be there. They also found more cult symbols with the body. This time they were inside the grave."

"Do they have any idea how she died?"

"Doesn't say."

"Heh. No one at the press wanted to make nonsense assertions ahead of the Medical Examiner for once?"

"I guess not. It says she was actually found days ago but the police and prosecutor refused to release the story to the news."

"I suspect they were trying to reduce the infamy these satanists are acquiring."

"That would make sense. Are you still going to do your usual graveyard hacky sack or whatever else this Halloween?"

"Yeah. Why do you ask?"

"Um, because people are dying in cemeteries."

"Oh that. Well first off, you don't actually know that person died in the cemetery. She was just found there. Also, it hasn't really been that many victims so far, and they've been fairly spread out across time and cemeteries."

"So that makes it all safe? What if they pick Greenwood for Halloween?"

"They?"

"The witch cult people that are committing the murders."

"You really believe they're the ones doing the killings? Looks more like silly teenage girl drama to me. I mean, big deal. They graffiti stuff around town and apparently leave evidence of seances or something in graveyards."

"Plus, you know, kill people."

"Tell you what, if I see a bunch of broomsticks or cauldrons parked at Greenwood's entrance on Halloween night, I won't go in. How's that?"

"What exactly am I supposed to tell the police about you when someone finally makes a connection?"

"It's merely coincidental. I was spending my nights in cemeteries long before any of this started. You know that. If they want to connect me to anything more than just the locations, then they should be able to produce some actual evidence. What about all these body parts here in these jars, Phil?"Ryan pointed to the surgical specimens. "You seem to spend a lot of time hanging around this hospital, and I sometimes see you with scalpels and stuff. Plus there are all these people that leave here missing organs. Sounds suspicious and I think you're connected to all of it!"

"I am. I get paid to do this."

"Conspiracy! Organized crime! String him up!"

"You're connected to all these jars too, you know."

"I am. I get paid to do this."

"So you're a co-conspirator."

"Co-conspirator indeed!"

Chapter 49

Idelette hardly left her own home all the next day. She stared at her wrist often, and pondered what was to come of her? How did the bite heal as it did? Would she become a vampire? She didn't feel any craving for blood. And she wasn't dead, or, undead, as it were. Her conversation with the vampire whirled through her mind over and over again. She slept a lot, but when she was awake, she just relived the previous day's nightmare. She hardly ate or drank and her night was restless. She did not leave her house for any length of time until early the next morning, when she went to the forest to gather firewood. Her mind wandered constantly and she could hardly focus even on this menial task. When she returned, many stared at her strangely as she pressed silently through their midst toward the church.

"Where have you been all day, young lady?" Dom Calmet asked as she descended the steps to his office. He was still resting from the fall he sustained during her abduction. He was bruised and scraped, but not too seriously injured. His joints were sore but it would pass.

"In the forest gathering firewood. I wanted some time alone," Idelette replied.

"No one has seen you all day. I asked around."

She did not address this comment but sat down and got straight to the point which brought her there.

"Why don't you offer the cup to the parishioners, father?"

"Because it is the blood of Christ," the priest replied, somewhat startled at the change of subject.

"But aren't we commanded to eat the bread and drink the cup?"

"The priest drinks the cup on behalf of his church. Can you imagine if a drop of our Lord's blood were spilled due to a careless moment on the part of a parishioner? No, only the priest must handle the cup."

"But aren't we saved by the blood of Christ?"

"Yes, but—"

"So shouldn't we partake in the blood?"

"You partake of the body. And all bodies have blood. So you get the blood as well."

She had never heard this logic before. She thought for a moment, then shook her head. "But then why is there a cup at all if the bread embodies both the blood and the body? It doesn't make sense."

"What is prompting this line of questions, Idelette?"

"Is it sinful for me to desire the blood of Christ in addition to the body?"

"It is if the Roman church has settled the matter. The bread is the body. And, the body must contain blood. So you receive the blood when you receive the body. We do not offer the cup to parishioners as a matter of reverence to the blood of our Lord."

"But I want the blood of my Savior. I want to be cleansed from my sins and never thirst again. Just one taste of his blood and body and I can have eternal life."

"You have eternal life because you were baptized into the church catholic. Besides—."

"But we Christians could also have the true blood of Christ, father. Didn't he command his disciples to eat the bread and drink the cup? The cup must accomplish something independent of the bread," she interrupted again.

"You are sounding dangerously like a Lutheran. The Protestants are careless with the cup. You must submit to the Church's authority on this matter."

"I just want the blood becau—."

Conrad walked in on them. He looked worried and quickly sat down as though he were fatigued.

"Father, I have reason to believe the creature still lives."

"Nonsense. You told me you saw his ashen remains yourself. He was utterly destroyed," Dom Calmet rebuked.

"But was he, father?"

"Yes. Why should any of us doubt it?" he asked somewhat impatiently, still flustered from the previous exchange with Idelette.

"I met a man on the path this afternoon, in the forest. He said he was on a pilgrimage toward Rome and he claimed that he saw a sinister man deep in the forest."

"Such men abound on highways. Did he say more?"

"There was blood on the sinister man's clothes and about his face."

"But this stranger who reports these things to you was unharmed?"

"So it seems, but he was adorned with several crosses and saints."

"I see. I see." He reclined back in his chair, weighing the matter.

"The man I met is still on the path, father, now encamped with a fire and roasting a rabbit. It is not yet dark and there is still time. Perhaps you should go out to interview this man. I fear we are not out of danger, but I don't want to alarm our neighbors. I can tell you the paths to take, and you can go alone, returning with your report before the sun has set."

Dom Calmet reluctantly agreed to investigate the matter and followed the directions that Conrad gave him through the wood. He limped slightly as he left. Idelette attempted to speak with Conrad but their relationship was just not the same since she spoke with the vampire. Could it be that her beloved priest was involved as the vampire suggested? Could she confide in Conrad regarding the conversation she had with the creature? Did Conrad also suspect the priest and now Idelette too? She didn't know what to say or do. She felt so alone.

"How are you doing?" she asked for lack of anything better to say.

"I am well," he replied, somewhat indifferently. "You seem different since you were rescued from the vampire. You have remained aloof."

"I- I don't know. I suppose I am. Aloof that is. It was all so frightening, and my mind is so overwhelmed by all of it. I was taken by a vampire, Conrad. A vampire! And, thanks to your bravery, I survived. But it was all so terrifying. I hardly feel that I have returned to normal life."

"Continue to rest and focus on your daily work. It will pass. I must get back to work myself. I've lost too much of this day. Night will be here soon and work needs to be done."

Night was indeed upon them sooner than anticipated, and Idelette was in her home when she was startled by a commotion outside. She dressed and went out to see what was transpiring in the streets. A crowd was near the gate. As she approached, it became clear that Dom Calmet had not returned and people were arguing what to do. She asked if anyone knew where Conrad was but no one had an answer. The vampire had warned her against the priest but how could she believe a monster? Overcome by the thought that the man who had cared for her so closely all these years was not safely home yet, she opened the gate herself and rushed out to find him. She could not wait for Conrad.

The forest was darker than expected and the night was partially cloudy. Idelette tried her best to remember the directions Conrad had given to find the stranger on the road. She ran as quickly as her legs would carry her when she suddenly stumbled and fell to the ground. She brushed dirt and leaves off her clothes but stopped when she smelled fire. Rising in the benighted wood she realized there were coals from an extinguished road-side fire smoking beside her. Furthermore, she noted an uneaten rabbit near the fire. But did she smell blood in the grass? She shuddered with fear and turned this way and that, attempting to see or hear anything or anyone around her. Silence. But as she peered among the trees, she noticed something irregular among the ferns. She cautiously approached, confident what it was, but fearful who it might be. She was right, it was a corpse. It was apparently the stranger Conrad described. As she knelt over the body, she was suddenly grabbed from behind. She shrieked.

"What are you doing here?" Conrad insisted.

"Have you been looking for our priest too? I cannot find him."

"But you found this."

"Yes. I fear Dom Calmet is similarly dead! We must find him."

Her words had hardly passed her lips when the priest came walking up to Conrad and Idelette.

"Father, why are you still in these woods?" Idelette asked, without greeting him.

"I took a wrong turn on my way back to the village. I got completely turned around in the dark. As I worked my way back to familiar paths, I heard voices. Idelette, how is it that you are in the forest at night?"

"I was searching for you."

"With Conrad?"

"No. I don't know when he arrived."

"I found her here with the body," Conrad joined.

"It is the stranger you told me of. It was nearly dark when I finally found him. And he was already dead."

The three looked at each other with concern and suspicion for a moment. They were all putting the pieces together. Idelette had been in the forest all day when the man saw a sinister character. Conrad was the last to see the man alive, or so he claimed. Dom Calmet was alone in the dark forest claiming the man was already dead. Conrad found Idelette with the corpse. Conrad's whereabouts were unknown to the villagers when she left in search of Dom Calmet.

"Come. We must return," Conrad broke the silence. After another awkward moment they walked silently back to the village. By the time they were through the gate, Dom Calmet was struggling to walk. Several folks noticed his poor condition.

"My spirit is willing but my aging body is too weak for these things," he acknowledged their concern. "I am an old man and much has happened to stress my vitality these past few days. I must rest. Please bring me to the church so I may pray."

The two of them helped their priest back to the sanctuary. Once he was seated comfortably, they closed the doors and descended the steps to the path through the graveyard. Idelette and Conrad exchanged only a brief glance then he parted from her company toward his own home. She also proceeded to her house, but stopped at her door. She paused, thinking long and hard about all that had transpired. Not willing to rest, she turned and looked back to the church. Drawing a long breath and resolving to have her questions answered, she began the familiar trek back to her priest.

Chapter 50

Ryan wandered through neighborhoods toward Greenwood cemetery as trick-or-treating began to die down. People started to extinguish the jack o'lanterns on their porches, bring in candy bowls, and retire for the night. Once porch lights were off, and streets were dark, then it was safe to enter the cemeteries. Children were in their homes, and adults were still at bars. Teenagers were still partying and wouldn't start smashing pumpkins until well into the early hours of morning. Also, ghost hunters wouldn't arrive in the graveyards until much closer to midnight. Of course, with all that had happened around Grand Blanc recently, it would have to be a pretty courageous, or stupid, group of ghost hunters to brave the cemeteries this Halloween.

But Ryan had to examine the state of things in Greenwood. He felt there was a high probability that the witches would return to Greenwood on Halloween. Now that he knew who was involved, this was his opportunity to observe them, and try to figure out what they were really up to. With that knowledge, perhaps he could find a way to undermine Zoe, and return the grave robbing business back to normal, free of police inquiries and murdered friends.

Ryan walked slowly through the trees on the north side of the cemetery. He paused frequently to listen to his surroundings and make sure he was not followed. As he came to the open ground of the graveyard, he stopped inside the treeline, and watched. Several jack o'lanterns glowed in the distance, scattered amongst the headstones. But all else was inactive.

He stepped onto the path, but did not follow it. Instead, he crossed it to stay hidden among the graves. The leaves made it difficult to walk silently, and the barren trees offered little shadow from the moonlight above. But this was precisely what he was an expert at. He stealthily explored every section of Greenwood. Here and there, glowing orange faces leered at him, but whoever placed those pumpkins was long gone. Satisfied that he was alone, he allowed himself to step back out onto the path near the retaining wall on the south side of the cemetery.

Ryan was making his final pass through, walking down the main drive toward the circle, when he heard distant footsteps. They were fast, many, and all around him. These could not be police—they stay in their cars. They could not be ghost hunters—there were far too many and they were far too quiet. Nor were they vandals—again, too many and too quiet. As they passed between trees and stones he saw their shadowy shapes. These were certainly the witches. Ryan stopped right in the middle of the crossroads and waited.

The witches ran a counterclockwise circle that closed in around him. There were easily seventy-five of them, probably more. He recognized several of them as they stopped and crowded around him. As expected, Zoe emerged from the group and approached.

"'Then rushed in the shades of the night,' Ryan quietly observed to nobody in particular.

"Happy Halloween," Zoe said with annoyance.

"Happy Reformation Day. Fine widdershins, by the way. Aren't you all supposed to be having some weird orgy with Lucifer right now? And where are your broomsticks?"

Suddenly, something struck Ryan in the back of the head. He fell to the ground, unconscious and bleeding.

He woke in an unexpected, but familiar, place. It was the woods behind Ragner Park. He was sitting up against a tree and his hands were bound around it. His neck ached from his head hanging down unsupported. Worse though, was the sharp pain at the back of his head. There was blood still dripping down through his hair from the open wound on his scalp. Occasional drops made it into his mouth. He must not have been out for very long. As he painfully raised his head and looked around, he noted that all the same witches were there.

"I've lost feeling in my arms," Ryan observed.

"Shut your mouth! You're a murderer. You killed one of ours. You killed her," one of the girls shouted. It was the one he had confronted in Oak Hill several nights before.

"I most certainly did not."

"I said shut up!"

"I'm serious. I didn't kill anyone. Not this time."

"Liar," joined another—stepping forward was a Vietnamese girl with black hair and blue contact lenses. She had also been in Oak Hill that night.

"'This from a bride of Satan? What's your name, by the way?"

"It's Mary, but what does that matter to you? You're a dead man."

"You killed her. She was my friend and you killed her," the first girl rejoined.

"Not I."

"You're a liar, but you know what? It doesn't matter. Every death connected with us around this city will soon be put on you!"

"He said he didn't do it," Sarah stepped forward.

Ryan was speechless when he heard her voice and saw her among the coven. The look of confusion on his face must have even surpassed the feeling of betrayal he was contending with. It may have been a deeper wound than the one in his scalp.

Sarah began to speak, "I—"

"Shut up!" Zoe interrupted and pushed her away.

"I've lost feeling in my arms," Ryan observed again, this time to Zoe, still not sure what to say to Sarah.

"You won't ever need arms again. And she was right by the way. We've got it all arranged. Your little body snatching business is about to be exposed to the world. And what's more, you committed all of our crimes. You killed those people. You put the graffiti everywhere. You are the head of some bizarre crime syndicate. And tomorrow this city will know all about it."

"How do you figure?"

"You are going to confess."

"How do you figure?" Ryan spit out some blood that had run down into his mouth from his scalp.

"Oh, I can get you to confess. I have been developing my powers for quite some time. I'm on the cusp of something you can't even imagine. I am a necromancer and soon will have minions among the dead. Thank you, by the way for trafficking so many of those bodies for me. Soon this coven will raise an army of the dead. We have all that we need and I have the secret knowledge to make it happen. But for tonight you will be my puppet, and you will confess to everything right here, before killing yourself—and all on camera no less. Then you will be dead, and I will be unimpeded. I'm even taking your job in the morgue, by the way. Just as an added bonus. One from your grave robbing team is dead, the other is converted to one of us. She is ours now." (An insulted expression manifested itself on Sarah's face at Zoe's use of the word 'ours'). "So all you once had becomes mine. And you will lie dead. Anyway, we'll start shortly. I hope you're excited."

"I know I am," said the familiar voice of a woman from among the girls.

Everyone near her backed away sharply and stared at the stranger who had materialized in their midst.

"Happy Reformation Day, Ryan. Your hair smells intoxicating," Idelette added.

"You should taste it," he gave her a knowing look.

"No, I shouldn't." Then she turned to Sarah and said, "you need to leave. Now."

"In point of fact, I was just about to, even before you showed up." She scowled at Zoe as she walked away from the crowd, out of the woods, and out of Ragner Park.

Sarah had barely passed beyond the edges of the crowd however, when she heard the tumult begin. She didn't even look back.

Idelette grabbed one of the witches by the neck. Before the girl could react, the vampire effortlessly threw her against one of the other girls. The force of impact was so strong the two witches fell dead in a heap. Girls jumped back in fright, but they had hardly begun to process the situation when the vampire turned and ripped the head off of the next nearest witch. Her body fell at the revenant's feet and spurts of blood dumped into the dead leaves. That girl's body had hardly struck the ground when Idelette turned and threw the head at Zoe, knocking her off her feet and down the hill.

Pandemonium ensued. Witches scattered everywhere, though they parted around Idelette as she traversed the mob.

In an instant she had stopped behind the tree Ryan sat against. With a quick pull she broke the ropes which fettered him to the trunk. The diener's arms fell limp at his sides. He tried to move them but they were numb. He sat helplessly and watched the carnage which surrounded him.

Witches were tripping over each other and getting snagged in branches and thorns as they tried to flee. The vampire waded through them with ease. She slaughtered many, working her way around the perimeter of the group, forcing them back in on themselves. Few managed to escape her. Blood sprayed this way and that. She dented and debarked tree trunks with their heads. She tore off limbs and opened throats. She tread upon some and impaled others on branches. The screams for help from any one of them were answered only by the agonal cries of others.

Ryan eventually rose to his feet as the spectacle ebbed to a halt. He looked upon the dozens which lay dead all around him. Walking to the edge of the hill, he nearly tripped over the heaps of corpses. He looked down the slope for Zoe. But he knew that she and her closest minions were long gone. "'A thousand shall flee at the threat of one,'" he muttered.

Idelette's voice came from behind him again. "So they flee. It hardly matters. Compulsion will drive them back to Greenwood."

"I know that feeling," Ryan sighed, now looking the other direction, thinking about Sarah. Having regained use of his arms he felt the back of his head. Still-oozing blood warmed his fingers. "My head hurts," he winced. But when he turned to face Idelette, there was no one there.

Chapter 51

There was still tremendous and ongoing celebration throughout the unsuspecting village over the execution of the vampire. People congratulated one another and songs were already being composed. Some burned effigies. But everyone noticed that Idelette would not partake in the festivities. Several people—including Kurt, who had been watching her interactions with Conrad—stared at her suspiciously tonight, looking to see if she would join the crowds this time. But she did not. Instead, after she and Conrad parted ways and returned to their homes, she immediately hurried back to find Dom Calmet in the church. She paid no attention to the graves around her as she tread the path to the church doors. The hinges creaked loudly and announced her entrance as she stepped into the sanctuary.

Dom Calmet rose from a pew when she approached. He looked nervous. But neither were admitting their apprehensions about one another. Though she had come with questions, he began interrogating her first.

"Is it really you who returns to us after your time with the undead?" he asked.

"Yes."

"How have you lived?" he seemed determined to investigate the matter.

"You know I was saved by the villagers."

He paused and chose his words. "But surely the creature—"

"I am unharmed."

"And so you have returned to us unaffected. God be praised."

"God be praised. Amen."

"What troubles you young lady?" Relenting the previous topic.

"How have you come to know so much about vampires?" Idelette commenced her own investigation.

"Study and travels, of course."

"But I still do not understand. What books contain such knowledge? Where have you travelled to learn about vampires?"

"Many pious and learned men have written on the topic. I had access to innumerable such books during my years of catechesis. I travelled to no exotic places. I have merely encountered diverse and sundry stories between here and France."

"Have you no personal experience with vampires, then? No secret knowledge?"

"Child, what is prompting these questions?"

"She suspects you," Conrad interrupted. They both turned in surprise. "When she was with the creature he must have told her more than she has admitted to us. He has put some idea in her head—rousing suspicions within us."

"But we don't even know if the creature is dead now," she interrupted. "The man in the forest, surely—"

"But," Conrad interrupted, "you think there is other evil among us. Some more sinister and hidden evil. Someone among us." He paused and drew a long slow breath. "And you are right."

Here he stared at the priest. But with that last remark he grabbed Idelette by the shoulder, and with superhuman strength, threw her behind him across the church. She crashed against some pews. Dizzied and confounded, she struggled to recover.

"Conrad?" the priest began.

But before Dom Calmet could say more, Conrad thrust his fist into the priest's abdomen. Staring him in the eye he whispered, "Yes. Me." Then he let him fall and walked toward his next victim. He reached down unsympathetically to lift her up. She dodged his hand and sprinted to the front of the church. He let her go and watched for a moment. There was plenty of time.

Idelette knelt over the body of her beloved priest. Tears poured down her cheeks but she had no words nor even breath to sob. Conrad approached her from behind.

"Stupid old man," he muttered.

Idelette burst into loud sobs at the insult.

"Very well, then. Cry for your priest. I'm not unfeeling. I absolutely care that you have your opportunity to utterly despair before I kill you too. In fact, it is so important to me, that I'll just go lock the door, so we can share this sad and final moment together uninterrupted."

As he walked to the other end of the church, Idelette noticed a slowly growing pool of blood begin to seep out from under the priest's body. The deep red was enchanting. The smell was overcoming. She felt the most insatiable desire begin to grip her. It was strange and horrible and exciting. She lowered her head and licked the blood from the floor. It was incredible. Intoxicating. Inadequate. She was voracious now. She drank all she could as fast as she was able. The unquenchable thirst and the invigorating energy that was exploding inside her defied words. And it was all happening so fast. She shuddered with disgust as she paused to take a breath. Tears ran down her cheeks as she looked at her dear priest. Then she enthusiastically drank more. Her tears still flowed, but she could not restrain herself. Her hair dragged in the pool of blood and tears. But she drank.

"When this is all done," Conrad explained as he walked back from the church door, approaching her from behind, "I'll simply tell everyone that you actually were bitten that night in my father's house—oh, did I mention that part?—and that you killed the cleric. Half the village already suspected it anyway when we found you. I'll tell them I had to kill you. You turned into a monster—a blood thirsty vampire."

And with that remark he bent down and grabbed Idelette's arm but found she did not easily budge. She quickly reached across with her other hand, clutched his wrist, and broke it. He recoiled in pain and sudden confusion. Invigorated by her sanguinary meal, she rose and faced him. His confusion rapidly turned to rage and he charged at her in fury. She struck him with a blow she did not know she could produce. He tumbled over some pews. She pursued before his body had even come to rest. Suddenly though he was up and had her by the hair. He struck her head with his knee and she fell to his feet. Recalling her previous success with his wrist, she grabbed his ankle and fractured that too. Down he fell and she was up.

The commotion had been heard by several people outside. They were pounding at the door. Idelette grabbed Conrad by his already fractured ankle and threw him against the church door. That stopped the pounding. He rose and grabbed a candelabra. She broke a massive fragment from a pew. He rushed at her with the candelabra. She threw her piece of sacred timber and it struck him in the jaw. As he momentarily fumbled, she was instantly upon him. She grabbed his hair and yanked his head back, pulling until the skin on the front of his neck began to tear. He glared at her with palpable hatred for just an instant, but she thrust her free hand into his abdomen, as he had done to Dom Calmet. The blood flowed swiftly from his neck and stomach. Idelette drank, as his muscle tone declined and he became limp. The torrent of blood eventually slowed, and at last she let him fall to the floor.

Rising with a disgusted shudder she walked back to Dom Calmet and knelt by his side once more. She picked up the Bible that was still in his dead hand and pondered it for a moment. Tears began to form in her eyes. Unexpectedly though, her beloved priest whom she thought was dead, whispered to her in an agonal voice.

"Dear girl, what have you become?"

"I don't know. I did not seek this. It was inflicted upon me."

"I am dying. But am I now to do so knowing that you are a minion of Satan?"

"Am I to abandon every hope, father? What penance can I possibly do? Or was every sin atoned for on Calvary? Even iniquity such as this?"

"Dear child," he began, but then he seemed to stare through her, his pupils dilated slightly, and he was gone.

Idelette cried fiercely for several seconds. But between her wailings she could hear the voices outside. She wiped the red-tinged tears from her eyes, arose, then walked to the church doors and unlocked them. But she paused and looked at Conrad with such conflicted emotions she could not decide what to feel or think. Rage contended with sorrow, but betrayal was perhaps the strongest of all. She shuddered again and gripped the Bible tighter. With a sigh, she opened the doors and walked slowly out into the churchyard. Some people came running to join those already in the graveyard. Many recoiled in fear when they got close. Some gasped. Some crossed themselves. Regardless, every one of them stared.

"Idelette," Kurt began, but her glance stopped his tongue.

Some gripped torches and weapons, apparently contemplating an attack, but none dared. The people directly in front of her slowly backed away, out of her path, as she passed them by. She did not stop to acknowledge or even try to explain. They beheld her as an abhorrent spectacle. And she felt like a shadow—alien and intangible. As she passed beyond the graves and out of the churchyard, some people rushed inside behind her to behold the welter in their church. Commotion ensued from within and Idelette continued down the path. The words of the psalmist crept into her mind: "I have become a reproach, especially to my neighbors, and an object of dread to my acquaintances; those who see me, flee from me. I hear the whispering—terror on every side!" She quickened her pace as she passed through the gate of her village and across the fields. She did not look back but broke into a full run. The dense forest lay ahead of her, towering to a cloudy sky bleakly above.

Chapter 52

The four remaining witches ran for their lives out of those murderous woods and out of Ragner Park. Through shadows and street lights they fled. The October wind seemed to carry them and the falling leaves twirled about them. They looked back occasionally as they ran, hoping they were gaining ground. The sidewalk was uneven and their stride was not graceful. Zoe turned a hard left across Ragner Boulevard before reaching Byron and broke through underbrush into the trees. The other girls followed immediately. The high grass and underbrush slowed their pace considerably, and the darkness left them even more uncertain. Branches whipped across their hands and faces as they stumbled and ran. The moon was faint through thin clouds, but their eyes soon adjusted and they moved more steadily, though no less fearfully. They were almost through the trees and into the back of Greenwood.

At that same moment, unbeknownst to the witches, Idelette crossed Leonard Street and walked into Greenwood from the south.

Back in Ragner Park, Ryan finished prying the ropes off his wrists, gathered his things, then pursued the witches west down the boulevard. It was no mystery where they had gone. He jogged steadily but conserved his energy. There was time enough.

When their boots struck the mools from out of the northern trees, and the array of headstones lay before them, the witches scattered. Lady continued straight south, Becca cut hard left down the path toward the empty northeast corner, Liz followed Zoe as she broke off right, running hard toward the circle, but then deviated south into the headstones before getting there.

Lady tumbled down a slope, sliding along leaves and flat grave stones. Her knees, wrists, and elbows bled but she did her best not to cry out from the sudden pain. She was just down the east hill from the crossroads. She cast about for a moment as she sat up, trying to decide what to do next, when she looked up and saw her. Standing atop the hill was Idelette, looking right at her. How did she get there? Lady was on the road in a single bound and running south again. She crested the slope toward potter's field when suddenly she felt a grip upon her shoulder and her feet felt no ground below them. She crashed down among leaves and branches fifty feet into potter's field. She rolled over onto her back grimacing with pain. Coming to her senses she opened her eyes and looked all around. She was alone. On open ground. Stay? Run?

She ran. Lady was almost out of Greenwood and into the neighboring school ground when she was suddenly flung right back into the middle of potter's field. She screamed in fear and pain. But this time when she opened her eyes, she was certainly not alone. Idelette grabbed her by the ankle and dragged her up the slope toward the Jewish section. Lady screamed and frantically grasped at tombstones as Idelette walked to the top of the hill. In her groping she happened upon a fist-sized stone.

She seized it and threw it as hard as she could at Idelette. It struck her in the back of the neck. Stopping immediately, the vampire looked the witch in the eye. Lady realized her mistake and screamed all the more, but it was futile. The revenant raised her upside down by the ankle, reached down to grab her hair, then let her foot fall. Lifting her up by the hair, Idelette grabbed the girls jaw and tore it free from her face. The screams were immediately quenched with blood gushing down the front of her. Idelette wanted desperately to drink, but she let it pour out on the ground, then dropped the witch's corpse into the coagulating puddle at her feet.

Zoe had pulled Liz down to the ground behind a large tombstone as they listened to the screams echoing from the other side of the cemetery.

"Get out there and look around," Zoe demanded.

"Are you crazy? Why me?"

"Because you're the one who's scared and because I said so."

"No way."

"DO IT!" Zoe screamed and gave Liz a push.

Liz crept toward the crossroads.

Becca had heard it all too. All she wanted was to run out of the graveyard and right into one of the neighboring houses. She weighed her options. But as she looked she saw Ryan walking into the cemetery from between those houses. Seeing she was trapped in Greenwood, she rose and ran toward the circle. But what was that sneaking among the headstones in the distance? She froze. Then the thing stood. It was only Liz. The two met on the path then quickly ducked into some trees.

"Did you hear that?" Liz whispered first.

"Yeah. I thought it might have been you."

"I was with Zoe. We thought it was you or Lady. It must have been Lady."

"Maybe she killed the other woman," Becca sheepishly suggested.

"Don't be stupid. Where do you think she is?"

"I don't know. I think maybe near the office building. What do we do now?"

"Maybe the woman left. Maybe she caught Lady and figured the rest of us were long gone by now. Maybe we're alone."

"Maybe."

"We're right by the road. If she were nearby, she'd have us by now. Come with me. Zoe is over there. Let's go tell her it is safe for now. We should go while we can."

"There's something else." Becca stopped Liz. "I saw Ryan in here too. Right after the screaming stopped. He walked in from over there."

"Do not tell Zoe! She won't leave if she knows he's here."

Meanwhile, Ryan had walked the eastern edge of Greenwood and was rounding the path up to the office building. When he got there, he saw Idelette walking toward the wall. She glanced back at him. He followed.

"I was hoping to have this taken care of before you got here," Idelette said as she sat down on the wall and looked down at Leonard Street.

"Not a chance. I heard the screams. I think some of the neighbors did too. It won't be long before police come. Who was it?"

"The punk rock one."

"Where is she?"

"Top of the hill between potter's field and the Jewish section. The others are still here. And if Zoe knows you're here, they're not leaving."

"What's the plan?"

"Zoe will try to organize the other girls. They will try casting spells against us. Only Zoe truly believes. The others just want to run away I think."

"So…what's the plan?"

"Kill them all before the cops get here." Just as she said that, a police car drove by. Ryan rose and walked straight north into the depths of the graveyard. Idelette stayed and watched the cop car. It almost vanished over the hill when it suddenly braked and turned around. No doubt it was coming to investigate reports of a disturbance in the cemetery. 'Just kids' the officer must be thinking. The vampire rose. Time was short. As she walked toward the circle, she heard the police cruiser pull slowly into the cemetery.

Ryan heard it too. He stayed off the road. He could dodge police just fine. He had done it a million times before. Though, there might be a lot of them tonight. But so be it. He had dodged a lot of police before too.

"We're not leaving!" Zoe insisted as Becca and Liz tried to persuade her to go. "Here comes a cop car. We need to act smart and act fast. Stay in the trees and the graves. Work around it."

"Let's go to the circle then," Liz suggested.

"No good. The cops won't find us there, but we can't get out when Ryan shows up. He intends to put us in the ground. But I've got spells in mind."

"What about the other woman?" Becca interrupted.

"I think she's gone. We would know by now if she were here," Zoe replied. "Look, the cop is spotlighting the west side now. Let's go into the trees north east of the crossroads. But go separately."

As they began to creep between tombstones, Ryan stalked behind them. Liz was in back. He closed in on her, took three or four quick steps, and grabbed her from behind with one arm around her arms and torso, the other covering her mouth and nose. He pulled her to the ground, flipped her over, and stared straight into her eyes as he knelt over her. Her lip trembled slightly as he reached into his coat with his right hand.

Suddenly she was yanked right out from under him, being dragged toward the circle. Liz let out a shriek that was quickly silenced. Ryan stood and watched as Idelette ran, amazingly fast, dragging Liz in tow. She stopped just before she stepped onto the road, lifted Liz up to look at her, then repeatedly dashed the side of her head against the corner of a tombstone until her head was misshapen. She thirsted for the last few pulses of her carotids but refrained and threw the corpse up the hill, through the trees, and into the circle—easily forty yards, through branches.

She turned and said to Ryan as he approached, "'For we know that no murderer has eternal life abiding in him.' Keep your hands clean of these girls' deaths. I am condemned already."

Then he watched as she did something unexpected. With a burst of speed, she ran again, alighted, and landed hard on the hood of the police car. The officer slammed on his brakes but she was gone as quickly as she came. Undoubtedly, he was now calling for backup. Ryan turned to follow Zoe.

"Is Liz behind you?" Zoe asked as Becca met her in the trees, just as they had agreed.

"Yes, I think so."

"Ryan must be close. We need to find Liz and form a circle fast," she said as she pulled her spell book from her coat pocket.

"I saw the police way over there. It looked like they stopped suddenly. Maybe Ryan is over there. Maybe they already have him," she sputtered, betraying her lack of confidence in the naively optimistic suggestion.

"I hope not. This is not a police matter. I want him dead so I can make him my minion."

"What do we do if they have him already though?"

"I seriously doubt they have him. And where is Liz?"

"Gone," Ryan replied as he approached.

The two girls whirled around and there he was. Becca trembled. Zoe looked defiant—like a trapped animal.

"The police are already here," he continued, "and I'm sure more are on their way. There is no way out of this for you. So here you die."

As he spoke, Idelette dropped down right in their midst. She grabbed Zoe by the shoulder as she struck Becca across the face—the girl flew several feet and hit her head on a tree. She lay motionless in the leaves. She raised Zoe up off the ground and held her out at arm's length.

"What are you?" Zoe gasped.

"I am the way of all flesh."

"Why are you helping him?"

"I'm not. I'm just stopping you."

Then Zoe muttered some unintelligible words blended with a few English phrases. When nothing happened an expression of confusion and defeat briefly betrayed her thoughts. Then with a look of rage and resolution she turned toward Ryan and blurted out, "I loved you!"

Ryan raised a quizzical eyebrow. Idelette turned to look at him.

"Oh yes. But you never noticed me. How long were we friends? What was so terrible about me? Why could you not love me back?" As she spoke she struck Idelette in the side of the neck. Idelette dropped her and the witch fled. The vampire pulled a small folding knife out of the side of her neck. There was surprisingly little blood. She handed the knife to Ryan. He immediately recognized it.

"I gave her this. Many years ago."

"Loved you?"

"I don't buy it. I think she was just creating a distraction."

But the revenant had already turned to pursue Zoe. She was approaching the office building.

Ryan turned to see Becca was waking. He picked her up, put her on her feet, held her by the back of the neck, and looked her in the eye.

"Please please please don't kill me!" she sobbed.

"Zoe will be dead in a moment. You are the last. The police are going to be swarming through here in the next couple of minutes."

"I just want to go home. I don't even want to remember any of this. Please let me live!"

"Get out of here. Turn from these evil ways. Maybe go to church this Sunday." He paused. "I should do the same." Then he let go of her.

She cried and fled Greenwood, stumbling on roots and grave markers as she went. Ryan watched her run out the east side of the cemetery. She never looked back.

Zoe glanced back as she neared the office. No one was following her. She had wounded it for sure. Maybe it was dead. But as she rounded the corner of the building she was suddenly struck in the face. She writhed flat on her back. Idelette's boot came down hard on Zoe's stomach. She tried to scream but had no air. She rolled onto her side and spit out some blood. The vampire picked her up and held her against the building. Zoe feebly tried to swat at her, flailing her arms futilely. Idelette caught her hand and broke it. Zoe shrieked in pain and kicked violently. Idelette pressed herself against the witch so she could not move.

"Repent your sins, girl. The grave below is all astir to meet you at your coming. And you have only seconds left." Then after a brief pause to stare deep into her victim's eyes, she turned Zoe's chin upward and tore her throat wide open with her bare hand. The smell of blood was intoxicating and it poured all over the two of them. Zoe looked as though she wanted to scream but merely mouthed some silent words as her eyes stopped and her pupils fixed into a dead stare. Idelette dropped her to the ground, felt a disgusted chill creep up her spine, and palpated the Bible in her pocket. As she did, three police cars rushed in through the Leonard Street entrance right behind her. She grabbed Zoe's corpse and vanished into the shadows. They passed her by. Then, once they were deeper into the cemetery, she hoisted Zoe's body up into a tall tree, tied her hair around a branch, and let her corpse dangle high over the main drive between the office building and the Leonard Street entrance. The police would find it when they came back around.

Meanwhile, Ryan was sneaking through the graves, dodging police cars all around, trying to get to the office building. Idelette met him before he made it there.

"It's time to leave," she said.

Ryan knew it was done.

"This place is going to be busy for the rest of the night and perhaps well into morning. But things will likely calm down after a day or two. Meet me at the crossroads in one week, just before dawn."

"November 7 before dawn. Agreed," Ryan said.

Then the two scattered in opposite directions. Ryan went out through the north woods, turned west on Ragner Boulevard, and fled south.

"Get this photographed and get it all cleaned up before light," the sergeant said as he and two other officers stared up at Zoe's dangling corpse. We've got detectives on these cases. Get them here."

"They just found two more bodies deeper in the cemetery, sir."

He sighed. "Process the scene. Do it right, but do it fast. I don't want any of this left at daylight. No press. No public onlookers. Get it done! And get the Medical Examiner's Investigator here!"

Idelette crawled into the sump pump pit near the office building and whiled away most of the night. She was desperately thirsty. Her skin was starting to crack and peel but did not bleed.

She could barely feel the Bible she was holding. The night dragged on and slowly the commotion of the police died down. Finally, she managed to fall into dreamless sleep which lasted several days and nights. Around sunset on the evening of November sixth she arose and dragged herself out of that hole. She had little strength to stand on the path. But it was not yet night, so she ambled a pointless and redundant route through the graveyard. As she approached the crossroads she saw a group of three teenage girls sitting at the base of a tree. One of them had a book. She turned toward them and they saw her approach. Immediately, the girls rose and fled before her, out of the cemetery and into the neighborhoods. She did not pursue.

Large areas of her skin were split and denuded. The bones of her fingers were fully exposed. She was tired and weak. The thirst was powerful, but she did all she could to ignore it as she dragged her boots through the leaves and among the stones. The night crawled its circuit above her and dawn seemed to resist coming. In extremis she whiled away the darkness in aimless ambling and broken prayer. Her hand constantly on her Bible, she waited for the knell of sunrise. The stars above were slowly fading in their courses. The tombstones were cold but the bones of her fleshless fingers felt nothing when she touched them. Her steps were slow and she could hear the corpses below stir in their respective graves as she approached and passed over each one. Their writhing settled though as she stepped off the grass and walked down the main drive to the bench opposite the Jewish section. Lying down and looking up into the atmosphere, she wondered if her thoughts could ever be so clear. Her right hand gripped her pocketed Bible, but she could not feel it. Finally the eastern sky began to hint of the coming dawn and with a last desperate prayer to the God of salvation, she sighed and waited to die.

Chapter 53

Greenwood was unusually still in the cold gray light before dawn on November 7. Ryan walked through the trees, into the graveyard again, and watched cautiously for anyone—police or passersby, but mostly for his only remaining friend. He carefully proceeded to the crossroads, but saw no one. Only scattered jack o'lanterns were watching, still grimacing where they had been left. Then, he noticed something strange. A few gray specks floated by. They looked like ash. Then he noticed a couple more. They all came from the south. He looked down the road and there in the distance he saw her lying on the bench. She stared at him lifelessly, but definitely saw him. Her skin was pale and cracking. Her blonde hair streamed down to the ground and there were scattered leaves settling on her black coat. The occasional ashy fragment broke free as the eastern sun shone upon her left side. She was starting to skeletalize, and clearly beyond help. Ryan sighed and slowly approached her corpse. One of the jack o'lanterns moldered beside her. He had no words, nor did he even truly know how to feel.

As he looked down on her regressing corpse, he realized she was still alive when suddenly her cloudy eyes glanced past him. He turned and saw a man near the crossroads, walking toward them. Ryan felt like he recognized him, yet couldn't quite recall how or where he had seen him before. He watched for a moment, then looked back at Idelette, deciding whether or not he needed to flee the scene. Being found with a dead body was contrary to his instincts. He could argue that he just came upon it—that would be true—but it seemed too dangerous to associate himself with any of this. The investigation might unravel everything. He was just about to tell Idelette he was sorry that he needed to desert her in her dying moment when he noticed her expression had changed. It resembled fear. He looked back at the man, who was still far off but walking toward them.

Suddenly Ryan felt sharp pain in his wrist, and looked down to see Idelette had sunk her teeth into him and was sucking his blood. He pulled his arm away, but she grabbed it back and continued. He pulled it away again and this time she let him. Ryan watched as the wounds closed up immediately.

"What have you done?" he asked in an accusatory tone. She merely laid there.

"What's all this then?" the man said from behind Ryan.

"I don't know. I just came upon her a moment ago," Ryan replied as he turned to face the man.

"Is that right?" he responded after a moment of eye contact.

"Do we know each other?" Ryan asked.

"No. We have not met. But I know this dying woman," the man responded as he turned back to look at Idelette. Ryan watched as the man's expression immediately changed. He appeared to be overcome with fury. Ryan looked down at the bench. It was empty.

"That's weird. You agree there was a dead lady here a moment ago, right?" Ryan said.

"Yes. Yes, I do," the man turned back to him in rage.

"Well, I don't. I never saw any body, and if the police ask, I don't know who you are, what you're talking about, or where you got these crazy ideas that I was ever in Greenwood with a dead body. What dead body? I never saw a dead body. What man? I don't know any man. Who are you anyway? I don't know you." Ryan stalled.

"His name is Conrad," Idelette answered from behind them.

Just then Ryan noticed an owl swoop out of the trees across the graveyard. It was daylight now, but Ryan could have sworn there was a slight glow about the bird.

The man turned. "Hello, Idelette."

With that remark, she was immediately upon him, biting into the left side of his neck. The taste put her in a frenzy and she tore at the wound with her teeth—desperate for every drop. He threw her off him, but she leaped right back again, intent to drink all she could. He pried her off once more and kicked her across the drive. She was on her feet in an instant and their eyes met momentarily.

Conrad turned to consider Ryan, but the diener only looked bewildered. Conrad grabbed him by the shirt and threw him down onto the bench, which cracked in half beneath him. He lay there for a moment assuming he was paralyzed, or dead, but gradually realized he was essentially unharmed. Before he could do anything more, Idelette had grabbed Conrad and thrown him into a nearby monument. The giant stone cracked but did not yield.

In an instant Conrad was up. He gave a momentary look of confusion at Ryan, who was somehow still alive. The look quickly turned from confusion to resolve. They ran for each other. Conrad struck a hard blow to Ryan which he was not ready for. But as Conrad's guard was down, Idelette was upon him again.

He hit her hard across the face. She fell to the ground on her back. Grabbing his leg, she pulled it out from under him. She could feel her strength still gathering as the blood she had tasted coursed through her. Conrad tried to rise, but Idelettee pulled him back down. Leaping to her feet, she stomped on his chest. He screamed in hate and blood sprayed from his neck. She dove upon the crimson torrent and began to drink again. Conrad threw her off from him once more and jumped to his feet.

They stood for a moment staring at each other. Ryan seized the opportunity. He took hold of Conrad's arm, which distracted him just long enough. Immediately, Idelette lunged upon him again. She grabbed his head and pulled it back toward his spine. The bite mark she had previously made tore open even further, spraying all over her. As Conrad tried to struggle, only breaking free of Ryan, she lifted him from the ground with her left hand, letting him dangle by the neck. With a look of hatred, she thrust her hand into his stomach and tore his abdominal wall down toward his pelvis. His vitals spilled out between his legs. Then, pulling his head back, she thrust her hand down through the front of his neck into his chest, grabbed whatever she felt—which was warm and pulsatile—and pulled it up and out. She dropped his body to the ground, stood on his now-hollow chest, tore his head off his shoulders, and dashed it against a nearby headstone several times. Viscous fragments of brain tissue dripped out of the neck. She dropped the head and turned toward Ryan.

They stared at each other for several silent seconds and then Ryan looked at his healed wrist where she had bitten him. He looked back up.

"What have you done?"

"I'm sorry," she whispered with tears forming in her eyes.

Ryan had no words.

"I'm so sorry," she cried. "I'm so sorry! Goodbye!" And with that remark she reached her right hand into her coat pocket, thrust the Bible into Ryan's hands, and fled.

He stood there staring down at it for several seconds. At last he opened it. Of course it was in Latin. When he looked up again, he scanned all around, but he knew she was gone and he was alone.

"What happened here?" Mike suddenly spoke from behind.

"I couldn't say," Ryan whispered.

"We could have a real problem on our hands if anybody sees this," he shook his head in disapproval. "You know, we never used to have these kinds of messes when Phil was doing this. Then you came along and things have really escalated," Mike sighed.

Ryan said nothing but looked at him with his mouth slightly agape. Then he too shook his head and looked down at his wrist again.

"Are you alright?" Mike asked.

"I don't know. I don't think so. Let's just get this cleaned up."

The two of them worked diligently side by side but Ryan said nothing. His thoughts were completely chaotic. Between his incredulous thoughts about Phil, his desire to know where Idelette had gone, and his misery about his new situation which she had inflicted on him, he simply did not know what to say to his friend as they cleaned up the clotted gore. They hosed off the grass and replaced headstones and the broken bench to their proper places. They would have to repair them at a later date, however. No sooner had they finished when Detectives Malli and Jameson drove in the Byron Street entrance.

Mike gave the diener a knowing look while the police were still far off. Ryan nodded and left Mike to intercept them. He had placed Idelette's Bible into his own coat, and his right hand seemed to naturally go to it as he walked past the retaining wall and out of Greenwood cemetery. He was just about to step out onto Leonard Street when he looked across the road and saw Sarah approaching him. They paused and stared at one another while cars passed between them. Ryan crossed over to her at last. The pair turned east and proceeded down the sidewalk together.

"You weren't at home or work," Sarah broke the silence.

"Thank you for searching for me. Probably smart to stay out of Greenwood for a while," Ryan added. "The police are in there right now."

"I heard Halloween was quite the blood bath," Sarah replied, looking over her shoulder and across Leonard into Greenwood. "Sorry I left. But I felt you were in safe company."

Ryan looked at his wrist again, but withheld his thoughts about safe company with Idelette. "Yeah, there were dead people everywhere before it was all said and done. I'm sorry you missed it. Idelette tore them all to ribbons. I didn't even do anything."

"Where is she now?"

"I don't know. But I desperately need to find her." He pulled Idelette's Bible from his pocket and handed it to Sarah. "And I have a lot to tell you along the way, if you care to join me in this pursuit."

Acknowledgements and Gratitude:

Feedback for the original publication of this novel in 2020 was very positive and encouraging. The following year I was asked to write a spin-off for a miniature book to be published by Booksby Press in limited edition. That book is titled Knowing Good and Evil and was written as a bonus chapter to The Grave Below. As I am now writing the sequel to the novel (which I had declared I would never do), I was increasingly motivated to re-release the first novel with Knowing Good and Evil incorporated into it. Chapter 22 of this edition is a slightly modified version of Knowing Good and Evil. Since I was doing an update anyway, I seized the opportunity to improve upon other parts of the novel. I cleaned up the writing, shed some underdeveloped ideas and other baggage, improved the pace, and even eliminated a minor character entirely. I feel this is now a far better version of The Grave Below, and gives much stronger foundation to build the sequel upon.

The initial motivation to write this novel stemmed from a statement made by Ed Uthman, MD. In his document (freely available online) titled The Routine Autopsy (version 1.003, August 1996), he makes the following personal observation:

"(Dieners) enjoy a much greater degree of autonomy than most workers at their pay grade...they are somewhat secretive...and one gets the idea that they have a lot more going on in their lives than they tend to let on. It is not uncommon for them to receive a variety of strange visitors in the morgue, some of whom have a less than savory appearance. For fiction writers, I think there is a lot of character development potential for dieners."

I first read that in 1999 and I became a diener in 2001. In 2003 I wrote the short story that anticipated this larger work. The larger plot idea sparked in 2006 during a conversation with my friend and mentor Chuck Schwallier. In 2009 I wrote the poem and the initial chapters which finally, after years of festering, grew into this novel. Eleven years later it was complete. And so here it is, at long last. I have included the original poetry at the end of this book for the curious who might enjoy seeing the primordial ideas which developed into The Grave Below. There are eleven unnamed characters who cross paths in a graveyard. And since the novel took eleven years to complete, I retrospectively titled the poems The Eleven. I make no claims about the quality of my poetry.

This work could not have been completed without the support of many persons who helped me along the way:

Eternal thanks to my Lord, the author of my salvation, Jesus Christ, one with the Father and Holy Spirit. One God, in trinity and unity, who redeemed me from my sins.

Many thanks to my wife, Jenni Hansma who did all of the graphic design and typesetting.

Thanks also to those who rendered assistance to the writing process (largely by reading draft chapters from numerous earlier manuscript versions): Jenni Hansma, Claire Mutch, Charles Sorrell, Rachel Martindale (2024), and Lanette Caudill.

Thanks to Terry Syrek, whose song Emberfall set the tone of the poems on which this novel is based (vide infra). Thanks also to Dream Theater for Overture 1928/Strange Déjà Vu, which became much of the soundtrack for writing this novel.

To all others, and I suspect you know who you are (even if I don't), what more could I possibly say here?

Patrick Hansma
July 26, 2020
March 14, 2024
חָנֵּנִי אֱלֹהִים

The Eleven – November Night

The sun is setting before a November night;
  when blood-letting's signaled by golden light.
The ventriloquist—wind—keeps speaking
  through the autumns dead linguists—seeking
  their place on the terrestrial sphere—
  to cover the earth (for death is near).
November progresses and with it on
  walks the restless one—*le revenant,*
  rustling the leaves and touching the stones
  pondering her fate—cold and alone.
No blood flows from her broken skin
  exposing the bone which once was within.
Her fleshless fingertips feel not the pain—
  nor the cold—nor November (October's remains).
Her boots drag through the rustling leaves
  and the corpses below—she slowly perceives—
  share, like her, the dead leaves condition—
  just like her—though void of volition.
With this thought the vampire, without beginning,
  stops to wonder if she is sinning
  just by surviving in a death without ending
  just by surviving, for fear of descending....

Now the last rays are fading into night
and the moon hastens its silver plight.
Seduced by the darkness, the immortal accursed
turns from her thoughts and begins to thirst—
just as she has—ever and anon—
through lifetimes, though tonight, she presses on.
Walking calmly to a cold marble bench
while denying a thirst she never can quench
in that November night she quietly lies
on the moon-lit marble and she decides to die.
Somber and pallid, her beautiful face
reveals the loneliness no time could erase
As quietly she looks—to the ephemeral spheres
turning eternally the evanescent years.
The moon recalls to her the heaven of the light
that she lingers to see beyond the waning night
which will finally end after ages of grief—
this November night—with everlasting relief.
The leaves rustle loudly as she softly decays
there on her death-bed, and she dares to pray
to the God of salvation, just before she dies
despairing in the darkness, the vampire sighs.

The Eleven–Halloween night

Walking past another pumpkin glowing on a grave
The ghost hunters began to feel a little less brave.
But it was Halloween night and the veil was so thin
Between this world and the next—and the dead within.
They had come with equipment to document the sight
Of ghosts and orbs and shadows in the graveyard tonight.
They had come with assumptions about what they would find.
Keeping the local stories at the back of their minds.
This thrill-seeking couple was looking for a good scare
Thinking they were alone and doing something so rare.
From outside the cemetery things looked so serene
It was haunting and spooky—perfect for Halloween.
They felt so bold and brave when they passed Greenwood's stone walls
But there was movement!—(surely just a leaf as it falls)
And the darkness was close! And then the horrible screams
That scattered the silence below the moons silver beams!
And the pumpkins that appeared—lit by no human hand—
Moldered in the leaves over the headstone-dotted land!
Feeling surrounded and like someone was watching them
They decided to leave and cut their fears at the stem

But they were far from where their car was foolishly parked
And eyes were upon them—lurking in the ghoulish dark.
So swiftly they turned and through the graveyard they both ran
But at once were stopped by a woman pallid and wan.
She was silent and lovely but her deep meaning eyes
Were void of expression—empty, unholy, and wise.
They felt their souls whither as they were frozen with fear
Watching as she walked, rustling the leaves so crisp and sere.
She was calm when she grabbed them suddenly by their throats
Then buried her fangs in their flesh—their blood sprayed her coat.
When having drank to satiety she let them fall
And there among the headstones the leaves would be their pall.
Turning from their corpses she went back through the dark night
While the wind in the branches hid the bodies from sight.

The Eleven–All Hallows Eve

The moon glowed softly through the gusty trees
And cast moving shadows over the dead
Who stirred at the sound of the rustling pleas
Of the withered leaves tormented over head

One by one they fell in the sullen night
To the paths and the grass among the mools
One by one fell amid the spectral plight
Of the living shadows of Halloween ghouls

Into this terrible melancholy
A solitary vampire calmly walked
Amid these graves, so haunted—unholy—
Seeking ghosts, yet seeing none, two others talked.

While entranced in just such an illusion—
Really the limits of their feeble sight—
While enslaved to their lies and delusion—
Into the graveyard rushed the shades of the night

Three returned again for this final year
As they had for so many years before

To haunt the graves among the leaves, so sere
And continue what was passing into lore

With great haste they raced the heavenly spheres
Which roll on toward the dismal November
Their foot falls echoed through the tombs of years
As they crafted fear for all to remember

Crunch! went the leaves beneath their darkened feet—
The vampire silently listened in awe
The ghost hunters stopped and looked to retreat—
They could not believe what their eyes never saw.

The three labored among them in shadows
The headstones echoed inhuman screams
They marked their presence with the soft sad glow
Of ghastly pumpkins with dead, unblinking beams.

Each lantern—carved from a pumpkins nightmare—
Motionless and lit by no human hand
Appeared on its own and flickered and stared
Causing emotions it seemed to understand.

The moonlight revealed some subtle motion
In the thick darkness and between the stones
But the others were lost in commotion
And feared that they actually were alone!

All around them was horrible shrieking
And the pumpkins were all that they were shown
The three shades gave them what they were seeking
But now they feared that they really were alone!

The Eleven–November Evening

From far off the witches heard her coming.
It was too cold to practice anyway.
With pallid fingers, already numbing
They gathered their books—they could not stay.

The girls had settled on the graves this night
To practice their evil art
Amongst the mools, far from the public sight
The dead would play their part.

Four of them then sat in the evening sun
At the close of a cold November day
With candles and books they had just begun
Their wicked rite as the sun rolled away.

They cast their spells among the rotting dead—
Costing them their teenage souls.
While on fallen leaves, all withered and red,
Fed the fungi, worms, and moles.

The Gate of God, opposite that of Man,
The setting sun, the rising moon and spheres
Were falsely worked into the witches' plan—
Until her footsteps fell harsh on their ears.

Her boots dragged through the leaves on the graves.
The dead below her all stirred.
In her was a longing for blood which saves
Her from thirst—and from God's Word.

Struck with terror the witches all trembled
Like cowardly girls alone in the cold
Forgetting why they even assembled
They gathered their spell books—useless and old.

They fled from the vampire's deathly approach—
Filled with horror they ran.
They felt their own weakness and the reproach
Of their own pathetic plan.

The Eleven-November morning

The sun was rising on a November day
    And the light chased the dark phantoms away
The old caretaker—so hardened and cold—
    Sighed at the clouds that listlessly rolled
    On the harsh cold wind brought by witchy November—
    Just like every year that he could remember.
Kicking his boots against the trunk of a tree
    To knock off whatever ageless mud he could see
He sighed at the thought of his endless chore
    Then he went to work looking for human gore.
Some mornings there would be none at all—
    But that was rare this late in the fall.
So he set out early each morning to find
    Whatever remains were left behind
    By untold terrors roaming in the night—
    Seeking victims before the morning light
And when he found them all mangled and cleaved
    He would dig them out from under the leaves
    And drag them back behind the cemetery
    Into the woods—and each he would rebury.
But this morning as he searched the grounds
    He was suddenly struck by what he found—

It was a woman—blonde and all in black
    Laying motionless there on here back
She was lying on a bench in the distance
    And he could see she was beyond assistance
No blood issued from her broken skin
    And he could see the bone that once was within.
Somber and pallid, her beautiful face
    Admitted a loneliness no time could erase
    And in death she had set her eyes on
    Some far and uncertain horizon
As he approached he could see her decay—
    He sighed at the sight which was slipping away—
His thoughts wandered as he studied her death
    He wondered what she prayed with her last breath
With this dismal thought he turned to walk away
    And harden his heart to the November day
But he was stopped by something there on the ground
    A ghastly pumpkin—sinister and round—
    Was lurking there—right by the caretakers foot
It's extinguished grin was black with candle soot.

END NOTES

Ch 3

- Lamentations 1:11
  Douay version

Ch 4

- The De Monarchia of Dante Alighieri, edited with translation and notes by Aurelia Henry
  The Riverside Press, Cambridge, 1904
  (public domain)
- Ephesians 4:27 (paraphrase)
- Rituale Romanum, 1772

Ch 5

- Isaiah 47:12
- Summers, Montague. The Vampire: His Kith and Kin. Barnes & Noble Publishing, 1991

Ch 6

- Benivieni, Antiono. De abditis nonnullis ac mirandis morborum et sanationum causis, 1507.
  Pare, Ambroise. The Workes of that Famous Chirurgion, Ambrose Parey. 2nd English ed. 1649.
  Calmet, Antoine Augustine. Dissertation Upon the Apparitions of Angels, Daemons, and Ghosts, and conceerning the Vampires of Hungary. 1st English ed. 1759.
- 1 Peter 4:7, NIV

Ch 8

- Job 36:20, ESV, slightly modified
- Lamentations 3:1
  Isaiah 57:15, NIV
  Lamentations 3:4 & 6

Ch 12

- Augustine, City of God
  (in turn, quoting Virgil's Aeneid)
  The Works of Aurelius
  Augustine, Bishop of Hippo
  Translation by Rev Marcus
  Dods, Edinburgh 1871
  (public domain)
- Isaiah 47:12
- Lamentations 3:7
  Isaiah 57:15, KJV
  Lamentations 3:8
- Psalm 31:10
  Lamentations 3:16-18

Ch 16

- 1 Thessalonians 4:11 (allusion)
- Isaiah 46:10 (allusion)
  Ephesians 4:27 (paraphrase)
  Matthew 10:28 (allusion)

Ch 22

- Ecclesiastes 1:2, Vulgate
- Matthew 26:41

Ch 30

- Revelation 20:11 (allusion)

Ch 33

- Genesis 3:19, KJV (modified)

Ch 34

- John 1:5

Ch 39

- Edgar Allan Poe, Ligeia, 1838

Ch 40

- Leviticus 19:26 & 31, Leviticus 20:6 & 27, Exodus 22:18, Deuteronomy 18:9-12, Micah 5:12, Galatians 5:19-21, Revelation 21:8 & 22:15 (allusion)
- Exodus 7:11 (allusion)
- 1 Samuel 28 (allusion)
- Acts 8 (allusion)
- Revelation 20:7 (allusion)
- Revelation 5:9 (allusion)
- 1 John 3:6 (allusion)
- Matthew 18:6 & Luke 17:2 (allusion)
- 1 John 3:6 (allusion)
- Romans 9:22 (allusion)
- 1 Samuel 2:34, Psalm 139:16 (allusion)
- 1 Corinthians 15:3, Romans 3:25, Ephesians 1:7, Hebrews 1:3 (allusion)
  Colossians 3:3

Ch 41

- Mark 5:9 (allusion)
- Isaiah 47:12 (allusion)
  Isaiah 28:15
- Isaiah 47:9 & 11
- Job 3:21 & 22
- Edgar Allan Poe, The Conqueror Worm
- Amos 6:9 (allusion)
- Exodus 22:18 (allusion)

- Isaiah 47:9
  Ephesians 4:27 (allusion)
- Hebrews 12:1
- Psalm 61:2, John 20:28, Jeremiah 7:10, Hebrews 12:1, Job 30:19
- Job 30:20 & 23, Job 35:6, Isaiah 59:12, Job 13:23, Isaiah 59:13
- Isaiah 29:4, Job 7:3, 5, 6, & 21, Job 10:3, Job 17:1
- Isaiah 28:18, 1 chronicles 16:35 & 36, Job 19:25, Psalm 90:9, Genesis 3:19, Job 19:27 & 27, John 11:27, Luke 18:13 (NIV), Revelation 22:21

Ch 42

- Psalm 66, Old English Psalms Dumbarton Oaks Medieval Library

Ch 44

- Augustine, City of God, (in turn, quoting Virgil's Aeneid)
  The Works of Aurelius Augustine, Bishop of Hippo Translation by Rev Marcus Dods, Edinburgh 1871 (public domain)
- The Collected Works of Edgar Allan Poe, Vol. I: Poems. Page 3, 1969, Thomas Ollive Mabbott
- 1 John 5:16, KJV
- John 6:52-58
- John 4:10
- 2 Corinthians 5:17 (allusion)

Ch 45

- Exodus 20:13
- 1 John 3:15 (allusion)
- Exodus 21:22 (allusion)
- Genesis 4:10 (allusion)

Ch 47

- John 8:44
- 1 Samuel 26:10
- Matthew ch 4 (allusion)
  Shakespeare, The Merchant of Venice

Ch 49

- Matthew 26:41

Ch 50

- Isaiah 30:17

Ch 51

- Psalm 31

Ch 52

- 1 John 3:15
- 1 Kings 2:2
- Isaiah 14:9, NIV

Ch 53

- Genesis 4:10

About the Author

Patrick Hansma is a forensic pathologist who lives in Michigan with his wife and three kids. He and his wife also own Patrick's Rare Books, LLC. He wrote this novel to fill his time and get these festering ideas out of his head. He swore there would be no sequel. But that proved untrue....

PatrickHansma.com

Patricksrarebooks.com

Printed in Great Britain
by Amazon

48286626R00209